THERE ARE
NO GHOSTS
IN THE
SOVIET UNION

Reginald Hill

THERE ARE NO GHOSTS IN THE SOVIET UNION

A Novella and Five Stories

A Foul Play Press Book

The Countryman Press, Inc.
Woodstock, Vermont

First U.S. edition, 1988

Copyright © 1987 by Reginald Hill

First published in Great Britain, 1987
by William Collins Sons & Co. Ltd.

Library of Congress Cataloging-in-Publication Data
Hill, Reginald.
    There are no ghosts in the Soviet Union.

    "A Foul Play Press book."
    I. Title.
PR6058.I448T45   1988   823'.914   88-16123
ISBN 0-88150-119-0

Printed in the United States of America

A Foul Play Press Book

The Countryman Press
Woodstock, Vermont
05091

CONTENTS

There Are No Ghosts in the Soviet Union   5
Bring Back the Cat!   76
The Bull Ring   108
Auteur Theory   122
Poor Emma   168
Crowded Hour   213

THERE ARE NO GHOSTS IN
THE SOVIET UNION

1

For Inspector Lev Chislenko, the affair began on Friday,
the thirteenth of July, in a graveyard, but he did not at first
think this unlucky.

A man had been spotted behaving suspiciously in the
Novodevichy Cemetery which is only a block away from
the Gorodok Building. Chislenko answered the call and
recognized the man immediately. His name was Starov and
he was a black marketeer. He was also a cocky little bastard.

'What are you doing in the cemetery, Starov?' asked
Chislenko.

'I like to go places where all men are truly equal,' replied
Starov. 'I'm thinking of joining the Party.'

'Why are you carrying two thousand roubles?'

'It's money I've been collecting for our local old folk's
holiday fund.'

'Why did you try to run away when the custodian approached you?'

'He didn't approach. He jumped out from behind a big
marble angel. It's Friday the thirteenth, remember? That's
a bad kind of date. I thought maybe he was a ghost or
something.'

'There are no ghosts in the Soviet Union,' said Chislenko
unthinkingly.

Starov guffawed and accepted the unintentional invitation
to complete the old joke.

'No, they've all been given exit visas to Israel!'

Starov was still laughing when Sub-Inspector Kedin entered. Chislenko had sent him to contact HQ on Petrovka
Street to find out what they'd got on Starov. But he returned
with other pieces of news.

First, a British tourist had collapsed during a tour of the

Novodevichy Convent. When his clothing was loosened to permit first aid, he was found to be wearing six pairs of jeans and twelve T-shirts.

That solved what little mystery surrounded Starov's intentions.

Secondly, there'd just been an emergency call from the Gorodok Building.

'A man fell down a lift-shaft from the seventh floor. Or perhaps he was pushed. It seems the caller wasn't very coherent. Usual emergency services have been dispatched, but I said if they wanted a senior officer in charge, you were just around the corner. Hope you didn't mind, Chief?'

Kedin was no fool. With Chislenko out of the way, he could claim this Starov case, all neatly tied up. It was a nice collar for an ambitious young officer.

On the other hand, Chislenko was not without ambition either. He knew that the Gorodok Building was the admin HQ of the important Organization of Machinery Supply, Maintenance and Service. A man who sorted out trouble there might get noticed by some very influential people.

It was a consideration Chislenko was later to recall with sad irony.

'OK, I'll go,' he said, knowing that if Kedin had volunteered him, he really had no choice anyway.

'Wrap him up nice and tight,' he ordered, nodding at Starov.

The black marketeer grinned and said, 'Say Inspector, you're not related to *the* Chislenko, are you? Used to play for Dynamo?'

'No. He's not related to me either,' retorted Chislenko sourly. He left, carefully not slamming the door.

When he arrived at the Gorodok Building he found the place in chaos. Whoever had made the emergency calls had certainly created a sense of emergency. A frenzy of firemen were trying to clear the building while a panic of police were trying to seal it off. The lift involved in the incident, which was on the south side of the building, was naturally out of use. Unfortunately so many cops, firefighters and emergency technicians had crowded into the north lift that it had broken down between the fourth and fifth floors. This meant that Chislenko, trying to establish order wherever he passed, had to labour up the stairs to the seventh floor. On the fifth landing he passed two medics giving the kiss of life to a third who had collapsed as the team sprinted upstairs to the emergency.

Chislenko did not pause but kept going to the seventh floor where by comparison things seemed almost calm. An elderly grey-faced man in lift-operator's uniform was leaning against a wall. An out-of-breath medic stood by him with a hypodermic in one hand and a jar of smelling salts in the other, but the liftman was taking his own medication from a battered gun-metal hipflask. The smelling salts could not mask the stink of cheap vodka.

A second medic crouched before the open lift making cooing and clicking sounds as if trying to coax a reluctant puppy out from under a low bed. Two firemen in green overalls stood indifferently by. Along the corridor, fractionally opened office doors were alive with curious eyes.

Chislenko advanced and looked into the lift.

There were two women in it. One of them was middle-aged and stout. She was sitting on the floor with her knees drawn up under her several chins and her body pressed as close as it could get to the back wall. In addition her fingers were gripping a length of ornamental ribbing along the wall with a knuckle-whitening tightness which might have made sense if she were perched on a narrow ledge overlooking a precipice. Her eyes were wide and round and terrified.

Beside her knelt the other woman, in her twenties, slim and pretty, her arms wrapped comfortingly round the fat woman's shoulders.

'All right,' said Chislenko in his best official manner. 'Let's get you out of there, shall we, madam?'

He stepped into the lift and reached down to pull the fat woman out on to the landing. Her reaction was startling. She opened her large, red, damp mouth, and started to scream.

'You bloody idiot!' yelled the younger woman, her face

still pretty in its rage. 'Sod off, will you? Get out! Half-wit!'

Baffled, Chislenko retreated.

The liftman was looking only slightly less grey than his gun-metal flask, but Chislenko was running short of sympathetic patience.

'You the one who made the calls?' he demanded.

'That's right, boss,' said the man. 'Muntjan. Josif Muntjan. Oh Christ!'

He took another drink.

'All right, Muntjan. What happened?'

The man shook his head as if this were a question beyond reach of any answer he could give.

'You reported a man had fallen down the lift-shaft, is that true?'

'Pushed,' said Muntjan. 'Not fallen. Pushed.'

There was a phone on the wall a little way down the corridor. Chislenko went to it, studied the directory sheet, and dialled the code for the basement.

A voice said, 'Hello?'

'Who's that?' said Chislenko.

'Who's *that*?' echoed the voice.

'Chislenko. Inspector, MVD. I'm in charge,' said Chislenko challengingly.

To his surprise the man laughed.

'You'll get no quarrel from me, Inspector. Brodsky, Fire Officer. How can I help you?'

'I assume you're examining the bottom of the lift-shaft. What have you found?'

'Fag-packets. Dust. Cockroaches. Spiders. I can send up samples if you like.'

'No body?' said Chislenko.

'No body. Nobody. No sign of any body or anybody. Not in the shaft or up the shaft. Oh, and before you ask, Inspector, we've checked the north lift too. The same. We've been hoaxed.'

Slowly Chislenko replaced the receiver. No wonder the man had laughed. It was a well-known injustice of the security service world that the man in charge of a wild goose chase usually ended up with bird-shit on his head.

8

'All right, Muntjan,' he said, putting on what he thought of as his KGB expression. 'Start talking. And this time I want the truth! What the hell's been going on here?'

Muntjan belched, then began to laugh. True, there was something hysterical in it, but Chislenko was growing tired of people laughing every time he spoke. He clenched his right fist. The medic looked away. Only a fool let himself become a witness to police brutality.

Muntjan saw the fist too and shrugged. Suddenly he was the sempiternal peasant who knows all things are sent to try him and resistance is pointless.

He began to talk.

By the time he'd finished, Chislenko wished he'd never begun.

According to Muntjan, the lift had been descending from the upper floors. In it were the two women and a middle-aged man.

On the seventh floor the lift had stopped. When the doors opened, there was one man waiting there.

'Going down,' said Muntjan.

The man hadn't moved. He didn't seem to have noticed the lift's arrival. Muntjan looked closely at him to make sure he wasn't anyone important. He was slightly built, in his mid-twenties, very blond, wearing a double-breasted suit of old-fashioned cut. He wasn't one of the Building's regulars.

Deciding he didn't look all that important, Muntjan said, 'If you're coming, boss, get your skates on. These folk have got places they want to be!'

Still the man didn't move. The middle-aged man in the lift cleared his throat impatiently. The two women went on chattering away to each other. And now someone else appeared, an older man in his early thirties who must have been wearing rubber-soled shoes, so silent was his approach. The first man glanced round at him with a smile of recognition. The newcomer responded by putting his arm round the first man's shoulders in what seemed a simple gesture of greeting.

And then he thrust the blond man violently into the lift.

9

The smile vanished from his face, being replaced by amazement modulating into terror.

He attempted to draw back, teetering like a frightened child on the edge of a swimming pool. But his centre of balance was too far forward and, willy-nilly he stepped into the lift.

And now Muntjan hesitated in his hitherto fluent and detailed tale.

'Go on,' prompted Chislenko.

Muntjan took a last suck at his flask. It was clearly empty. He shrugged and said, 'He went through the floor, boss.'

'Went through the floor?'

Chislenko stepped up to the lift again and looked inside. The two women had not changed position. The floor on which he had stood in his vain attempt to get the fat woman out looked as solid as it had felt. He went back to Muntjan.

'Went through the floor!' he said angrily.

'You've got it, boss. Went through it like it didn't exist. Clean through it, flapping his arms like a fledgeling too young to fly. And that was it. All over in a second. Clean through. No trace, except . . .'

'Except what?' said Chislenko, eager for something—anything—to get a hold of.

'I thought there was kind of a long shriek, tailing away, but very distant, like a train at night, a long long way off, you know what I mean?'

'No,' said Chislenko. 'I don't know what you mean. I don't begin to know what you mean.'

He returned to the lift. The two pairs of eyes looked at him, one pair terrified, the other angry.

'Right through?' he said. 'You mean, here?'

He pointed down.

'That's right, boss.'

Gingerly he stepped forward on to the solid floor, rocked gently from heel to toe, and finally jumped a foot in the air and crashed down with all his weight.

This experiment had an unexpected bonus. The fat woman shrieked out loud and swooned away, releasing her grip on the ribbing.

'You insensitive bastard!' exploded the young woman in a new extreme of fury which still did not touch her beauty.

Chislenko stepped back and said to the medics. 'For God's sake, get that lump out of there!'

Once they had dragged her into the corridor, the medics started ministering to the recumbent woman and the firemen started examining the lift. The younger woman looked as if she was ready for another explosion, but Chislenko had had enough.

'Papers,' he said, snapping his fingers.

She glowered at him, but said nothing as she opened her bag. The ritual of examining identity papers has assumed an almost sacramental status in Moscow and employees of the state know better than to risk any official blasphemy.

'You are Natasha Lovchev?'

'Yes.'

'Employed in the Organization of Machinery Supply, Maintenance, and Service?'

'Yes.'

'As a secretary/typist in the Engineering Resources Division?'

'As personal assistant to the Deputy Chief Costings Officer,' she retorted indignantly.

Chislenko was amused but didn't show it.

'It says secretary/typist here,' he said.

'Yes, I know. It was a recent promotion and I haven't had my papers changed yet.'

Chislenko allowed himself to look dubious and the girl continued, 'I have an office of my own; at least, I only share it with one other assistant. It's on the eighth floor. I was showing it to my mother here before we went to lunch.'

'Ah. This lady is your mother,' said Chislenko, looking down at the fat woman who now opened her eyes and looked around in bewilderment.

'Yes. She's here in Moscow visiting me. Please, Comrade Inspector, may I now take her home? You can see she is not well. All this has been far too much for her.'

These were the first truly unaggressive words she had addressed to Chislenko and he was touched by her filial concern, and also by her big brown eyes which were as lovely in appeal as they were in anger. But there was still work to be done.

'All *what* has been too much for her?' he inquired. 'Perhaps you could give me your version of what happened here, Miss Lovchev.'

'You want to hear it again?'

Chislenko's heart stuttered.

'Again?'

'Yes. I heard Josif here tell you all about it just now.'

She gestured at the liftman, who nodded at the mention of his name and said, 'There you are, boss,' defiantly.

'You mean you confirm what this . . . fellow has just told me? About a passenger being pushed into the lift and going through the floor?'

'Yes, of course I do. I don't pretend to understand it, but that's what happened,' she retorted, defiant in her turn.

'Then please tell me this, Comrade Personal Assistant to the Deputy Chief Costings Officer,' said Chislenko sarcastically. 'Where is this man? There's no one down the lift-shaft because we've looked there. So where is he? Come to that, where's the man who pushed him? And didn't you say there was another man in the lift, Muntjan?'

The lift man nodded.

'Did you see him too, Miss Lovchev?'

'Of course I did,' snapped the girl.

'Then where is *he*, too?' demanded Chislenko. 'Tell me that, if you can!'

He paused to enjoy his rhetorical triumph, but it was spoilt almost instantly by Muntjan who said, 'He's there, boss. That's him,' and pointed over Chislenko's shoulder.

The Inspector turned. Three men had appeared at the head of the stairway next to the lift-shaft. Two of them were uniformed policemen flanking the third, a man of middle age, bespectacled, carrying a briefcase and slightly out of breath after his ascent.

'Yes, that's him,' said Natasha. 'Now can I get my mother out of here?'

She knelt beside the fat woman, angrily waving the medics

12

aside. The newly arrived trio came to a halt. Chislenko had a sense of things slipping out of control. There were far too many spectators for a start. Doors which had been opened just a crack were now wide ajar as those behind them grew more confident. He had no doubt the stairs were jammed with inquisitive auditors from other floors. He really ought to clear everyone away and start from scratch, in an empty room, seeing individual witnesses one at a time. But in some odd illogical way he felt this would make him lose face in the eyes of the young woman.

'Report,' he barked at the policemen.

'We caught this one trying to escape out of the back of the building, sir,' replied one of the officers.

'Rubbish,' said their prisoner calmly.

'Speak when you're spoken to!' snarled the policeman.

'Certainly. You've just spoken to me, haven't you? I said, rubbish. Far from trying to escape, I merely walked at a normal pace out of a normal exit from this building. And far from being caught, I stopped the moment you addressed me and returned here at your request without demur.'

'Identification,' rapped Chislenko.

The man produced a set of papers which identified him as Alexei Rudakov, a mechanical engineer currently working at a high level in the planning department of the new Dnieper dam project. Also he was a Party member. Chislenko's eyes drifted from the papers to Rudakov's person, to the good cloth of his well-cut suit, to the soft leather of his shoes.

'Thank you, Comrade,' he said courteously, returning the papers. 'Would you mind answering a few questions?'

'If I must,' sighed the man.

'First of all, can you confirm that you were travelling in this lift when the . . . er . . . incident occurred.'

'I can,' said Rudakov.

'I see,' said Chislenko. 'Now I find that very curious, Comrade.'

'It *was* curious,' said the man.

'No. I mean I find it curious that a man of your standing, a Party member too, should have left the scene of an . . . er

13

... incident so rapidly when you must have known it was your duty to stay.'

'I heard the operator here ringing the emergency services,' offered the engineer in what was clearly only a token excuse.

'Nevertheless.'

'Rudakov sighed again.

'I'm sorry. Yes, of course, you're quite right. I should have stayed. But for what, Comrade Inspector? You put your finger on it just now. I *am* a man of standing and reputation, both in my profession and in the Party too. That's just what I was thinking of when I left. Let me explain. In my job, I deal with facts and figures, with exact calculation, with solid materials. The Party too, as you well know, is based upon figures and facts, on historic inevitability and economic practicality.'

He paused to permit Chislenko and most of the others present to nod their grave agreement. The kneeling girl, however, permitted her filial feelings to overcome her patriotism to the point of rolling her lovely eyes to the ceiling in exasperation at all this male verbiage, and one of the firemen, who had finished their examination of the lift and lit cigarettes, broke wind gently.

Chislenko suspected this was an offence, but he already felt ridiculous enough without pursuing a charge of 'farting against the State'.

'So, Comrade Inspector,' resumed the engineer, 'you can see how unattractive I found the idea of having to wait here and bear testimony to something as bizarre as this ... incident. Duty is not the only imperative. Suddenly I found myself walking down the stairs. I'm sorry, but I'm sure that an intelligent man like yourself will sympathize and understand.'

Oh yes! thought Chislenko. You're so bloody right, Comrade!

He looked with loathing at the escorting policemen. If only they hadn't been so fucking conscientious! This whole ridiculous business was beginning to smell like bad news for clever Inspector Chislenko's bright future. Up to this point, things had remained manageable; just! The testimony of an

14

hysterical woman (in official terms, Mrs Lovchev's hysteria was abundant enough to cover her daughter also), and of a drunken and superstitious peasant (in official terms, this description fitted anyone in an unskilled job whose testimony did not suit the police), could have been easily disposed of. But how the hell was he to deal with this pillar of respectability? One thing was certain; his previous instinct had been right. He must get away from all these inquisitive eyes and ears.

He said carefully, 'It is, of course, every citizen's duty to act in the best interests of the State, as he sees them, Comrade. Let us see if we can find somewhere quiet to take your statement.'

'No!' exclaimed the girl, Natasha, beautifully angry once again. 'Let him tell what he saw here, in front of everyone like the rest of us!'

There was a murmur of agreement the whole length of the corridor, stilled as Chislenko glared angrily around. Who the hell did these people think they were dealing with?

But before he could let them know quite clearly who was in charge here, Rudakov cut the ground from under his feet by saying, 'The young lady may be right, Comrade Inspector. I wished to remain silent and uninvolved, but your efficiency has prevented that. Now that you've shown me my duty, the least I can do is to tell you simply and without prevarication what has taken place. So here goes.'

It was disastrous. He confirmed in precise unemotional tones every detail of what the others had said.

Chislenko let out a deep sigh. There was only one thing left to do, pass the buck upwards and hope to be agile enough to dodge out of the way when as usual it came bouncing straight back down.

2

There had been two days of silence from the Procurator's office and Chislenko was beginning to hope that his initial report had been allowed to sink to the bed of that ocean of paper which washed around the basement of Petrovka, the Moscow Headquarters of the MVD.

Unfortunately he himself did not dare let things lie. Official procedure required the making of follow-up reports, each one of which increased the risk of drawing unwelcome attention. It was necessary, for example, to visit Mrs Lovchev to get her version of events once she had recovered sufficiently to speak. He found her clearly enjoying the role of convalescent, sitting up in bed in her daughter's apartment, eating cream chocolates. The apartment was tiny and Natasha had given up the bed for the duration of her mother's visit and moved on to a narrow, age-corrugated sofa. Mrs Lovchev's version of events differed from the others only in style. It was colourful, melodramatic and drawn out beyond belief and tolerance by family reminiscence, folklore analogy, and in-depth analysis of the lady's own emotions at each stage of the narrative.

The positive side of the interview was that it gave him a chance to get to know Natasha Lovchev rather better. He'd checked her records in the State Employees computer, of course, and found nothing against her. It had been necessary to mention in his report that she had had no official authority for inviting her mother to see her new office, but he pointed to this as evidence of the extremely lax security at the Gorodok Building rather than dereliction of duty on Natasha's part. After all, pride in one's work and love of one's mother were both figured in the official list of virtues published by the Committee on Internal Morale and Propaganda each year.

Natasha was present during his interview of Mrs Lovchev. From time to time she interrupted, but Chislenko didn't mind, especially as her interruptions, which were at first defensive of her mother, became increasingly more embarrassed and irritated as that good lady rambled on and on, till finally she rescued the Inspector from the little bedroom and led him out in to the equally small living-room, closing the door firmly behind her.

She didn't apologize for her mother and Chislenko admired her for that. Children should never apologize for their parents. But her offer of a cup of tea was clearly compensatory and conciliatory. And as they drank and talked, Chislenko found himself aware with his male receptors of what he had already noted with his policeman's eye, that Natasha was very pretty indeed. Not only pretty, but pleasant, interesting and bright. Chislenko felt able to relax a little, and enjoy the tea and her company and a brief moment off duty.

'What do you really make of all this?' he asked her. 'Now you've had time to think about it. Off the record.'

'Off the record?' She regarded him with an open scepticism and then shrugged and wiped it off with a stunning smile. 'Well, off the record, it has to be a ghost, don't you think?'

'A ghost?' he echoed. He must have sounded disappointed.

'All right, I'm sorry,' she said. 'I know that's what my mother's been going on about for the past half-hour and you hoped for something more original from me. Perhaps I could dress it up for you. *A para-psychological phenomenon*, how would that sound in your report? Or perhaps you prefer a *delusive projection produced by localized mass-hysteria, perhaps relatable to repressed claustrophobia triggered by the lift.*'

'Now I like the sound of that,' he said, only half joking. So far, until his reports were complete, he had avoided anything like a conclusion, opinion or recommendation. This kind of phraseology sounded just the ticket.

Natasha snorted derisively.

'Use any jargon you like,' she said firmly. 'In my book, any human figure which passes clean through a material barrier is a ghost. Go back in records and look for an accident happening in that lift-shaft. The past is where your investigation should be, if you've got the nerve.'

She was mocking him, but the gibe struck home. The idea had actually occurred to him, but he had dismissed it at once, and not merely because it was absurd. No; an ambitious thirty-year-old inspector of police knew that his every move was scrutinized with great care, and he had no desire to find himself explaining that he was examining old records in order to test a ghost hypothesis!

He covered his discomfiture with a smile, and returning mockery for mockery, he said, 'Why the past? What's wrong with precognition? If you believe in ghosts, surely you believe in visions too? Perhaps this was an event which has yet to happen.'

'Oh no,' she said sombrely. 'It's happened.'

'How so sure?'

'The clothes,' she said.

'The clothes?' He cast his mind back to the witness statements. 'Yes, I recall, there was something about an old-fashioned suit. But, good lord, Moscow's full of old-fashioned suits! Who can afford a new-fashioned suit these days?'

The question was rhetorical since any attempt to answer it would almost certainly have involved a slander of the State.

She said, 'It was more than that. It was, well, a *new* old-fashioned suit, if you follow me. And he was wearing a celluloid collar too. Now, old-fashioned suits may be plentiful still, but you don't see many celluloid collars about, do you? And he had button-up shoes!'

'Now there's a thing!' said Chislenko. 'So what kind of dating would you put on this outfit?'

She pursed her lips thoughtfully. It would have been very easy to lean forward and kiss them but Chislenko was not letting himself relax *that* far. Not yet anyway; the thought popped up unexpectedly, surprisingly, but not unwelcomely.

''Thirties, late 'twenties, somewhere around then, I'd say,' she said.

He laughed out loud and said, 'Now that *is* interesting. When you go to work in the morning do you ever look up?'

'Look up?' She was puzzled.

'Yes, *up*.' He raised his head and his eyes till he was looking at the angle where the yellowing paper on the walls met the flaking whitewash on the ceiling. 'Or is it head down, eyes half closed, drift along till you reach your desk?'

18

'I'm very alert in the mornings,' she retorted spiritedly.

'I'm glad to hear it. Then you must have noticed that huge concrete slab above the main door. The one inscribed. *The Gorodok Building. Dedicated to the Greater Glory of the USSR and opened by Georgiy Malenkov in June 1949.*

'Nineteen forty-nine,' she echoed. 'Oh. I see. *Nineteen forty-nine.*'

'Yes. Part of our great post-war reconstruction programme,' he said, rising. 'A little late for celluloid collars and button-up shoes, don't you think? Thank you for the tea, Comrade Natasha. I'm sure we'll meet again, I'll need to keep in touch with you till this strange business is settled.'

He offered his hand formally. She shook it and said, 'And I'll be very interested to learn how you manage to settle it, Comrade Inspector.'

He smiled and squeezed her hand. She returned neither squeeze nor smile. He didn't blame her. Only a fool would allow a couple of minutes' friendly chat to break down the barriers of caution and suspicion which always exist between public and police.

And Natasha, he guessed, was no fool.

Checking Josif Muntjan, the liftman, wasn't half as pleasant but just as easy. The State makes no social distinction in its records. Menial or master, once you come into its employ, you get the womb-to-tomb X-ray treatment.

Muntjan came out pretty clear. There was a record of minor offences, all involving drunkenness, but none recent, and nothing while on duty. Indeed, the supervisor, who didn't look like a man in whom the milk of compassion flowed very freely, spoke surprisingly well of him. He expressed surprise rather than outrage at the mention of the hip-flask.

'It's not an offence to own one, is it?' he said. 'No need to report it, though, is there? I'll see he doesn't bring it to work with him again. He'll take notice of what I say. Jobs aren't easy to come by when you're old and unqualified.'

Chislenko nodded; the man's sympathetic understanding touched him. He clearly knew that if Muntjan were tossed

19

out of his job, he probably wouldn't stop falling till he landed in one of those shacks on the outer ring road where the Moscow down-and-outs eked out their perilous existence. Or rather, non-existence, for of course in the perfect socialist state, such degraded beings were impossible.

Crime too was impossible. Or would be eventually. The statistics showed progress. Chislenko defended the statistics as fervently as the next man, knowing that if he didn't, the next man would probably report the deficiency. But falling though the crime rate might be, there was still a lot of it about and Chislenko resented the amount of time he had to spend on this unrewarding and absurd business at the Gorodok Building. The only profit in it was that it had brought him into contact with Natasha Lovchev, but that relationship was still as uncertain in its outcome as a new Five-Year-Plan.

He turned his attention from Muntjan to Alexei Rudakov. Here the computer confirmed his own first estimate. Rudakov was a man to be treated with respect. Only his initial foolishness in leaving the scene of the incident made him vulnerable to hard questioning. The trouble was, the harder the questioning, the firmer his story.

Finally Rudakov said, 'Comrade Inspector, clearly you want to hear this story as little as I want to tell it. In a few days I shall be returning to the Dnieper Dam. Rest assured, I shall not be making a fool of myself by repeating this anecdote there. In other words, if you stop asking questions, I'll stop giving answers!'

It made good sense to Chislenko. The best way to deal with this absurd business was to ignore it. He only hoped his superiors would agree, and he gave them their cue by writing a final dismissive report, this time risking a conclusion couched in the kind of quasi-psychological jargon Natasha had mockingly used.

Then he crossed his fingers, and waited, and even said a little prayer.

The authorities were right to ban religion.

The following day he was summoned to Procurator Kozlov's office.

3

Of all the deputy procurators working in the Procurator General's office, Kozlov was the one most feared. Unambiguously ambitious, he took lack of progress in any case under his charge as an act of personal sabotage by the Inspector involved, and his own advancement was littered with the wrecks of others' careers. His legal career had begun in the attorney's department of the Red Army, and on formal official occasions Kozlov always wore the uniform of colonel to which his military service entitled him.

He was wearing the uniform today. It was not a good sign.

So preoccupied was Chislenko by this sartorial ill-omen that at first he did not notice the other person in the room. It was only when he came to attention and focused his eyes over the seated Procurator's head that he took in the unexpected presence. Standing by the window looking down into Petrovka Street was an old gentleman (the term rose unbidden into Chislenko's mind), with a crown of snow white hair, a goatee beard of the same hue, cheeks of fresh rose, eyes of bright blue, and an expression of almost saintly benevolence.

Procurator Kozlov did not look benevolent.

'Inspector Chislenko,' he rasped. 'This business of the Gorodok Building. These are your *final* reports?'

He stabbed at the file on his desk.

'Yes, sir,' said Chislenko.

'And you recommend that no further inquiry is needed?'

'I can see no line of further inquiry that might be useful,' said Chislenko carefully.

The Procurator sneered.

'No line which might be fruitful if pursued in the indolent, incompetent and altogether deplorable manner in which you've managed this business so far, you mean!'

The unexpected violence of the attack provoked Chislenko to the indiscretion of a protest.

'Sir!' he cried. 'I resent your implications . . .'

'You *resent*!' bellowed Kozlov, his smart uniform stretching to the utmost tolerance of its stitching.

'Comrades,' said the old man gently.

The speed with which the Procurator deflated made Chislenko look at the old gentleman with new eyes. Wasn't there something familiar about those features?

'Let us not be unfair to the Inspector,' he continued with a friendly smile. 'He has done almost as much as could be expected, and his desire to let this matter die quietly is altogether laudable. However . . .'

He paused, came to the desk, picked up the file and sifted apparently aimlessly through its sheets.

'Do you know who I am, Inspector?' he said finally.

Desperately Chislenko searched his memory while the old man smiled at him. Honesty at last seemed the best policy.

'My apologies, Comrade,' he said. 'There is something familiar about you but I cannot quite find the name to go with it.'

To his surprise the old man looked pleased.

'Good, good,' he said, beaming. 'In my work, as in yours, not to be known is the best reputation a man can look for. I am Y.S.J. Serebrianikov.'

It was with difficulty that Chislenko concealed the shocked dismay of recognition. Of course! This was the legendary Yuri the Survivor, that shadowy figure who had started his career under Beria and survived his passing and that of Semichastny, Shelepin, and Andropov, in the process making that most dangerous of transitions from being a man who knows too much to live to being a man who knows too much to destroy. Now nearly eighty, he was officially designated Secretary to the Committee on Internal Morale and Propaganda, which sounded harmless enough, but this was not a harmless man. Either through flattery or blackmail, he always picked his protectors well and for many years now he had been under the ægis of the powerful Minister of Internal Affairs, Boris Bunin, which explained his presence but not his purpose in the MVD Headquarters. Bunin at 65 was young enough to have very large ambitions. Serebrianikov with his vast store of knowledge and his still

22

strong KGB connections must have been, and might be again, a tremendous help to him.

Chislenko bowed in his direction.

'It is an honour and privilege to meet you, Comrade Secretary,' he intoned.

'Thank you, Comrade Inspector,' replied the old man. 'Now in the matter of this trivial and absurd incident at the Gorodok Building, you are perhaps wondering what my interest is? Let me tell you. I am old now, and should (you are perhaps thinking) be spending my time in my dacha at Odessa, watching the seagulls. But some old horses miss their harness, as perhaps one day you will find, and the Praesidium—in their kindness and to satisfy an old man's whim—permit me to preserve the illusion at least of still serving the State.'

This was dreadful, thought Chislenko. No man could be so humourously self-deprecating except from a base of absolute power.

'What I do is sometimes watch and sometimes listen and sometimes read, but mainly just sniff the air to test the mood of the people. *Internal morale* is the fancy name they give it. I watch for straws in the wind, silly rumours, atavistic superstitions, anything which may if unchecked develop into a let or hindrance to the smooth and inevitable progress of the State.'

'But surely this silly business at the Gorodok Building could hardly do that!' burst out Chislenko, winning an angry glare from the Procurator, but an approving smile from Serebrianikov.

'Possibly not, in certain circumstances,' he said. 'Had, for instance, the initial response not been so attention-drawing. I do not hold you altogether responsible for the other services, but is it not true that your policemen sur-rounded the building and arrested everyone trying to leave?'

To explain that this had not been his idea at all was pointless; only results counted in socialist police work.

Instead Chislenko countered boldly, 'Had we not done that, Comrade Secretary, we should not have apprehended the witness, Rudakov.'

'True,' said the old man. 'But with hindsight, Comrade Inspector, do you not think it might have been better if you *hadn't* caught Comrade Rudakov?'

This precise echo of his own feelings was perhaps the most frightening thing Chislenko had heard so far.

'At least the Comrade Engineer appears a man of discretion,' continued Serebrianikov. 'Unlike Muntjan who is a drunken babbler, and the woman, Lovchev, who is a garrulous hysteric. Yet there might have been means to restrain these, too, if you had avoided conducting the initial interrogation in public!'

'In public! No!' protested Chislenko.

The old man took out a small notebook and held it before him, like a Bible aimed at a vampire.

'Would you like me to recite a list of those who *admit* to overhearing the whole of your initial interviews, Inspector.'

Chislenko remembered the firemen and the medics, the corridor draughty with open doors, the stairways crowded with curious ears.

I wish I were dead! he thought.

'I apologize most sincerely, Comrade,' he said formally. 'My only excuse is that I was misled into thinking a serious incident had taken place in a government building.'

'I should have thought that those circumstances would have urged greater discretion, not less,' murmured the old man.

'No, Comrade, what I meant was that, realizing I had been misled, perhaps even hoaxed, I momentarily lost sight of the need for discretion. Indeed, Comrade Serebrianikov, with permission, I would like to say that even now I am at a difficulty in understanding what all the fuss is about. I mean, if there *had* been an incident and there *had* been any need to hush things up, well, not to put too fine a point on it, I'd have made damn sure that everyone in the entire building, in hearing distance or not, knew that if they didn't keep mum, they'd have their balls twisted till they really had something to make a noise about!'

The transition from formal explanation to demotic indignation took Chislenko himself completely by surprise, and made the Procurator close his eyes in a spasm of mental pain.

Serebrianikov only smiled.

'You are young and impetuous and see your job in terms of fighting the perils of visible crime,' he said. 'That is good. But when you are as experienced and contemplative as age has made me—and the Procurator here—' this came as an afterthought—'you begin to appreciate the perils of the invisible. Let me give you a few facts, Inspector. It is now a week since this alleged incident. What will you find if you visit the Gorodok Building? I will tell you. So many of the personnel working there refuse to use the lift in question, which is the south lift, that long queues form outside the north lift. When a directive was issued ordering those in offices on the south side of the building to use the south lift, many of them started walking up the stairs in preference. Furthermore, this incident is still a popular topic of conversation not only in the Gorodok Building but in government offices throughout the city, and presumably in the homes and recreational centres of those concerned.'

Chislenko started to speak, but Serebrianikov held up his hand.

'You are, I imagine, going to dismiss this as mere gossip, trivial and short-lived. I cannot agree. Firstly, it panders to a particularly virulent strain of superstition in certain sections of our people who, despite all that education can do, still adhere to the religious delusions of the Tsarist tyranny. But there is worse. All families have their troubles and these can be dealt with if kept within the family. Our sage and serious Soviet press naturally do not concern themselves with such trivia, but several Western lie-sheets have somehow got wind of the story and have run frivolous and slanderous so-called news items. And only last night at a reception to celebrate the successful launching of our Uranus probe, I myself was asked by the French ambassador if it were true that ghosts were being allowed back into the Soviet Union. The man, of course, was drunk. Nevertheless . . .'

The pale blue eyes fixed on Chislenko. He felt accused and said helplessly, 'I'm sorry, Comrade Secretary . . .'

'Yes,' said Serebrianikov. 'By the way, Comrade Inspector, you're not related to Igor Chislenko who used to play on the wing for Dynamo, are you?'

'I'm afraid not,' said Chislenko.

'A pity. Still, no matter,' said the old man with sudden briskness. 'Procurator Kozlov, I think we understand each other, and I have every confidence this young officer can establish the truth of this matter, explode the lies, and bring the culprits to book. I shall expect his report by the end of the week, shall we say? Good day to you.'

With a benevolent nod, Serebrianikov left the room, his step remarkably light and spry for a man of his age.

The Procurator remained at his desk, his head bent, his eyes hooded. Chislenko remained in the posture of attention to which he had belatedly snapped as he realized the old man was leaving. After perhaps a minute, he said cautiously, 'Sir?'

Kozlov grunted.

'Sir, what is it precisely that the Comrade Secretary wishes us to do?'

The Procurator's head rose, the eyes opened. The voice when it came was almost gentle.

'He wishes *you* to scotch all those wild stories about what happened in the Gorodok Building,' said Kozlov. 'He wishes *you* to show that not only was there no supernatural manifestation, but also that the whole affair has been stage-managed by subversive elements, encouraged and supported by Western imperialist espionage machines operating out of certain embassies, with the ultimate aim of bringing the Soviet state into disrepute.'

'But that's absurd!' protested Chislenko. 'I don't mean the bit about Western imperialist espionage, of course. I'm sure the Comrade Secretary is quite right about that. But what's absurd is expecting me to set about disproving a ghost!'

Kozlov smiled.

'Do you wish me to inform Comrade Serebrianikov that his confidence has been misplaced?' he asked, almost genial at the prospect.

'No! No indeed, sir!'

'Then I suggest you get to work! And you would do well to remember one thing, Chislenko.'

'What's that, sir?'

'There are no ghosts in the Soviet Union!'

4

When a Soviet official is given what he regards as an absurd and impossible task, he knows there is only one way to perform it: *thoroughly!* Whatever conclusions he reaches, he must be certain at least that no matter how finely his researches are combed, there will be no nits for his superiors to pick at.

Chislenko saw his task as dividing into two clear areas. First: disprove the ghost. Second: find a culprit.

It might have seemed to a non-Soviet police mind that success in the latter would automatically accomplish the former. Chislenko knew better than this, because he knew what every Russian knows: that when it comes to finding culprits, the authorities have free choice out of about one hundred and thirty million candidates.

In this case, of course, there was a short-list of four. And here was another reason for delaying the hunt for the culprit.

Rudakov looked pretty invulnerable. Even his attempt to leave the scene of the incident pointed to his innocence. Unless he'd managed to get up someone important's nose, he looked safe.

Mrs Lovchev was even safer. Who the hell could accept a fat old widow from Yaroslavl as a subversive? In any case it would be impossible to implicate her without dragging in her daughter also.

Natasha was a pretty good bet, regarded objectively. Young upwardly mobile professionals were just the group that tended to throw up the dissenters, the dissidents, the moaners and groaners about human rights. Serebrianikov would probably be delighted to be given one to squeeze publicly to encourage the others.

Chislenko shuddered at the thought. It mustn't happen.

27

The KGB mustn't be allowed even a sniff of Natasha. If there had to be a culprit, he would do all he could to make it that poor bastard, Josif Muntjan.

Meanwhile, he had to accomplish task one and scotch the ghost. It was of course absurd that the State should need to disprove physically what it denied metaphysically, but there was no doubt that the best way of convincing that great mélange of logic and superstition which was the Russian mind that there'd been no ghost in the Gorodok Building was to prove that there was nothing for there to be a ghost of!

The strength and the weakness of Soviet bureaucracy is a reluctance to throw away even the smallest scrap of paper. The whole life of the Gorodok Building was there to be read in the archives of the Department of Public Works.

There were two ways of gaining access. One was to write an official request which would be dispatched to the office of Mikhail Osjanin, the National Controller of Public Works. The request, of course, would never get anywhere near the Controller himself, who had far more important things to do (mainly, according to rumour, brown-nosing top Praesidium people, in pursuit of his own high political ambitions). But one of his minions would doubtless consider it, ask for clarification, consider again, and finally accede. It might, if Kozlov countersigned the request, go through in only a week.

The other way was for Chislenko to check his own mental archives, which were in their way merely an extension of this same Soviet bureaucracy.

Yes, there it was, the half-remembered scrap of information. Six months earlier he had interrogated several men detained after a raid on a gay bar near Arbat Square. It was not a job Chislenko liked and he was easily persuaded that most of those he questioned had been in the bar accidentally or innocently. One of them had been called Karamzin and he had given his job as records clerk in the Department of Public Works.

Chislenko went to see him.

The frightened little clerk nearly fainted when he recognized the Inspector, but once he grasped the reason for his visit, his cooperation was boundless, and within minutes rather than days, Chislenko had at his disposal all he required.

The Gorodok Building had been projected in 1947, approved in 1948 and erected in 1949, under the guiding hand of a project director called M. Osjanin.

'This Osjanin, is that the same one who's your boss now?' inquired Chislenko of the hovering clerk.

'Ultimately, I suppose,' said Karamzin. 'In the same way as Comrade Bunin's your boss.'

Chislenko knew what he meant. The only time he ever saw the Minister for Internal Affairs was on television when he stood in the rank of hopefuls on the saluting platform in Red Square.

'I take your point,' he answered.

'Naughty boy,' said the clerk coquettishly, then a look of such consternation spread over his face that Chislenko almost laughed out loud.

'What about the building's maintenance history?' he asked.

'Over here.'

They spent an hour going over this. There was no reference to anything other than routine maintenance with regard to the lifts or indeed to any other part of the building.

He thanked the clerk formally, resisting a strong temptation to wink, and continued his researches among the records of the emergency services, principally fire and police. Again nothing. Finally he composed a memo to the Chief Records Officer, KGB, beginning it *further to an inquiry authorized by Y.S.J. Serebrianikov*, and sent it across to the Lubyanka, uncertain whether it would produce the slightest effect. To his surprise, a reply came back within the hour. KGB records had nothing on file about any sudden death or violent incident in the Gorodok Building during its whole existence.

The speed of the reply confirmed one thing. Comrade Serebrianikov was no old buffer put out to grass till he went to the Great Praesidium in the sky.

His task now finished so far as scotching the ghost was concerned, Chislenko drafted out the first part of his report. It was a job well done, but now the time had come when he could no longer delay beginning the second part of his investigation. The proof of Serebrianikov's continued authority in the KGB had been a salutary warning of just how delicately he would have to tread in keeping Natasha Lovchev safely out of the official eye. He made a vow to himself that, whoever else might suffer, he would at all costs protect Natasha.

An hour later he found himself arresting her.

It happened like this.

Deciding that it made sense to start his new inquiries with the Lovchevs (and also feeling a sudden longing to see that all-weather beauty again), he set out for the girl's tiny apartment. When he got there, he found Mrs Lovchev preparing to return to her home in a village close to Yaroslavl on the banks of the Volga, about two hundred and thirty kilometres away. She greeted him like an old friend and demanded to know if he'd found out anything more about 'the ghost', adding that she'd always thought Moscow folk a bit stand-offish, but since she'd started talking about her experience in the local shops, she'd found them just as friendly and curious as the folk back home.

'And she can't wait to get back home and tell them there that it's not all motor-cars and concrete here in the big city, can you, Mother?' laughed Natasha.

She looked and sounded delightful when she laughed, but Chislenko was too horrified at what had just been said to fully appreciate her beauty. Surely he'd warned them to keep quiet about the incident? Fears for the Lovchevs' and for his own future mingled to make him speak rather brusquely to the garrulous old woman. Natasha intervened sharply, the laughter dying in her eyes. He replied with equal sharpness in his best official tone, but this only provoked her to a slanderous if not downright subversive attack upon the MVD and all its works.

Jesus! thought Chislenko. If Procurator Kozlov could hear this . . .'

And then the dreadful thought occurred that perhaps worse people than Kozlov could be listening. What more likely than that Serebrianikov would have arranged for all those involved in the Gorodok Building affair to be bugged?

It was at that point that he arrested Natasha.

White-faced—with anger, he guessed, rather than fear—she let herself be thrust into the passenger seat of the little official car he was using. Normally 'pool' cars were as hard to come by as Western jeans, but in the last few days he'd found one permanently set aside for him, proof again of the strength of the Serebrianikov connection.

After he had been driving a few minutes Natasha burst out, 'Where are you taking me, Inspector? This isn't the way to Petrovka?'

'No, it's not. But we'll get there, never you fear,' said Chislenko grimly. 'I just want a quiet word with you first. I'm going to give you some advice and I think you'd be wise to take it.'

'What do you mean?' she said, looking at him with contempt. 'You scratch my back and I'll scratch yours, is that it?'

'What do *you* mean?' he demanded in his turn, growing angry.

'I've seen the way you look at me, Comrade Inspector,' she retorted. 'But I warn you, I'm not one of your little shop-girls to be frightened out of her pants by an MVD bully!'

The suggestion horrified Chislenko. Was this really how his admiration of Natasha's lively spirit and gentle beauty had come across—as unbridled lust?

Holding back his anger with difficulty, he said, 'Listen, Natasha, for your mother's sake if not for your own. This business at the Gorodok Building, it's not wise to talk about it. It's certainly been very unwise of your mother to go spreading tales of ghosts and ghouls all over Moscow, and it would be even unwiser for her to fill the Yaroslavl district with them too.'

'Unwise for her to tell what she saw?' said Natasha

indignantly. 'How can that be? And I saw it too, don't forget!'

'I'd try not to be so sure of that,' said Chislenko.

'What are you trying to tell me, Inspector?' demanded the girl. 'And why do I have to be driven all over Moscow to be told it?'

She still thinks I'm going to park the car somewhere quiet and invite her to take her skirt off, thought Chislenko.

He swung the wheel over and accelerated out of the suburbs back towards the centre of town.

'It would be wise to admit the possibility of error, Comrade Personal Assistant to the Deputy Costings Officer,' he said coldly. 'It would be wise for your mother to do the same.'

'Wise? Give me one good reason?'

He slowed down to negotiate the turn from Kirov Street into Dzerzhinsky Square.

'There's your best reason,' he said harshly, nodding towards the pavement alongside which loomed a massive, ugly building. In many ways this was the most famous edifice in the city, out-rivalling even St Basil's. Yet it appeared on no postcards, was described in no guide books.

This was the Lubyanka, headquarters of the KGB.

They drove on in silence.

After a while the girl said in a blank, emotionless voice, 'What now, Comrade Inspector?'

Chislenko said, 'I take you to Petrovka.'

'So I *am* under arrest?'

'I said so in your apartment, Comrade, and I'm not sure who may have been listening there. So I take you to Petrovka. I ask you some questions. The four most important ones will be: *One*, who was closest to the lift door when the lift stopped on the seventh floor? *Two*, what were you doing at that moment? *Three*, are you quite sure the man waiting for the lift did not merely change his mind and walk away? *Four*, who was it that made all the fuss and insisted on calling the emergency services?

'Your answers will be: *One*, Josif Muntjan. *Two*, I was engaged in close conversation with my mother. *Three*, it's possible as my mother and I didn't take much notice till the liftman started yelling. *Four*, Josif Muntjan.

'Do you follow me, Comrade?'

'Yes, Comrade Inspector,' she said meekly.

'Good. Then I will make out a report saying that the Comrade Personal Assistant after some initial misunderstanding was perfectly cooperative and I have every confidence she and her mother will behave as good citizens should. You meanwhile will make your way home and take your mother for a walk and persuade her to hold her tongue when she gets back to her village.'

'Don't I get a lift home?' she said with a flash of her old spirit.

Chislenko smiled.

'That would be out of character for the MVD,' he said. 'There might be others beside yourself looking for an ulterior motive.'

She flushed beautifully.

'I'm sorry I said that,' she said. 'It was a stupid thing to suggest.'

He glanced at her and said drily, 'No, it wasn't,' and she flushed again as they turned into the official car park at Petrovka.

That evening Chislenko visited Alexei Rudakov in his room at the Minsk Hotel on Gorky Street.

'You again,' said the engineer ungraciously. 'I was hoping for an early night. I leave first thing in the morning.'

'I know. That's why I've called now,' said Chislenko. 'I won't keep you long. I wouldn't be troubling you at all except that Comrade Secretary Serebrianikov of the Committee on Internal Morale and Propaganda has taken a personal interest in the case.'

He paused. Rudakov's eyebrows rose as he registered this information. Chislenko returned his gaze blankly.

He said, 'So if you could just confirm the following points. You were standing behind the liftman, Josif Muntjan, when the lift stopped on the seventh floor?'

'Yes.'

'Next to the two Lovchev women who were engaged in lively conversation?'

'That's right.'

'So their conversation would probably have distracted your attention just as Muntjan's body must have blocked your view?'

A slight smile touched Rudakov's lips.

'Quite right, Inspector,' he said.

Chislenko phrased his next question carefully, 'If the man waiting to enter the lift had stepped forward, then changed his mind and retreated, stumbling slightly, and if then Josif Muntjan had started shouting that there was an emergency, you would have accepted his assessment, would you not?'

Again the smile.

'As an expert in my field, I've always learned to accept the estimates of other experts, however menial,' the engineer replied.

'You mean, yes?'

'I mean, if that had been the case, yes.'

'And is it possible, in your judgment, Comrade, that that might have been the case?'

This was the key question.

'Of course one could say that anything is possible . . .'

'So this too is possible?' interrupted Chislenko.

'Yes . . .'

'Good,' said Chislenko. 'That's all, Comrade. If you would just sign this sheet, here. I think you'll find it's an accurate digest of our conversation.'

Rudakov hesitated. Chislenko admired the hesitation but was glad when it developed no further.

With an almost defiant flourish, the man signed.

'Thank you, Comrade,' said Chislenko, putting the paper into the copious file on the affair he was lugging round with him in his battered briefcase.

'Official business over?' said Rudakov. 'Would you like a drink before you go, Inspector?'

'That would be kind,' said Chislenko.

The engineer poured two glasses of excellent vodka.

'Here's to a successful conclusion to your inquiries, Inspector,' he said.

'I'll drink to that,' said Chislenko.

'So Comrade Serebrianikov is interested in this business,' Rudakov went on. 'A fine man.'

'Yes. You know the Comrade Secretary, do you?'

'Oh, not personally,' said Rudakov. 'I don't move in such exalted circles. But naturally I know of his high reputation. It's men like him that have made the State the magnificent, just and efficient machine we enjoy today.'

Chislenko smiled to himself. Rudakov had clearly decided not to take any risks. Being haughty with a mere copper was one thing, but now there was a hint of a KGB connection, the man was underlining his credentials.

'And what is Comrade Serebrianikov's assessment of the affair, may I ask?'

Chislenko looked at him quizzically across his glass.

'Comrade Serebrianikov does not believe there are any ghosts in the Soviet Union,' he murmured.

'No, of course not,' replied Rudakov, a trifle uneasily. Then, recovering, he added, 'It must have been an odd case for you to work on, Inspector.'

'Pretty routine, Comrade,' said Chislenko.

'Ghost-hunting is routine?'

'I thought we'd agreed there are no ghosts,' said Chislenko menacingly. He was rather enjoying this.

'Yes, of course, I didn't mean . . .'

Chislenko tired of the game quickly and said, 'But it *was* routine. Even if there had been the possibility of a ghost, which there couldn't be, of course, there'd have had to be someone whose ghost it might have been, which there wasn't. I checked back all the way to nineteen forty-nine. That's where the routine comes in, Comrade. We even check out the impossible.'

'Why 1949?' said Rudakov.

'That's when the Gorodok Building was completed,' said Chislenko, putting down his glass.

'Really? I'd have said . . . but no, it hardly matters. Another drink before you go?'

'No, thanks,' said Chislenko, recognizing the tone of dismissal. But he also recognized the tone of something unsaid and his natural curiosity made him add, 'What doesn't matter, Comrade.'

'Sorry?'

'You seemed surprised at something about the date. Nineteen forty-nine is what the records say.'

'And no doubt they're right. The building itself certainly belongs to that post-war period, but it just occurred to me now, while you were speaking, that . . . well, I dabbled in many branches of mechanical engineering before I got on to power stations. I was involved in various kinds of building projects, domestic and commercial, and I'd have said that the lift in the Gorodok Building predated nineteen forty-nine by quite a bit. German manufacture too, at a guess, though I'd need to see the actual machinery to be certain of that.'

'You're sure of this, Comrade?' said Chislenko.

Rudakov laughed and said mockingly, 'In this affair it seems I must wait for you to tell me what I'm sure of, Inspector. So, no, I'm not sure of anything except that I must get on with packing. Good night to you.'

'Good night, Comrade,' said Chislenko.

Slowly he made his way back to the high-ceilinged room in the old apartment house which was his home. Here he had another glass of vodka, much cheaper but also much larger. It would have been nice to slip into bed with nothing more troublesome than a few erotic fantasies about Natasha filling his mind. But to a good policeman, there are imperatives stronger even than sex. Unsatisfied lust can be dealt with either by a warm hand or a cold shower, but unsatisfied curiosity is not so simple to remove.

In addition, if it turned out he'd missed something, however unimportant, it could mean a black mark against his name.

It was a long time before he got to sleep.

5

When the gay little records clerk arrived at the Public Works building the following morning, he was alarmed to see a figure lurking in the side entrance he used. He was not at once reassured when he recognized the waiting man as Inspector Chislenko.

'The Gorodok records,' snapped the weary-looking Inspector. 'Hurry.'

Delighted that it was his files not his friends that interested the Inspector, Karamzin scurried to obey.

The records were as meticulous as one would have expected in a project supervised by a man who had since risen to the imposing heights of public responsibility that Mikhail Osjanin now occupied. Everything was listed and costed, down to the last pane of glass and concrete block. The lifts in the building had been manufactured and supplied in 1948 by Machine Plant No. 242 situated in Serpukhov, sixty miles south of the capital.

So much for Comrade Engineer Rudakov! thought Chislenko with some relief as he noted the details. Even experts could be wrong.

Now all that remained for this particular expert to do was close the trap on poor old Muntjan. Not that such a job required much expertise, only authority and the will. Chislenko found he had little stomach for the job and the only sop to his conscience was that if he didn't do it, someone else with far less concern for the liftman's well-being would. At least he, Chislenko, could do his best to see that the case against Muntjan was couched in terms of alcoholic delusion rather than political subversion. Surely even Serebrianikov would agree that it was absurd to present a broken-down old man like Josif as an agent in the employ of the West?

When Chislenko arrived at the Gorodok Building, he discovered that Muntjan was making his task easy. The liftman had taken a few days' sick leave immediately after the incident, only returning the previous day. There was still a significant boycott of the south lift by many workers, but those who were using it soon had cause for a different complaint, namely that Muntjan refused to let the lift stop on the seventh floor.

Finally the staff supervisor was informed. He had given Muntjan a public dressing-down and ordered him to answer every summons to every floor.

Josif obeyed. But so nervously debilitating did he find the experience of stopping at the seventh floor that he needed to fortify himself from his hip-flask every time it happened. By the end of the day, the supervisor was once more called to deal with the situation.

'I sent him off straightaway, no messing,' said the man sternly.

'You mean, you sacked him?' said Chislenko.

'Well, not exactly sacked,' said the supervisor, his sternness dissolving slightly. 'To tell the truth, Inspector, I'm a bit sorry for the old fellow. He's getting on and this business has been a real shake-up for him.'

The supervisor's attitude puzzled Chislenko a little. He didn't look like a naturally kind man, and the Inspector now recalled being surprised by his compassionate attitude to Josif at their first encounter. He felt he might have missed something and there was enough residual irritation from the business of the dating of the lift to make him react strongly.

'Listen,' he growled, putting on his KGB expression. 'Isn't it time you told me the truth? It'll sound a lot better in my report if it comes straight from you. So give!'

The supervisor glowered at him angrily for a moment, then suddenly he seemed to exhale all his resentment in a long, deep sigh.

'It's my wife,' he said.

'Yes?'

'Muntjan's her uncle, well, sort of half-uncle, really. But she's got an overdeveloped sense of family responsibility. I tell her I've got my responsibilities too. I told her when I got Josif the job that if he didn't do it properly, he was out. I meant it, believe me, Inspector.'

'And what did your wife say to that?'

'She said she understood. I was quite right. I had my job to think of. Only . . .'

'Only?'

'She said if Uncle Josif got the sack, he'd never find another job, and he'd not be able to afford to keep his room, so he'd have to come and live with us.'

That must have sounded like the ultimate threat! thought Chislenko. He looked with pity at the unhappy supervisor. The man had more cause for worry than he knew. He'd just offered himself as another sacrificial victim to Serebrianikov. The only difficulty in presenting Muntjan as an advanced alcoholic in the grip of the d.t.s had been in explaining how he kept his job. Now all was clear. The poor bastard was in the trap beyond all hope of escape.

But why should he be feeling this degree of sympathy? Chislenko asked himself. The case he was building up against Muntjan was surely not only the best, but also the only possible explanation of the incident! Natasha was mistaken; her mother was mistaken; Rudakov was mistaken. They must all have been mistaken, mustn't they?

Of course they were, he told himself angrily. He was absolutely certain of it. All that remained now was to go and arrest Muntjan.

He said to the supervisor, 'I'd like to examine the south lift. Can you arrange for it to be stopped and put out of use for half an hour?'

'Yes, of course, Comrade Inspector. But couldn't you examine it just by riding in it?'

'I want to look in the shaft, and at the winding machinery too,' said Chislenko.

The supervisor clearly thought he was mad but was wise enough to hold his peace. Chislenko too began to think he was mad as he got covered with dust in the shaft and stained with oil in the machine cabin. What he was looking for, he admitted to himself in that tiny chamber of his mind he reserved for his most lunatic admissions, was some mark of manufacture, preferably one which would indicate that the lift had been produced in Machine Plant No. 242 in Serpukhov in the year 1948.

For a long time he found nothing. After a while this began to worry him. There were places where perhaps a name or a number might have been expected to be stamped, but when the dust and oil were rubbed away, only a smooth surface appeared; but something about the smoothness was not quite right. Was it his imagination or had something been filed out of existence here? He could not tell. He must be mad, playing about up here when he should be arresting poor Muntjan, the drunken bum who'd started all this brouhaha!

Then he found it, screwed with Germanic thoroughness to the underside of the brake-lock housing, a small plate packed so tight with a cement-like mix of dust and oil that he had to chip at it with his pocket knife before the letters slowly emerged.

Elsheimer GmbH Chemnitz, and a reference code, *FST 1639–2*.

Carefully he copied them down in his notebook before triumphantly emerging from the machine cabin at the top of the shaft. The supervisor looked at him in horror.

'Would the Comrade Inspector care to wash his hands?' he asked carefully.

Chislenko examined his hands. If the rest of him was as filthy as they were, then it was a hot bath and a dry-cleaner's he really needed.

'Thank you,' he said.

The supervisor started the lift once more and they descended towards his quarters in the basement. On the way down, the lift stopped at the seventh floor and Chislenko felt a dryness in his mouth as the door opened. But his apprehension turned to surprise when he saw it was Natasha standing there.

'Good lord,' she said. 'What on earth have you been doing? You're filthy.'

'More to the point, what are you doing?' he demanded. 'You don't work on this floor. You're on the eighth.'

She flushed.

'That's right. But I had to go down to ground floor for something and the lift was marked *Out of Order*. Well, to tell the truth, I've tended to use the stairs anyway rather than get in by myself. But I heard it start moving as I reached the seventh landing and I thought, this is stupid, I'm not a child to be frightened of ghosts in broad daylight, so I came along here and pressed the button.'

She spoke defiantly as if challenging him to laugh at her. When she looked defiant, she still looked beautiful. It was perhaps at this moment that Chislenko realized he was in love with her.

He said, 'Well, get in if you're getting in. We can't hang around here all day.'

Gingerly she stepped inside. When the lift stopped at the ground floor, he said formally, 'I may have some more questions to put to you later, Comrade Lovchev. I would like you to be available for interview this evening.'

'This evening is not possible, Comrade Inspector, but at the moment, I have no plans for tomorrow evening,' she said pertly. 'So try me then. Who knows? You may be lucky!'

The supervisor shook his head as she walked away.

'Give 'em a bit of status and they think they're boss of the universe, these young ones, eh, Inspector? What that one needs is a randy man to satisfy, and half a dozen kids to bring up, what say you?'

'What I say is, why don't you keep your stupid mouth shut,' said Chislenko.

Half an hour later, relatively clean, he was back at Petrovka. There was a bit of a setback when he could find no reference to a German town called Chemnitz in his up-to-date World Gazetteer. That know-it-all Sub-Inspector Kedin, solved the mystery.

'Try Karl-Marx-Stadt,' he said. 'The name was changed in 1953.'

So at least the town was in the Democratic Republic which would make cooperation easier once the initial contact had been made. That was where the real difficulty lay. An Inspector of the MVD might just get away with mailing an official request for help to the police force of a friendly country, but telephoning, which was what Chislenko wanted to do, was impossible without higher approval.

He asked to see Procurator Kozlov.

41

'I don't see any point in it,' said Kozlov after he'd listened to Chislenko's report. 'Muntjan is obviously at the centre of this business. I'm not certain Comrade Serebrianikov is going to be happy that it's all down to drunkenness. He seemed certain there must be a Western connection somewhere, but I've no doubt he can track that down for himself once he has Muntjan. This supervisor seems a likely contact to me. Check him out thoroughly, Chislenko.'

Chislenko shuddered. Poor old Uncle Josif! Poor old nephew supervisor!

Kozlov continued, 'As for this lift business, I don't see what difference it makes. There's probably some simple explanation. Perhaps it's you that's got things muddled, Inspector. Don't think I've forgotten that it was your muddle that got us into this in the first place!'

'Yes, sir,' said Chislenko, admitting defeat. 'I'll put my report in writing, then.'

'I'd appreciate that,' said Kozlov sarcastically. 'And stick to the relevant facts, will you? Nothing about lifts and Germany, understand?'

Chislenko left and returned to the Inspectors' office. Half an hour later he was summoned back to Kozlov's room. The Procurator was writing at his desk and did not once look up as he spoke.

'I've been thinking, Chislenko. I don't like loose ends. You have permission to contact the authorities in Karl-Marx-Stadt in pursuance of your inquiries. Thoroughness in small things, that's what makes the State great, you'd do well to remember that. Dismiss!'

Chislenko dismissed. It was clear to him that the change of heart had not been Kozlov's. He must have reported to Serebrianikov and that terrible white-haired old man had given the go-ahead.

Suddenly Chislenko wished he'd kept his mouth shut. A man should be careful in his choice of masters. True, at the head of the MVD was Minister of Internal Affairs Bunin who was known to be Serebrianikov's protector. But it would be a comfort to know for certain that the Comrade Minister knew for certain what the Comrade Secretary was up to.

On the other hand, that burning curiosity to learn the causes of things which had taken him into the police force in the first place demanded to be satisfied in this matter.

He sent for Sub-Inspector Kedin who knew everything.

'I bet you speak good German, Kedin?'

'Pretty fair.'

'I thought so. Sit here with me. I may need you.'

It took three phone calls spread out over the rest of the day to get things under way.

The first established contact and brought the information that there was no machine manufacturing company called Elsheimer currently operative in Karl-Marx-Stadt.

The second confirmed that yes, there had been a firm called Elsheimer, founded in 1885 and foundering in 1932.

The third revealed that rather than simply foundering in 1932, Elsheimer had been taken over by Luderitz GmbH, a subsidiary of Krupp, and thereafter had diverted to the manufacture of armaments. This in its turn had been taken over first by the Russians in 1945, and subsequently by the Democratic Republic itself, and still survived in a much developed and expanded form as State Machine Factory (Agriculture, Heavy) Number 364 AK.

With not much hope, Chislenko gave the details of the lift. They sounded slight, the story sounded feeble, the task impossible. He could almost hear the incredulity at the other end of the line as Kedin translated his request that the Karl-Marx-Stadt Polizei should check to see if any old records of the Elsheimer company remained and if they contained any reference to the lift in question.

Such a request to a Russian official would, he knew, have been tossed into a pending tray; a couple of months later, after two or three reminders, a token search might have been made, and the negative response sent through the slowest of official channels some few weeks later.

German efficiency—plus the desire to impress these Russian peasants with that efficiency—might speed things up in this case. But after all this time, it didn't really seem likely the response could be anything but negative.

Early the following morning the phone rang. This time he did not need Kedin. The East Germans—clever bastards—had got their own Russian speaker who told him in a studiedly matter-of-fact voice that the records of the Elsheimer company had been found intact and that the lift in question was one of a pair manufactured in the spring of 1914 and shipped to St Petersburg (as it was then), shortly to be renamed, first, Petrograd (because after 1914 St Petersburg sounded too Germanic), and finally, in 1924, Leningrad. The order had been placed in 1913 by a St Petersburg construction company and the lifts were intended for a new hotel in the city to be called (the interpreter allowed himself the ghost of a chuckle) the Imperial.

These details would be confirmed in writing within the next few days, with photocopies of the relevant record sheets. If the Comrade Inspector required any further assistance, he should not hesitate to ask.

Chislenko smiled as he recognized the triumphant insolence behind the measured correctness.

'We are most grateful,' was all his reply. He didn't grudge them their triumph. But once again he found himself wondering about the wisdom of the course he had set himself on.

But to turn back now was impossible. This information was official. When the written confirmation arrived, it would be on the record. He had to proceed, even though now he was beginning to guess where his progress would take him.

He picked up the telephone and asked to be put through to MVD Headquarters in Leningrad. The traditional rivalries between the two cities—Muscovites regarding natives of Leningrad as peasants and being regarded in their turn as barbarians—unfortunately extend even into official circles. Chislenko did not want to be messed about, so he cut through any potential delaying tactics with the sharpest instrument at his disposal.

'This is an inquiry authorized by Comrade Secretary Serebrianikov of the Committee on Internal Morale and Propaganda,' he declared baldly. Then after a pause to let the implications sink in, he made his request.

The promised return call came midway through the morning.

The Hotel Imperial no longer existed. Indeed it hadn't really existed as the Hotel Imperial at all. Planned for completion at the end of 1914, its construction had been suspended at the outbreak of the war and it wasn't actually finished till 1922. It occurred to someone shortly afterwards that Imperial was perhaps not the most suitable name for this revolutionary city's most modern hotel, and the name was changed about the same time as Petrograd became Leningrad. It must have seemed a name for all time when they decided to christen it after the Father of the great Red Army and re-named it the L.D. Trotsky Building. The name survived Trotsky's expulsion from the Party in 1927—rehabilitation perhaps still seeming possible—but not his exile two years later, when it was rechristened, uncontroversially, the May Day Centre. During all these vicissitudes it was used as an administration and accommodation centre for visiting officials and delegations from all over the country. Moscow might be the official capital, but Leningrad was, and would always be, the historical centre of the great revolutionary movement . . .

Chislenko interrupted the threatened commercial brusquely. 'And what happened to the place, whatever you call it, in the end?'

'It was hit by German shells in 1943,' came the reply in a rather hurt tone of voice.

'Hit? You mean destroyed?'

'It was rendered unusable, that's what the records say.'

'And it was never reconstructed as such.'

'No, Comrade. That area of the city, like many others, was cleared and totally rebuilt in the great post-war reconstruction programme.'

'Is there in the records a list of those who were in charge of that particular site in the clearance stage of the reconstruction programme?'

For the first time the MVD man in Leningrad let a hint of impatience sound in his voice.

'We've no list as such, but I suppose I could go through the minutes and progress reports and see which names turn up.'

'That would be kind. The Comrade Secretary would, I am sure, appreciate that,' said Chislenko.

The names were soon forthcoming. In fact it wasn't too long a list, and one name dominated the rest. Clearly this was the man on the ground who was in direct control of the day-to-day work.

Chislenko noted it without comment. He'd already written it down on his jotter with a large question-mark next to it. Now he crossed out the question-mark.

The name was Mikhail Osjanin.

6

That evening in Natasha's apartment with the radio turned up high just in case he was right about KGB bugs, he told the girl about the two reports he had left in the Procurator's office that afternoon.

One of them had been long and very detailed. This was the one which showed there was no possible historical basis for a ghost, then went on to give the new and revised accounts of events from Natasha, her mother, and Rudakov, ending with the conclusion that a combination of heat, fatigue, stale air and a little restorative alcohol had combined to make Josif Muntjan hallucinate so strongly that his hysteria had communicated itself to those around.

Chislenko then declared boldly that he could find no evidence of subversive intent and recommended that Muntjan should undergo a medical examination to test if he were fit for his job. If, as seemed likely, he failed this, he should then be pensioned off to be looked after by his niece who happened to be the supervisor's wife.

Natasha whistled.

'That's bold of you, isn't it?'

'Is it?'

'Yes. You could just have tossed him and the supervisor to the wolves, couldn't you?'

'Don't think that I wasn't going to do it,' said Chislenko drily.

Then he told her about the second report.

It had been very short.

In it he said that it appeared that the lifts in the Gorodok Building had been manufactured in Chemnitz, Germany, in 1914 for the Hotel Imperial in St Petersburg. This building had been damaged in 1943 and the site had been cleared in 1945 under the supervision of M.R.S. Osjanin.

'I don't understand,' said Natasha.

'You would if you could see the photostat documents accompanying the other report. The full history of the Gorodok Building's there. Plans, costing; material and machines; purchase, delivery; everything. All authorized and authenticated by the project director, who has since risen to the rank of Controller of Public Works, one Mikhail Osjanin.'

Natasha digested this.

'You mean Osjanin was on the fiddle?'

'Possibly,' said Chislenko.

'But a couple of lifts . . . how much would they cost, by the way?'

'I forget the exact costing, but a lot of roubles,' said Chislenko. 'The point is, of course, how much else was there?'

'Sorry?'

'How much other material cannibalized from demolition sites and officially written off did Osjanin and his accomplices recycle into the reconstruction programme? And what else has he been up to? A fiddler rarely sticks to one fiddle!'

Natasha studied him earnestly.

'This is dangerous, isn't it?' she said softly.

'Could be. That's why I've put these reports in separately. By itself the second one is pretty meaningless. I even left the old names in—Chemnitz, St Petersburg, the Hotel Imperial. You could drop it in a filing cabinet and no one would look at it for a hundred years. But set it beside the documents on the Gorodok Building attached to the other . . .'

'I see. You make no accusations, draw no conclusions. That's for someone else.'

She sounded accusing.

'Right,' he said.

'And will conclusions be drawn?'

'Osjanin's a youngish man, mid-fifties. Rumour has it he feels ready for even higher things. It all depends whether Oscar Bunin, my MVD Minister, sees him as an ally or a threat. If he's a threat, then Bunin will almost certainly set Serebrianikov on him.'

'Otherwise he'll get away scot-free?' said Natasha indignantly.

'Certainly,' smiled Chislenko. 'But, at least, giving the Comrade Secretary *that* has put me in credit enough to dare recommend that poor old Josif Muntjan gets let down lightly.'

She thought about this for a moment, then leaned forward and kissed him.

'You're a nice man, Lev Chislenko,' she said.

'No, I'm not,' he said bluntly. 'I'm a policeman.'

'Yes, you're that too. I've been wondering about that. You shouldn't be telling me all this, should you? Why are you doing it?'

He took a deep breath.

'Because I'm in love with you,' he said. 'Because I've nothing to give except what I am, (which I'm not ashamed of, by the way) and that means telling you things you shouldn't hear, telling you things you won't want to hear. It's called trust, I believe.'

She sat very still, then said, 'You're taking a hell of a risk, you know that?'

His face lit up with a kind of delight.

'Yes. I know that.'

'Suppose I can't love you?'

'I could persecute you.'

'I could blackmail you.'

'Yes,' he said.

She leaned forward and kissed him again. He tried to take her in his arms but she drew back.

48

'You're not related to the Chislenko who used to play for Dynamo, are you?' she asked.

'No, I'm not,' he said.

'Good. I hate football,' she said leaning towards him once more.

The wireless was still blaring when he woke up in the middle of the night. It was dark and Natasha was warm beside him under the coarse linen sheet. She was awake.

'Lev,' she said.

'Yes.'

'I was thinking.'

'Yes.'

'All that stuff about there being no one for that man to be a ghost of. Because no one had died in the Gorodok Building since it was erected.'

'Yes.'

'Well, it's not true now, is it? I mean, if the lift was made as far back as 1914, anything could have happened in it, couldn't it? And those old-fashioned clothes he was wearing, they would make sense now. Have you thought of that?'

He didn't tell her, *yes, of course I've thought of all that,* because no one loves a know-it-all policeman, and he desperately wanted this girl to love him. Instead he turned towards her and began kissing her breasts and after a while had the satisfaction of knowing he'd put all thoughts of the strange events in the south lift of the Gorodok Building out of her mind.

Putting it out of his own mind in any permanent sense proved much more difficult.

Every instinct told him that his wisest policy was now to shun the whole affair completely. If Serebrianikov and Bunin decided that nothing should be done about Osjanin, then it would be very silly to let himself be discovered apparently still paddling in these muddied waters. Particularly as his only excuse could be that he was still hunting for a ghost!

What he wanted to do was contact Leningrad again, or better still to go there, but there was no way he could hope to conceal even a simple telephone call, let alone a journey. So he compromised by paying yet another visit to the Records Office.

'Hello, Comrade Inspector,' said Karamzin, the clerk, with a simpering smile of welcome. 'Do we want to rifle my records again?'

Good Lord! thought Chislenko. Can it be that the vain little bastard's beginning to imagine my frequent visits have got something to do with *him*!'

He said, 'Is this really a *Central* records office? I mean, do you have records of other buildings—in Leningrad, say?'

'Oh yes,' said the clerk confidently, then modified his certainty to, 'At least, some of them. As long as it's post-war, that is.'

'This would be pre-war,' said Chislenko.

'A public building?'

'A hotel that was taken over by the State, more or less,' said Chislenko. 'So in a sense it was a public building.'

'What year?'

'I've no idea,' said Chislenko. 'It's the Hotel Imperial, to start with. Then it becomes the L.D. Trotsky Building, and it ends up as the May Day Centre.'

The clerk left the room rolling his eyes as if to say, if all he wants is my conversation, why does he have to invent such bloody inconvenient excuses? He was away for thirty dusty minutes, but his face was triumphant beneath the smudges when he returned.

'Here's something,' he said. 'It's not much, but at least it shows we're willing.'

He simpered again.

Chislenko ignored him and studied the musty file. Basically it was a record of maintenance expenses. Once the Imperial became the property of the State, it was State money that was required to replace broken windows, make good storm damage, renovate the heating system. Once again, he blessed the bureaucrats. His practised eye quickly scanned the sheets. There was nothing of interest till he reached 1934.

And there it was, July 1934, a sum of money, and typed alongside it, *repair to lift*.

'Thanks,' he said to the clerk. 'Thanks a lot.'

'My pleasure,' said the clerk to the policeman's rapidly retreating back. 'Entirely, it seems.'

Now one thing remained to do. Again, a telephone call to his MVD colleagues in Leningrad would probably have been the quickest way, but the same objection remained as before. So instead he took a calculated risk and drove down Leningradsky Prospekt till he reached Pravda Street, where the offices of the great newspaper of the same name were situated.

His application to examine copies of the paper for July 1934 was greeted with the bored resentment which is the Muscovite's conditioned response to almost any request for help or information, but at least he was not required to produce any authorization other than his MVD card.

Seated at a rough wooden table, he began his search.

His first discovery was that in 1934 the thirteenth of July had also fallen on a Friday.

He found the report he was looking for printed three days later. Probably in the impatient West it would have been in the very next edition, but wise Mother Russia always takes time to weigh carefully what her children may safely be told, what is best kept from them.

This was a small report, easily missed. It merely stated a man had been killed in an unfortunate accident at the May Day Centre on July 13th. For some reason the lift had jammed between the ninth and tenth floors, but the indicator had continued to function. Thinking the lift had arrived, the accident victim had opened the outer door on the seventh floor and stepped into the shaft before he realized his error. The lift had then started to function again and medical evidence was not clear whether the fall had killed him or whether the descending lift had crushed him to death in the basement.

Chislenko swallowed hard. But it was not just the ghastliness of the story which twisted his stomach. It was the man's name.

He was a rising light in the Leningrad Party, a valued friend and associate of the famous Sergei Kirov.

His name was Fyodor Bunin.

Chislenko called for the man in charge of the archives.

'Do you have a copy of the *Encyclopædia of Historical Biography*?' he asked.

The man looked as if he'd have liked to deny this, or at least to say that it was nothing to do with him if they'd got one or not. But something in Chislenko's expression made him reply with only token surliness, 'I expect so,' and go and fetch it.

It was the latest edition, though there was nothing to show that there had been previous editions. Anyone who had a full set would be able to chart all the ebbs and flows of the great power struggles which had shaken the State since its inception nearly seventy years before. But as private ownership of the work was forbidden by edict, private owners were few and far between.

Chislenko thumbed through the bulky tome till he found *Bunin*. It was a sign of something, he didn't know what, that Bunin the novelist and Nobel Prize Winner, who chose to live in Paris after the Revolution, actually merited a few lines. This contrasted with a page and a half on Boris Bunin, Head of the MVD, the Ministry of the Interior. His star was clearly in the ascendant, so much so that its light had spilled over to illuminate the brief life and minor eminence of his elder brother, Fyodor, whose promising career had been nipped off by a tragic accident.

According to the *Encyclopædia*, in the atmosphere of growing distrust in the early 'thirties between Stalin and his powerful henchmen, Sergei Kirov, Party Leader in Leningrad, Fyodor Bunin's voice had been one of the few influences towards conciliation and compromise. Young though he was (only 25 at his death) he had the ear of both leaders and was widely regarded as one of tomorrow's men. With his death any vague possibility of reconciliation between the opposing forces had disappeared, and a few months later

Kirov's assassination had signalled the beginning of the Great Terror.

Chislenko finished reading and closed the volume with a snap that made the archivist purse his lips in irritation. On his desk a telephone rang and the man glowered at Chislenko as if that too was his fault, but the Inspector did not notice.

Everything in this case seemed to lure him into greater peril. To be found pursuing a ghost as if he believed in it would do his career no good at all, but to offend the sensibility, as well as the sense, of his own MVD Minister by suggesting that this was the ghost of his own dearly beloved brother might well destroy it.

The best, the *only* thing to do was to tiptoe quietly away and never again mention the Leningrad accident.

'Inspector!'

He realized the archivist was digging his finger into his shoulder as if he'd been trying to attract his attention for some while.

'Yes?'

'It *is* for you,' said the archivist triumphantly.

He evidently meant the telephone.

Chislenko rose and went to it.

'Chislenko,' he said.

'Kedin here. Look, you'd better get back, quick as you can. Serebrianikov's in the Procurator's office and he wants to see you.'

'I'm on my way,' said Chislenko. 'Hold on though, Kedin . . .'

'Yes?'

'How did you know where to contact me?'

'Serebrianikov said we would get you at the *Pravda* building. Why do you ask?'

Chislenko didn't reply but gently replaced the receiver.

So much for all his precautions! He should have known from the start that men like Serebrianikov didn't let their watchers go unwatched. What was perhaps more frightening was the arrogant casualness with which the man tweaked the thread to bring him back to hand.

He returned the papers and the *Encyclopædia* to the archivist's desk and watched the man cross out his name. It felt like a symbolic act.

'Chislenko,' said the archivist. 'Are you . . . ?'

'No,' said Chislenko. And went to meet his fate.

7

'Well, here he is, the hero of the hour!' proclaimed Serebrianikov. 'Come in, sit down. You'll take a drink with us? Procurator, a vodka for Lev. You won't mind an old fogey like me calling you Lev, will you?'

Chislenko stood at the threshold, mouth agape, convinced he must be the victim of some hallucinatory nerve-gas. Serebrianikov, looking like the incarnation of old world benevolence, clapped his hands together in glee and said, 'I can see you're too hard on your Inspectors, Kozlov. They're not used to kind words in this office. Look at poor Lev here, not certain whether this is madness or mockery!'

Suddenly he became serious.

'I'm a hard man myself, Lev, when the need arises. But I've always believed, merit should be acknowledged and rewarded. You've done well. We all think you've done well. The Minister is very impressed. He wants to see you personally. We'll be off in a moment, but there's time for that drink first.'

'Comrade Bunin wants to see me?' said Chislenko incredulously.

Kozlov thrust a large glassful of vodka into his hand, saying, 'That's right, er, Lev,' (stumbling only slightly on the name). 'He's very pleased with the way *we* have handled this case.'

'Yes, he is,' said Serebrianikov a trifle sardonically. 'You've done well too, Procurator, and your reward is still to come. But Lev's the man of the moment. I give you Inspector Lev Chislenko!'

He raised his glass in salutation. Kozlov followed suit. Chislenko raised his in acknowledgement. Then in perfect unison the three men tossed the hot round spirit to the back of the throat, and because fifteen centilitres of straight vodka at that brief moment of initial epiglottal contact monopolizes all thought and feeling, for the first and probably the last time in their lives the trio felt and thought as one.

Then they were three again.

'And now,' said the old man, 'we must not keep the Minister waiting.'

Chislenko had imagined he would be escorted to the Minister's official chambers in the highest reaches of Petrovka where his own minor rank did not permit him to penetrate. Instead they went down to the street and climbed into an oldish but still luxurious Mercedes with a plain-clothes chauffeur.

'You like the car?' said Serebrianikov, noting his impressed glance. 'My enemies say it is unpatriotic to use a German car, but I reply that historically it has always been the duty of the patriot to flaunt the trophies of victory.'

Chislenko, who knew a little about foreign cars through gently envious study of confiscated magazines, wondered what particular victory over the Germans Serebrianikov had won in the late 'sixties.

He said, 'They make excellent machinery, the Germans.'

'Yes. Cars. Guns. Lifts even. They build to last, as Comrade Osjanin realized. A very clever man, Comrade Osjanin.'

The compliment sounded genuine. Chislenko risked a direct question, though still keeping it as ambiguous as he could.

'Is further action contemplated, Comrade Secretary?'

The old man smiled in acknowledgement of the easy route offered him to switch the subject from Osjanin, but replied, 'Oh yes, Lev. But you will have guessed that this business of the lifts was probably not a unique aberration. There have been suspicions before. You have given us our first sound evidence and now we shall dig and dig. There is corruption here on a huge scale, I would guess. Many, many millions of State money must have been diverted into the Comrade Controller's pocket, and the pockets of his accomplices. Perhaps you would like to help in the digging, would you, Lev?'

55

Chislenko must have looked so alarmed that Serebrianikov chuckled with glee.

'What a cautious man you are! I like that; it is a good
quality in an Inspector, caution. And discretion too. You
have shown them both, Lev. Now you must show them
again. Tell me, what did you discover in the *Pravda* records?'

Was he being invited to demonstrate his powers of caution
and discretion? Or was this a time for openness? It occurred
to him that he had no idea where the car was headed.
Perhaps at the end of the journey two KGB thugs with guns
and spades were waiting if he gave the wrong answers.
Sudden terror squeezed his heart for a long moment.

'Indigestion?' said Serebrianikov. 'It is my fault. Vodka
in the morning, without some *zakuski* to chew on, is all right
for tough old guts like mine, but you modern youngsters!
Here, have a peppermint.'

The old man sounded genuinely concerned.

Chislenko took a mint. As he put it into his mouth, he
wondered neurotically if perhaps it was drugged, then grew
very angry with himself. These were silly fantasies. If anything, he was safer in this car than anywhere. In a sense,
the car, he decided, was a time-capsule. Outside the car,
all the old rules applied. But inside, it was truth-time.
Serebrianikov had shown the way.

He took a deep breath and said, 'I found out that the
Minister's brother, Fyodor Bunin, died in an accident in
what was possibly the same lift on Friday, July 13th, 1934.'

'Possibly?'

'There were two lifts, Comrade Secretary. The records do
not show whether the one in which the accident took place
in Leningrad fifty years ago was used as the north or the
south lift in the Gorodok Building.'

The old man nodded approvingly.

'Good, good. You are using your intellect, Lev. Go on,
go on.'

Go on *where?* wondered Chislenko. He found he was
surprisingly eager to continue to impress the old man but
his brain was groping in a fog of vague possibilities. He tried
to focus on what he knew. Fyodor Bunin. The *Encyclopædia*

article. Because Boris Bunin was important, Fyodor Bunin was treated as important too, because . . . there was some kind of syllogism to be completed here . . . *because Fyodor was important to Boris!*

He said with calm assurance, 'The Minister loved his brother dearly.'

Serebrianikov nodded.

'Yes. It is not always so with brothers. There were almost ten years between them and such a gap can make brothers strangers. But young Boris hero-worshipped Fyodor. You must excuse me if I talk familiarly, Lev, but I know the family, you see. I talk of what I actually saw. Let me tell you this because I trust you. The official histories will tell us that the Comrade Minister was a dedicated young socialist, concerned with questions of public duty from his earliest school days. They will be wrong. Boris Bunin was a likeable child, but idle, dilatory, concerned only with football and cowboy films till adolescence started to add girls to the list. He showed no sign of ambition further than expressing a wish to be an airline pilot so he could fly to foreign countries and do all the delightful things he believed were commonplace there. It was often predicted that he might prove a considerable embarrassment to Fyodor if his political career fulfilled its promise. But I couldn't agree. Boris's love of Fyodor was the one area of complete seriousness in his young life. And in fact it was Fyodor's tragic death that changed Boris. After the funeral he was a different person. It was almost as if he were trying to keep Fyodor alive by *becoming* him. Do you understand what I am saying to you, Comrade Inspector?'

'Yes,' said Chislenko with utter confidence. 'You are telling me that the Comrade Minister has never forgotten his brother. You are also telling me that this devotion must have been common knowledge to everyone acquainted with the Minister. And you are finally telling me why, when this alleged incident of a man falling down a lift-shaft from the seventh floor on Friday the thirteenth of July exactly fifty years after Fyodor's death came to your notice, you were immediately so concerned and interested.'

'You're right, Inspector. I scented a plot of some kind. Was someone trying to remind the Minister of his brother's accident, to revive the pain? I could see no reason why this should be so, but the Minister himself had noticed the coincidence and it had indeed caused him some small agitation. So I decided it must be investigated by a clear, uncluttered mind. And I was fortunate enough to get you, Lev.'

To Chislenko's amazement and embarrassment Serebrianikov's hand rested on his thigh and squeezed. Perhaps it was the little clerk at the Records Office he should be talking to!

He said, 'But I didn't uncover any plot.'

The hand withdrew.

'Oh yes you did,' said the old man, a touch testily. 'Come now, Lev.'

Chislenko thought hard.

'You mean this Osjanin business? Let me see. That would mean this whole thing was set up to draw our attention to the lifts themselves, so that we would discover there'd been a fiddle when the Gorodok Building was constructed? In other words, it was all a simple tip-off!'

'You sound doubtful, Comrade Inspector.'

'Well, it's just that a straightforward anonymous phone call would have been a lot simpler,' said Chislenko.

'Now you're thinking like a policeman! This is not petty crime we're talking about, Inspector. This is corruption on a huge scale, involving important people in high places. An informant would run tremendous risks, so it is not surprising that he should use roundabout methods to distance himself from the results of his action. The stakes are high, Lev. You, of course, are acquainted with the penalty for corruption at this level?'

'Yes, Comrade,' said Chislenko. 'Death.'

Serebrianikov laughed.

'Indeed. Death. Or promotion, Comrade Inspector. That's always a possibility too! We are almost there. Be careful what you say to the Comrade Minister. Stick to the facts, Lev, and your future is bright.'

The car came to a halt. They had driven out of the city along the road to Archangelskoye and were in the driveway of a medium-sized villa set in a lovely garden. Standing in the open doorway to greet them was a man Chislenko recognized as the minister himself.

It did not take Chislenko long to acknowledge the wisdom of Serebrianikov's warning. Despite his own attempts to stick to the facts, and despite the old man's attempts to keep the Osjanin corruption case at the centre of things—and, to be fair, despite also Bunin's own evident attempt to keep everything on a businesslike and official level—they kept on sliding sideways towards the question obviously racking the minister's heart: could there really be any possibility of a supernatural manifestation?

Finally, with a resigned glance at Chislenko, the old man gave way to the inevitable and went for confrontation.

'Minister,' he said, 'it seems to me you are still bothered by the thought that perhaps something inexplicable really did happen here. In other words, there was a ghost. Your brother Fyodor's ghost.'

Chislenko began to rise, feeling that he should not be present if the conversation was to become so intimate. Bunin too rose and began to pace around the room. He was a grey-haired man with a strong, normally rather wooden face, but now it was working with emotion.

'If I thought there was a chance, Yuri, however remote . . .'

Serebrianikov seized Chislenko's sleeve and drew him back into his seat.

'Boris, believe me, there is no chance,' he said. 'It is a cruel deception, accidentally cruel, I believe, but that does not help ease your pain. But you must recognize that this charade was mounted by some enemy of Osjanin to draw attention to his crimes. This excellent young man I have brought with me will confirm this.'

He looked commandingly at Chislenko who said, 'Yes, Comrade Minister. All the evidence points that way.'

'Does it? Which evidence?' snapped Bunin.

Chislenko gulped. Frankly he didn't blame Bunin. He

59

found much that was still inexplicable in the whole business, but suddenly he had an inspiration.

'The second man,' he said.

'The second man?'

'Yes. All the so-called witnesses said there were two men. Now, your brother was alone when he had his accident, all the testimony points to that, so this can hardly have been a supernatural projection of what happened fifty years ago. No, what I believe is that two men were necessary to the charade so that one could be thrust forward into the lift and then jerked rapidly back and sideways, out of sight, allowing Muntjan, the lift-operator, who was obscuring the view of the passengers, to start his hysterical outburst which quickly infected the others.'

He paused. Serebrianikov beamed at him with approval.

'See, Boris, these are the facts. Believe them. Accept them. Your future may depend on it. Skeletons in cupboards are one thing; no one achieves power without a few of these; but ghosts in the mind! Any hint of that outside these walls could be fatal to your great future.'

Bunin stood quite still in the middle of the room, his whole body tense as an athlete's before some great explosion of effort. Then perceptibly he relaxed.

'You're quite right, Yuri,' he said gently. 'I am being foolish. Forgive me, Inspector Chislenko. I hope you will find only comfort in the realization that those who lead you are human also.'

Chislenko made a non-committal choking sound. The Minister picked up a framed photograph from his desk and studied it.

'He was so dear to me, you see. So dear. And would have been dear to his country too, had he lived. He had much to offer, much more than I . . .'

Serebrianikov rose, gesturing to Chislenko to do the same, and advanced to stand by the Minister.

'There he is, Inspector, so handsome a young man. Those are our parents, that's me, sprawling on the grass, and there's our dear friend, Yuri, who has guided me so well during all these years.'

It was an informal group photograph with a man and woman seated in garden chairs; a blond-haired boy stretched on the grass before them with his tongue poked out at the camera; and behind them, standing, two young men, one an older version of the young boy, with his hands on his mother's shoulders and a smile on his lips, the other (presumably Serebrianikov, though little was recognizable apart from the watchful eyes) looking self-consciously solemn.

How useful the KGB man must have been to Boris Bunin in youth, and how useful Bunin must have been to Serebrianikov in age! thought Chislenko. Now perhaps they would both be useful to him. Or dangerous, if things fell out badly.

Bunin put the photograph down and suddenly he was himself again.

'To business then,' he said harshly. 'I've thought over what you said about letting Osjanin have a bit more rope. I think for once you're wrong, Yuri. He has too many friends. Let's grab him straightaway. Tomorrow he's due to attend a conference in Kiev. If we pick him up this evening, we can pretend in Moscow he's gone there and tell the people in Kiev he was taken ill en route and has been hospitalized at, let us say, Gomel. That way we can have him for a couple of days, perhaps even a week, before word gets round and the rats start worrying. Fix it, Yuri. Fix it now. You can use the secure phone in the office.'

Serebrianikov may not have agreed with this policy, but he clearly knew when to argue, when to defer.

He went out of the door, closing it gently behind him.

After a moment Bunin said, 'Comrade Chislenko, you've been recommended as a man of discretion. Does that mean you tell nobody anything, except Comrade Serebrianikov to whom you tell everything?'

'No,' said Chislenko indignantly. 'It means I do my job.'

'Is that what it means? Yes, I believe you. In that case, Inspector, as part of your job, I'd like you to do something for me.'

He twisted the clip which held the back of the photograph frame in place and slipped out the photo.

'I'd like you to show this to the witnesses in the Gorodok Building affair and ask them if they recognize the young man at the back with the fair hair. I'd like you to do this discreetly and report their answers only to me.'

He looked Chislenko straight in the eyes as he spoke.

'Will you do that?'

'Yes, sir.'

'No comments, Inspector?'

'Only that for the past half-hour I've been wondering how I could get hold of a picture of your brother, sir.'

Bunin suddenly smiled.

'Curiosity's a valuable quality in a policeman, I expect. Quickly now, put the picture away.'

Chislenko slipped the photograph into his side pocket as the door opened. Before Serebrianikov could re-enter, the Minister led Chislenko to the doorway, effectively stopping the old man from coming in and possibly noticing the empty frame.

With his hand on Chislenko's shoulder, the Minister said, 'I was just asking the Inspector here if he was related to the Chislenko who used to play for Dynamo.'

'No, he's not,' said Serebrianikov confidentially. 'Are you, Lev?'

'Actually,' said Chislenko, 'he's my half-cousin. Only it tends to annoy me when everyone keeps asking, so I usually tell lies.'

'Except to Ministers,' said Bunin, smiling.

'Except to Ministers,' said Chislenko smiling back.

8

On their journey back to town the old KGB man was very quiet and Chislenko did not make the mistake of prattling nervously to break the silence.

He'd like to know what the Minister said to me when we were alone, he told himself almost gleefully. And he knows that I'll either volunteer to tell or hold my tongue.

The Mercedes halted outside Petrovka and Serebrianikov said, 'Goodbye to you, Comrade Inspector. I expect we will meet again fairly soon, but for the moment at least, your job is done.'

Was there a note of warning in his voice?

'Will there be charges against the lift-operator?' asked Chislenko.

The old man said, 'Probably not. It is best to let that affair die quietly, isn't it? To make a successful court case out of it would probably require you to prove the complicity of one or more of the other witnesses, wouldn't you agree?'

Chislenko tried to keep the alarm out of his face. Did the old bastard know about him and Natasha? The answer almost certainly was yes!

'The foreign press will have a much tastier morsel to slaver over when they get wind of the Osjanin case,' continued Serebrianikov. 'They like nothing better than an opportunity to show that our society is as corrupt and depraved as their own.'

'It doesn't seem to worry you, Comrade Secretary,' said Chislenko daringly.

The old man smiled.

'We'll let them gloat for a few days before we reveal that, as well as being a corrupt embezzler of public monies, Osjanin is also a paid agent of the CIA. Then watch them try to back-pedal!'

Chislenko was amazed.

'You mean there's a security dimension to all this? You never hinted at that before, Comrade Secretary.'

The old man chuckled musically.

'Maybe I just thought of it, Comrade Inspector,' he said as he pulled the door shut. 'Maybe I just thought of it.'

Chislenko watched the old Mercedes pull away.

Lev, my boy, he told himself, you're just a simple cop. Be wise; stay that way; keep your head down, your mouth shut, and do the job, nothing more.

'Are you all right, Lev?'

It was Kedin coming out of the building and finding him standing as if entranced on the pavement.

'Yes. Fine.'

It was, he realized, the first time Kedin had used his first name. But it was a mark of respect rather than presumptuous familiarity. Those whom Kedin wished to cultivate were usually clearly marked for the top.

Kedin's next comment confirmed this.

'Many congratulations, by the way. The whole place is buzzing with your great coup, though no one seems to know the exact details. Why don't we have a celebratory drink later and you can fill me in, give me a few tips, maybe?'

'That would be nice,' said Chislenko.

'Great. See you, Lev.'

'Yes. See you . . . er . . .'

Ivan. He remembered Kedin's given name as he reached his desk.

He spent much of the next couple of hours just sitting staring blankly into space, reviewing his dilemma.

The simplest thing to do was nothing. In a couple of days he could return the photograph to Bunin saying he had shown it to the available witnesses and none of them had recognized his brother. In the meantime he would avoid going anywhere near the Gorodok Building, or seeing Natasha, so that Serebrianikov would have no reason to suspect his instructions were being ignored.

That was what a wise young policeman with prospects and ambition would do.

Chislenko sighed, and the sigh was an acknowledgement that he was not a wise young policeman.

Quite simply, he had to know.

But that did not mean he was going to take unnecessary risks.

He went down to the departmental photocopying room a short while later, choosing the precise moment when the operator, a man of strict habit called Griboedov, would be preparing his afternoon mug of tea. In this wisest of States, private ownership of photocopiers was not possible and those in the public service were strictly monitored, with every copy being registered and counted.

'One document, suspect's record, one copy,' intoned Chislenko.

'You pick your fucking moments, don't you?' grumbled Griboedov, crouched at his ancient samovar which was as complex and as perilous as a nuclear power station.

'That's all right. I'll do it,' said Chislenko, walking past the reception counter into the photocopying room.

It was the work of a moment to slip the photograph from beneath the document he was carrying and run it through. Fortunately the copier was the very latest Japanese model and the reproduction was excellent.

Returning to the counter, he carefully filled in the book. Griboedov rose up with his tea, went to check the number on the copy meter and returned to countersign the entry.

'Nice machine,' said Chislenko. 'Japanese, isn't it?'

'That's right. Don't think the little bastards make samovars, do you?'

Laughing, Chislenko withdrew.

That night he had a date with Natasha. He broke it without contacting her.

The following morning he wrote his report to Bunin, enclosed it in a lightly sealed envelope with the photograph, and put it into the Inspectors' mail-out tray.

An hour later he returned to the tray with an internal memo he was passing on after initialling it. As he put the memo into the tray, he contrived to look at the envelope addressed to the Minister. It was now heavily stuck down.

The next day was Sunday. He put on his best, which was to say his other suit and went to visit Natasha, but when he got to her apartment there was no reply. He had been in the police business too long not to be alarmed at a sudden disappearance, and immediately he started banging on a neighbour's door.

A young woman in a thin cotton nightgown through which her huge dark nipples peered like a giant panda's eyes told him yawningly that Natasha's mother was ill and Natasha had gone off to visit her the previous day.

Chislenko went back in the evening, but Natasha had not returned.

He spent a restless night, full of fragmented anguished dreams in which Natasha and her mother ran down endless flights of stairs pursued by Serebrianikov in a lift shaped like a coffin. The following morning as soon as he got to Petrovka, he rang the Gorodok Building and asked for Natasha.

'Junior personnel are not allowed personal calls,' said the switchboard operator coldly.

'Chislenko, MVD,' he said, undercutting her by several degrees. 'Just get her on the phone if she's there.'

To his surprise and delight, she was.

'Natasha! It's Lev,' he said.

'Yes?' she said indifferently.

'How are you? How's you mother?'

'Mother's fine,' she said.

'And you? How're you? You sound tired.'

'Why shouldn't I? I got back very late last night and I didn't sleep much the night before either. As for the night before that . . .'

'Natasha, I'm sorry, I can explain . . .'

'Can you? I'm not sure if it's worth it. Now I have to go. I'm not allowed to take personal calls, not even from MVD Inspectors. Goodbye.'

The phone went dead.

'Oh shit,' said Chislenko.

He sat for a moment, then made up his mind.

When he got down to the car pool, he saw at a glance that his car, or rather the car he'd come to think of as his during the last few days, was gone.

When he inquired, the man in charge laughed and said, 'You're back in the queue now, Comrade. Special duty reservation was cancelled as from the weekend.'

'All right. What have you got?'

'Bugger-all at the moment, unless you want to push the thing yourself. Sorry. Put your name down and we might be able to do something for you, this afternoon.'

'Don't bother,' said Chislenko.

He set out for the metro on foot and, after an uncomfortably crowded and inexplicably delayed train journey, wished he'd continued the same way.

The first person he saw when he entered the Gorodok Building was Muntjan, lounging outside the open lift.

'So you're back,' he growled.

'I certainly am, boss,' said Muntjan happily. 'Doctor says I'm fit and well. Going up, boss?'

Suspiciously Chislenko sniffed the lift-man's breath. There was no trace of alcohol. Obviously the doctor had prescribed some more scientific salve for Muntjan's troubled nerves.

He stepped into the lift.

'Eighth floor,' he said.

The lift began to rise.

'Do you remember me, Josif?' he asked.

'I surely do,' said Muntjan, grinning broadly. 'You're the MVD cop who came when I had my nervous trouble.'

'Your nervous trouble?'

'That's right, boss. I saw my new doctor last Friday and he explained it all to me. Seems I'm highly strung, probably something to do with my distinguished war service, and so I'm more susceptible—is that the word?—to disorders-of-the-subconscious-imagination than ordinary folk. I made him write it down so I could get it by heart. Then he gave me these pills which he said would put me right and make sure I had no more of them delusions.'

'Delusions?' said Chislenko.

'Like I had when you came round that time. I'm sorry I caused all that trouble, boss, but it's all down to disorders-of-my-subconscious-imagination brought on by my distinguished war service.'

Serebrianikov tied up loose ends fast, thought Chislenko admiringly. If it hadn't been for the uncovering of the Osjanin corruption, poor old Josif would probably have been in the Lubyanka now, getting medical treatment of a very different kind. It was an ill wind and all that.

They arrived at the eighth floor. Chislenko paused before leaving the lift. He had the photograph in his pocket. Was it worthwhile casually showing it to Josif?

He looked at the smiling face before him and made up his mind. There was nothing to gain and too much to lose for both of them.

He said, 'Thank you, Josif,' and went in search of Natasha.

He found her in the tiny office she was so proud of that she'd brought her mother here to show it off. The girl she shared it with was at her desk also.

Chislenko glared at her sternly and said, 'MVD. I need to interview Comrade Lovchev privately.'

The girl rose reluctantly and left. Natasha meanwhile remained still and expressionless at her desk. She was pale and haggard. Like all other conditions, emotional and physical, it became her.

'Hi,' said Chislenko.

'Hello,' she said.

'Tell me about your mother.'

She looked faintly surprised by this approach and said, 'They found her lying unconscious in the kitchen. At first they thought she'd had a stroke, but by the time I got there, she'd woken up and it turns out she was clambering up on a stool to reach a high shelf and you know how stout she is, well, she'd overbalanced and cracked her head on the tiled floor. There was a bit of concussion, but nothing else, thank God. We're a hard-headed family, it seems, so she's really OK, thank you for asking.'

It came out in a rapid but coherent flow.

Chislenko said gently, 'I'm glad. But it must have been awful for you, travelling up there, not knowing. I wish you'd told me.'

'Told you? You'd have been there when I got the news if you'd bothered to turn up on Friday night!' she retorted. 'Yes, it might even have been a help and a comfort to have you there. But as you couldn't even be bothered to let me know you were breaking our date, I hardly felt much impulse to get in touch with you when I heard!'

'No,' said Chislenko. 'You wouldn't. I understand.'

'Do you?'

'Yes. Just as I know you'll understand when I explain.

But the important thing is your mother's all right and you're all right. I'm so pleased.'

'Is that what you've come to say, then?' said Natasha, shuffling some papers on her desk. 'I am rather busy.'

'Natasha, don't shit me around,' said Chislenko.

Her eyes widened in surprise at the coarseness of his phrase.

'Bad temper and common abuse I'll take,' he went on. 'But this cold sophisticated brush-off crap won't work.'

'For God's sake, where do you think you are, talking like that?' she cried. 'That might be OK down at Petrovka . . .'

'I love you,' he said.

'. . . but unless you can start sounding like a civilized . . .'

'I love you,' he said.

'. . . human being when you're in the outside world . . .'

He leaned over the desk and kissed her.

When he drew back she regarded him solemnly and then suddenly started giggling.

'Hark at me!' she said.

He kissed her again and this time she kissed him back.

When they broke apart he was breathless.

'Before this thing gets too serious,' he said, 'There's something I want you to look at.'

'I've seen it,' she said. 'Remember?'

'God, and you say I'm coarse! No, it's a photo. This man here, the blond, have you ever seen him before?'

He passed over the photograph and stabbed his finger at the face of Fyodor Bunin.

The effect was devastating. The colour which their embrace had brought to her pale cheeks now ebbed dramatically leaving them twice as pale as before. Her eyes rounded in fear and her voice when it came was shrill.

'That's him!' she cried. 'That's the man who fell through the lift. Lev, who is this? What does it mean?'

'God knows,' said Chislenko. 'I mean it literally. God alone knows.'

But the drama was not over. Natasha was still studying the photo.

'And that's the other one,' she said. 'Yes, definitely. That's him.'

'The other one?'

'The one who came up behind and pushed. Look, him there.'

Now her finger stabbed at the solemn face of the man Chislenko knew was that dear old friend of the Bunin family, Yuri Serebrianikov.

'But that's impossible!' he said. 'It has to be impossible! Please God, let it be.'

Behind him the door opened. He knew who it was even before he turned, but when he glanced at Natasha he didn't see any fear in her eyes to match his own.

'Yes? Can I help you?' she said impatiently.

Of course, he realized. There was no way that she could link the young man in the picture with the benevolent, white-haired old gent with his old-fashioned goatee beard standing quietly in the doorway.

He needed to explain this to Serebrianikov. He should have guessed the old bastard would still keep a close eye, and ear, on him. Such men did not survive what he had survived without a triple-barred caution at all levels at all times. But he had never suspected what might be at stake! How could he? How could anyone? Except perhaps Bunin. Had Bunin felt something, some vibration, which had made him persist in following up this matter despite all the good advice to the contrary?

Bunin had trusted him, and all he had got for his trust was a lie.

He suddenly realized that there was nothing he could say to Serebrianikov which was going to persuade the old KGB man to risk letting him survive to tell Bunin the truth.

But he had to try to do something for Natasha.

'She doesn't know,' he said. 'Even if she did, it doesn't make sense, does it? Leave her alone.'

Serebrianikov smiled.

'Give me the photograph, Comrade Lovchev,' he said.

Natasha looked in bewilderment to Chislenko, who nodded at her and said, 'Give it to him, Natasha.'

She handed it over and then demanded angrily, 'Just who are you anyway?'

Serebrianikov smiled and said, 'That's me there, my dear.'

And held up the photo, underlining his young face with his thumbnail.

Chislenko closed his eyes in pain.

Serebrianikov said, 'I have a couple of men downstairs. I'll send them up for you. Wait here, would you? Unless you prefer to run for it. That would make things even easier.'

He turned and left. Chislenko went to the door and watched him walk along the corridor to the lift. As he entered the old man glanced back and gave a friendly wave. Chislenko turned away.

Natasha came into his arms.

'What's it all mean, Lev?' she demanded. She was shivering as though a great coldness had gripped her.

'It means that fifty years ago that man murdered his own friend, the brother of the man who has protected him and kept him alive for God knows how many years.'

'But it can't be! I saw *both* the young men in the photo. They were ghosts or something, I've got to accept that. But *he's* alive! How can I have seen *his* ghost?'

She was beginning to sound hysterical.

'I don't know!' said Chislenko talking rapidly in an effort to soothe her. 'When I was young and clever I read Dante in translation and there's a bit in the *Inferno* where he meets the spirit of a man who's so evil that he's already condemned into hell while his body's still walking round alive on earth. Perhaps that's it! But I don't know. I don't understand any of it. Why's it happened? What's it mean?'

He realized that far from being a calming influence he was shouting too in his anger and despair.

And he was not the only one.

Distantly there was another voice raised up in a dreadful wail of horror and fear. Through the open door it drifted. Other doors opened along the corridor and someone said, 'Sounds like old Muntjan's been on the pop again,' and there was some laughter.

Muntjan.

'Wait here!' commanded Chislenko.

He ran out into the corridor. The noise was drifting up the stairwell. He sprinted down on to the next floor, the seventh. And there leaning back against the wall in the posture in which he had first encountered him, was Muntjan. His face too was the same colour and in his hand was the same hip-flask. Pills have their place, but in time of need a man flees to his oldest friends.

'Josif!' demanded Chislenko. 'What happened? Come on, man! Speak!'

'It was him, boss, it was him.'

'Who?'

'Him. That fellow again. We stopped at the seventh, just stopped, no signal or anything. The door opened and there he was, boss, same fellow, same clothes. I knew him soon as I laid eyes on him.'

He took another drink.

'What happened? What did he do?'

'He stepped into the lift, boss. Only this time he didn't go through the floor. The doors started to close. That's when I got out! I haven't moved so fast in years, boss, believe me. Like lightning I went, boss, straight out. Even then the doors nipped me, but I kept going, boss. I kept going!'

'And the other man. The old man in the lift?'

'That poor old gent? He never moved, boss. Never moved. He's gone down with that thing, whatever it is. They've both gone down together!'

Serebrianikov had felt no fear as the newcomer stepped into the lift on the seventh floor, only a great curiosity.

As the lift began to descend again, with the piercing wails of the hysterical Muntjan fading above them, he said calmly, 'Hello, Fyodor.'

'You're not going to dispute me, then, Yuri?'

'I don't think so. Though on the other hand it's always possible one of my more ingenious enemies is playing a curiously convoluted trick. Let's see.'

Serebrianikov put his hand inside his jacket and produced

a small automatic. Aiming it carefully, he kept his finger hard on the trigger till the nine shots it contained had all crashed into the woodwork behind his companion. The lift cubicle was filled with smoke and the smell of cordite, and the sound-waves of the shots bounced round the walls in deafening reverberations.

The old KGB man looked at the unmoved and unmoving figure before him and let the gun fall to the floor.

'So,' he said. 'What do you want? Explanation?'

'Explanation?'

'Yes. It was expedient. Joe was always going to win. I had to make a choice. You'd have gone with Kirov a few months later anyway, Fyodor, you must know that.'

'Yes, I must know that Yuri,' murmured the other, faintly mocking.

'So what is it you want?'

'I want nothing, Yuri. I'm not in the wanting game any more.'

'What then?'

'I am, you'll recognize the term, a sort of agent.'

'Agent? What for?'

The figure did not reply. Its voice had been like a faint breath of wind through a dark cypress tree and now it was stilled. Somehow Serebrianikov knew it would not whisper forth any more.

Above the figure's head the floor indicator had flickered down 5 . . . 4 . . . 3 . . . 2 . . . 1 . . . and now the indicator halted at B for basement.

But the lift did not halt. On and on it went, sinking further and further down.

And now at last, after all those years and all those deaths, Serebrianikov began to feel afraid.

When Chislenko got to the basement and forced open the lift doors which the impact of the bullets had jammed shut, he found the old man sitting in a corner with his head slumped on his chest.

Gently Chislenko raised it. The eyes were still open, but they were seeing nothing anyone living could see. He tried to close them but found it wasn't as easy as it always looked in the cinema, and in the end he gave up.

'Heart attack almost certainly,' diagnosed the doctor who arrived with the ambulance. 'He must have fired his gun to try to attract attention, but at his age there was never any hope, I'm afraid.'

'No,' agreed Chislenko. 'No hope at his age.'

He returned to the eighth floor, running up the stairs. The photograph he had removed from Serebrianikov's jacket was crumpled in his pocket.

Natasha was still in her office looking desperately and beautifully afraid.

'Lev, what's happening here? I don't understand anything!' she cried, jumping up as he entered.

He took a deep breath. It was good that she was afraid, except that probably she was afraid for the wrong reasons.

Her next words confirmed this.

'Josif's still saying he saw that ghost again and someone heard shots. Is it true that awful old man is dead? What's it . . .'

He seized her shoulders and shook her gently.

'There's been an accident,' he said.

'But, Lev . . .'

'There's been an *accident*,' he insisted. 'Comrade Secretary Serebrianikov has had a heart attack. He came here to meet me to discuss if any action needed to be taken against Muntjan.'

'But Josif saw . . .'

'Josif is very sick. He has been mixing tranquillisers and vodka. I've asked the doctor to give him an injection. When he is discharged from hospital, I expect he'll go and live with his niece. The Comrade Secretary had decided there were to be no charges against him. It was all a genuine confusion. He sent Josif to see me here, that's why he travelled down in the lift by himself.'

'But the man! The man Josif saw! The ghost . . .'

He drew her trembling body to him and crushed it tight.

'You're upset,' he said. 'The death of this great, patriotic and beloved old man has naturally upset you. You will feel

74

the need to weep for him. If anyone asks you any questions you don't know how to answer—especially anyone from the KGB—I dare say that your need to weep for the Comrade Secretary will overcome you very strongly at that moment. Won't it, Natasha?'

She felt calmer in his arms now. It was remarkable what a calming effect a lover's voice could have, especially when it was whispering the magic initials, KGB.

'Yes, Lev,' she murmured obediently.

'Good. That's very good. Just remember, darling, in all this there are only two things you must be absolutely certain of. Remember them and in the end you will come to no harm.'

'What are they?' she asked, eager for instruction.

'One is, that I love you.'

'You love me,' she said as though getting a lesson off by heart. 'And the other, Lev? What's the other?'

Chislenko laughed and spoke softly but firmly.

'The other is: there are no ghosts in the Soviet Union!'

BRING BACK THE CAT!

It was a cold, clear morning, shortly after ten, when Joe Sixsmith arrived at the house on Brock Wood Lane. He checked the number, then set out on the long walk up the drive. It was an imposing double-fronted villa whose bay windows proclaimed middle-class wealth like an alderman's belly.

An upstairs curtain twitched but it might have been a draught.

He rang the doorbell.

After a pause, the door was opened by a woman of about forty, good-looking, well dressed in a county kind of way, with an accent to match.

'Y . . . e . . . s?'

It came out long as a sentence. A death sentence.

'Sixsmith.'

'Sorry?'

He handed her his card.

'You rang my office,' he said.

She studied the card till he retrieved it. He only had one card and he wanted it to last.

'Ah, *that* Sixsmith. I was expecting . . .'

He knew what she was expecting. Paul Newman, or Humphrey Bogart at least. What she wasn't expecting was a balding West Indian in a balding corduroy jacket.

'Yes,' she said again. It was another sentence, suspended this time. She was making up her mind. Suddenly she closed the door.

At least once she'd made up her mind she didn't fuck around with conscience-cleansing excuses, he thought.

'You see, it works.'

He looked around. He was alone.

'You try it from your side.'

The voice came from between his feet. He looked down.

A small flap in the door at ground level was being swung on its hinge.

He stooped and said, 'Mrs Ellison?'

'Push it, Mr Sixsmith,' she said impatiently.

He studied her meaning for a moment, then pushed it.

'Again.'

He pushed it again.

'There, you see. It works both ways. Quite adequate for both ingress and egress, don't you agree?'

He said, 'Mrs Ellison, it certainly works. But I don't think I'm going to be able to make it. Also I don't know if . . .'

The door opened. Mrs Ellison looked down at him.

'Come in, Mr Sixsmith,' she said.

He went in. It was a long broad hallway smelling of lavender polish and hung with prints of *The Cries of Old London*. A girl of sixteen or seventeen was standing by a small table on which she was arranging a vase of flowers. She was rather plump and wore a tight sweater, short skirt and leg-warmers. She tore savagely at the flower-stems as if they had offended her.

A flight of stairs ran up from the hall to a landing, then turned back on itself. Sitting on the landing was a boy only slightly younger than the girl. His hair had blue highlights. He stared morosely at a spot between his feet.

'This is my daughter, Tittie. That is my son, Auberon,' said Mrs Ellison.

The boy didn't move but the girl said, 'Is he the new au pair?'

'Don't be ridiculous,' said Mrs Ellison. 'This way.' Sixsmith followed her into a large, airy lounge. An upholstered bench ran round the window-bay. A coffee table stood in the bay. Opposite the window was a mock Adam fireplace. In the grate before it stood a large well-cushioned cat-basket. A chintz-covered suite of three armchairs and a huge sofa rested on the pale blue fitted carpet. At one end of the sofa with his legs up sat a man in his forties, shirt-sleeved, unshaven, and reading a *Daily Mail*. He looked up, caught Sixsmith's eye, winked and said, 'Hello, Sherlock.'

The woman ignored him and led Sixsmith to the window-seat. He sat in the bay and she perched herself at the angle of window and wall.

'Mr Sixsmith,' she said, 'I would like you to investigate a disappearance. The disappearance of my cat.'

This was what Sixsmith had begun to fear. He rubbed his fingers across the worn ribs of his corduroy jacket and wondered how to react. He didn't have the kind of mind which made decisions or even deductions very quickly and he recognized this as a disadvantage in his chosen profession. But he liked to think that in the end he got it right.

'Well?' urged the woman.

He sighed and said, 'I'm sorry, Mrs Ellison. We've all got to draw lines. I draw mine at chasing stray cats.'

He began to rise. There was a snort of what sounded like suppressed laughter from the sofa. This hurt him. He thought he'd sounded rather dignified, even if what he'd meant was he saw no way of tracking down a stray cat, so didn't reckon there was much chance of squeezing his fee out of Mrs Ellison.

'Sit down, Mr Sixsmith,' she ordered peremptorily.

He paused in a semi-squat, neither rising not sitting. It wasn't the woman's tone that froze him. He'd long since developed tone-deafness to the accents of the bourgeoisie. The petrification derived from what he could see waiting for him through the open doorway into the hall. The girl, Tittie, stood there. She was regarding him sullenly and at the same time rolling up her tight sweater till it circled like a life-belt beneath her armpits. She wore no bra and lived up to her name.

Sixsmith sat down. The girl put out her tongue and turned away. Her brother appeared behind her and closed the door.

'What is hard to understand,' resumed the woman, certain it was her simple command that had done the trick, 'is why he should stray. Everything he wants or needs is here. He never goes further than the herbaceous border at the back or the shrubbery at the front. His little door stays open day and night. And as you saw for yourself, there's no chance of it sticking.'

From the hallway came the sound of a hand cracking hard across flesh and a female voice saying furiously, 'Piss off!'

'So what's your conclusion, Mr Sixsmith?' said Mrs Ellison, ignoring the interruption.

'Pardon?'

'You're a private detective. What conclusion do you draw from the facts I've just given you?'

He said, 'Oh yes. Look, Mrs Ellison, I don't have much experience of cats, I admit, but what seems likely to me is that either your cat strayed out on the road and got knocked down. Or maybe someone stole it. For one of those research places. I'm sorry.'

'Research places?'

'That's right. You know, medical research. Vivisection. There's a lot of pet-thieving goes on, I believe. Sorry.'

The woman rose now, her face twisted in grief.

'Vivisection? You mean . . . cut up? Oh no! I'd know . . . I'd feel it . . . how disgusting!'

There were tears in her eyes. She went to the far end of the room, where a couple of decanters and some crystal glasses stood on an authentic reproduction Jacobean cocktail cabinet, poured herself a drink and went out of the room.

The man on the sofa said, 'She weren't so bothered when she took him to be doctored.'

'Doctored?' said Sixsmith.

'Castrated. They smell like cats, else. That's two of us she's had done now.'

'You're Mr Ellison, are you, sir?'

Sixsmith spoke hesitantly. The man's appearance, manner, and broad northern accent jarred with this Hertfordshire stockbroker belt setting.

'That's me, son,' said the man. 'Surprised? Not as surprised as she were, I bet, when she clapped eyes on thee!'

Mrs Ellison returned. From the tintinnabulation of her glass she'd clearly gone in search of ice rather than solitude.

'Forgive me, Mr Sixsmith,' she said. 'There is something

79

of the Celt in me, emotionally speaking. I get upset very easily.'

It struck Sixsmith that she had not as yet acknowledged her husband's presence.

He said, 'You miss your cat so much, Mrs Ellison, I presume you've taken steps already to get him back?'

'True. I've advertised widely. I've contacted the RSPCA. I've even informed the police. They were not sympathetic.'

Ellison said, 'She contacted the cops in Bedfordshire, Cambridgeshire and Essex. We live in Herts, and she expects the cops in Bedfordshire, Cambridgeshire and Essex to be sympathetic!'

He shook the pages of his paper in angry disbelief.

His wife ignored him and said, 'I've also conducted a search of my own, Mr Sixsmith, though with limited resources and no assistance, it has not been easy.'

Sixsmith screwed up his face and tried to look professional.

'Did you search on a systematic basis, Mrs Ellison?' he asked.

'Yes. I've kept a record. Would you like to see it?'

'Please.'

She left the room again and Ellison emerged from his paper once more.

'You know how she's spent most of her spare time, which means most of her time, this past week?' he demanded. 'I'll tell you. She gets into her car and she sets off driving round the countryside. From time to time she gets out and she starts calling. *Darkie! Darkie!*'

'Sorry?' said Sixsmith.

'Darkie. That's the cat's name.'

Sixsmith scratched his nose, sighed, and said, 'Go on. She calls his name . . .'

'But that's not all. Oh no. Before she drives on, she removes some part of her clothing and lays it in a ditch or drapes it over a hedge. I bet half the police in Hertfordshire are out looking for the mad rapist of Baldock!'

'How do you know this, Mr Ellison? Do you accompany your wife?'

'No fear! No, my daughter went with her once. She told me.'

Mrs Ellison came back once more carrying a large desk diary and an Ordnance Survey map.

'I've got it all charted and recorded here,' she said.

'Thank you. Mrs Ellison, why do you leave items of clothing scattered round the countryside?'

She said, 'How do you know about that?'

Sixsmith sighed again and said, 'I'm a detective, Mrs Ellison.'

'I see. Well, it's smell, Mr Sixsmith. The framework of a cat's living space is smell. They lay a boundary of odour outside which they are in foreign territory. Darkie, wherever he is, is clearly lost. By leaving my garments where he might possibly find them, I am providing an oasis of familiarity in a desert of frightening strangeness.'

'Have you had any results yet?'

'How can I know? I leave the clothes for comfort, not as bait.'

Sixsmith said, 'I mean, have you caught a glimpse of . . . er . . . Darkie yet? Have you had any replies to your ads? Have the police or the RSPCA been able to help?'

'No. Nothing. The RSPCA keep me posted about any strays they get. The police, I fear, have done nothing. I've had several replies to my advertisements but they have so far either been frivolous or extortionate. Twice I have been offered cats which allegedly fitted the description. They were nothing like Darkie! The tricksters who tried to pass them off became quite aggressive when I told them what I thought. But it was clearly an attempt at fraud. Look, he is so distinctive, isn't he?' She handed him a colour photograph. It showed a cat rearing out of a wellington boot. It had a red ribbon round its neck. But it still managed to look dignified. And it was certainly distinctive, jet black except for a white patch on its head which involved most of its left eye and ear.

'Very nice,' said Sixsmith. It was time to talk business, he decided. When you were being hired by a wife who treated her husband as non-existent, it made sense to find who controlled the purse strings. He had a sliding scale, based on how much he felt the customer could carry and how much he needed the work. So far it hadn't slid off the bottom. This one was different.

He said, 'Mrs Ellison, before we go any further, let's put things on a firm professional basis. My terms are sixty pounds a day plus expenses, with two days' pay in advance. How's that grab you?'

She looked at him with the cold eyes of her class which admits silliness about anything except money. But before she could speak, Ellison said, 'Sixty quid a day? Jesus fucking Christ!'

That did the trick.

'That's perfectly agreeable, Mr Sixsmith. I'll give you a cheque before you leave,' said the woman.

'I'm a cash man, as far as possible,' said Sixsmith. 'And before I start would be better.'

He thought he'd gone too far, but after a moment she left the room once more.

'My God, you're cool for a darkie,' said Ellison. '*Darkie*! Hey, there's a thing!'

'Yes, sir, there's a thing,' agreed Sixsmith. 'Tell me, Mr Ellison, do you and your wife *never* speak, or is this just a lull in the storm?'

'Don't get cheeky, son,' said Ellison with no real resentment. 'And don't think just because she can dig up a hundred quid from her china pig that she's the banker round here. This is *my* house and it's *my* money that makes this family tick, God help us.'

'I believe you, man,' said Sixsmith. 'What do you do, Mr Ellison?'

'Apart from lying around here reading the paper, you mean? Precious little. I'd better tell you about myself, if only because I don't reckon you've been at this game long enough to nose around, asking question about me, without causing embarrassment. I had my own business up in Bradford till ten years ago. Then I got took over. I didn't complain, I made a packet and part of the deal was an executive directorship on the board of the boss company,

82

which meant a move down here, which pleased her ladyship no end. Last year, they managed to shuffle me out altogether. Golden handshake again, so I'm comfortably set up for life only I've not yet made up my mind what life is. That answer your question, son?'

'Great,' said Sixsmith, wondering among other things why Ellison should assume that pursuing his wife's cat should involve asking questions about his own background and character.

The door opened and the boy, Auberon, came in.

'Is Mum doing lunch?' he demanded. 'Tittie says she's not doing it again.'

'Why don't you have a go?' retorted his father.

'Jesus! This household's falling apart, you know that? Have we advertised or anything?'

'Only about the cat,' said Ellison. 'Now, shove off and make a few sandwiches, you don't need O-levels for that!'

Surlily the boy left, slamming the door behind him.

'You got kids, Sixsmith?' asked Ellison.

'Not to keep,' said Sixsmith.

'Bloody wise,' grunted the man.

'You having domestic trouble? I mean, with domestics?'

'Both,' said Ellison. 'We're what you call between help. Or do I mean beyond help? Time was when women could control a kitchen and their daughters were pleased to give a hand. We've grown beyond that, it seems. You don't cook, do you, Sixsmith?'

'That'd cost you another sixty, man,' said Sixsmith.

The door opened and Mrs Ellison returned carrying an envelope.

'When are we getting someone new to help in the kitchen?' demanded Ellison instantly.

This sudden rupture of their angry silence did not disturb the woman in the least.

'What's the matter? Finding your appetite again, are you?' she replied with icy scorn.

The answer meant a great deal more than it said, judged Sixsmith.

Mrs Ellison handed him the envelope.

'I think you'll find that in order,' she said.

He put it in his pocket.

'Not counting it?' said Ellison.

'Never got beyond ten,' said Sixsmith. 'Mrs Ellison, now I'm officially on the case, can I have a word in private?'

The woman looked at the man. He grinned ferociously and stretched himself out on the sofa.

'Follow me,' said Mrs Ellison.

She led him into the hallway. Through an open door he glimpsed the boy sawing at a loaf of bread in a high-tech kitchen. The girl had vanished but the distant thud of a stereo suggested she was upstairs. Mrs Ellison opened a door which gave him a glimpse of a small booklined room with a television set and a couple of deep armchairs.

'No,' she said, changing her mind. 'In here.'

They went back down the hall and into a dining-room.

Perhaps she believes we really do all have huge uncontrollable dicks and wants to keep a table between us, thought Sixsmith.

He was almost disappointed when she pulled out a couple of chairs and invited him to sit alongside her.

'Yes, Mr Sixsmith?' she prompted.

'Let's get down to cases, Mrs Ellison,' he said with what he hoped sounded like brisk professionalism. 'What do you really think happened to your cat?'

'I beg your pardon?'

'Lady, just because you're paying me to act clever don't mean you've got to act dumb,' he said in exasperation. 'Look. Your cat goes missing. Most probably it's strayed. That's what you work on, advertising and searching and such. But there's something else bothering you, and when you get no results, you call in a private eye. Me. Now, you're not paying me sixty a day and expenses just to find a stray cat, are you, Mrs Ellison?'

'It would be cheap if you could find him,' she answered. 'But no, you're right, of course. But I'm not sure how to put what I half suspect. It sounds so absurd . . .'

For a second she looked vulnerable enough for Sixsmith to glimpse her with a couple of decades peeled off. Twice the girl her pudgy daughter was, he guessed. He thought of those boobs and shuddered.

'You reckon someone's either stolen your cat, or maybe killed it, am I right?'

She nodded as if this were a less binding form of agreement.

'Right. Who's your money on, Mrs Ellison?' he said.

Immediately she was herself again, formidable and contained.

'My money is on you, Mr Sixsmith. Quite a lot of it,' she said. 'I suggest you start earning it.'

'All right,' he said, reaching into his inner pocket for a notebook and ballpoint. 'Let's get the facts. Mrs Ellison, when did you last see your pussy?'

For a woman plunged in such grief at a pet's disappearance, Mrs Ellison proved to be rather vague about her last sighting.

It had been a Friday almost three weeks earlier. Then she had been away for the weekend and when she returned on the Monday, Darkie had disappeared.

'Where was he when you saw him?' asked Sixsmith.

'Going out,' she replied promptly.

'Through the cat-flap, you mean.'

'Yes.'

'What time was that?'

'Late,' she said after a hesitation.

'Late. Before you went away for the weekend?'

'That I should have thought was a sixty-pence rather than a sixty-pound question,' she said acidly.

'Yes, right. Sorry. Was the whole family away with you, Mrs Ellison?'

'No,' she said shortly. 'I went by myself.'

'Uh-huh,' he said. 'Who took care of Darkie while you were away normally? Your husband? The children? The au pair?'

'I don't know,' she said.

That really surprised him.

'Don't know?'

'No, what I mean is, not being here, I can't be sure . . .'

'That's a sixty-pence answer, Mrs Ellison,' he grinned.

'Don't be impertinent!' she snapped. 'All I meant was that normally when I'm away, I leave strict instructions in writing for his feed and changes of water.'

'I see. And you leave these instructions with . . . ?'

'With the au pair normally,' she said.

'And did you do this on this occasion?'

'No, I didn't,' she said.

'Why not?'

'It wasn't possible. The au pair was not available.'

'You mean she'd left?'

'Yes. She'd left.'

Sixsmith digested this. Three weeks of looking after themselves! How had the Ellisons survived?

'So presumably the family looked after the cat that weekend,' he said. 'I'll need to talk to them, Mrs Ellison.'

'Of course,' she said.

'Presumably you've already questioned them.'

'To very little effect,' she said savagely.

'How little?'

'The children cannot distinctly recall seeing Darkie any time during the weekend.'

'And your husband?'

'I'll leave you to question my husband, Mr Sixsmith.'

So there it is, thought Sixsmith. Suspect Number One is Ellison. Two and Three, presumably the kids. And is there a Four?

He said, 'Neighbours. I may need to talk to them as well. To check on sightings. Will you mind?'

'*I* shan't mind,' she said significantly. 'You can confine yourself to the Bullivants next door. As you will have observed, Mr Sixsmith, to the rear and the left, this house abuts on to Brock Wood. Our sole immediate neighbours therefore are the Bullivants to the right. She is a rather silly but on the whole harmless woman. He . . . well, I'll let you judge for yourself.'

'They would know Darkie?'

'Oh yes,' she said significantly. 'They would know Darkie.

Bullivant and I have had many conversations about Darkie. That stupid man on more than one occasion has accused the poor dear of scratching up his seed-beds and even of damaging his cold frames. He has uttered threats, Mr Sixsmith, and doubtless will utter them again when you see him.'

Sixsmith scratched his bald spot with his ballpoint.

'You've spoken to him already, I suppose?' he said.

'Indeed,' she replied.

Jesus! He's going to love me! thought Sixsmith, beginning to wonder if he'd undercharged.

'Just one more thing,' he said. 'Brock Wood. Do you get many people in there?'

'Too many,' she retorted. 'There's a great deal of activity in there, day and night. Children mainly; courting couples —it can be quite disgusting! And shooting too. We frequently hear gunshot. Pigeons, I presume. Crows. Anything that moves. They're like Frenchmen round here. Frenchmen!'

Sixsmith wasn't clear if she meant the shooters or the lovers. He didn't ask, but said, 'Did Darkie ever get into the wood?'

'Never,' she said firmly. 'We have a heavy duty security fence between our grounds and the wood. Apart from our own private gate which is kept invariably locked when not in use, there is no way through, not even for a cat.'

Sixsmith doubted this, but again he held his peace.

'I'd like to talk to the children now, if I may,' he said.

'Auberon is in the kitchen. Tittie is upstairs, I think. I'll tell her you want to see her.'

'In a couple of minutes,' he said. 'I'll parley with the boy first.'

In the kitchen, Auberon was devouring a sandwich like a pair of badly laid bricks. The table on which he'd prepared it was a bomb site. Sixsmith sat down opposite and looked in vain for a place to put his elbows.

'Good, is it?' asked Sixsmith.

The sandwich was lowered momentarily and the chutney-ringed lips said, ''S all right.'

'Can't be much fun, making your own eats, though,' continued Sixsmith.

This question was treated as rhetorical.

'Your mum's upset about her cat,' said Sixsmith. 'What about you, Auberon? Are you upset?'

The boy swallowed.

'Not much,' he said. 'Always under your feet. Got locked in my room once and pissed in my wardrobe.'

'What did you do?'

'Put my boot up its arse, what do you think?'

Sixsmith pushed his chair back and studied the boy's feet. They were large. In fact, the boy was pretty large all over. The immature face and blue-tinted hair distracted attention from the fact that there was a man's body beneath them. Probably also a man's desire. Sixsmith recalled the slap he'd heard just after the girl had flashed her tits at him. He guessed the boy had tried to kop a feel. Christ, when you were that age and not getting it, you'd give one of your ears for a grope and both for a real bounce! Incest taboos didn't come into it.

Which was not to the point. What was to the point was that a good kick from one of those highly expensive bovver boots could break a cat's neck.

He said, 'Tell me about that weekend.'

'What weekend?'

The boy spoke aggressively but his eyes were on the defensive.

'You know,' said Sixsmith confidently.

'Nothing to tell,' said the boy, taking refuge in his sandwich.

Sixsmith let him chew, noting he had to help mastication with a slurp of milk straight from a bottle. Dry mouth, he told himself, feeling like a real detective.

'Start at the beginning. Friday. What did you do after your mother left?'

'Went back to bed,' said the boy sullenly.

Sixsmith was surprised.

'Hey, man, I know you're a growing boy and need your rest, but wouldn't that be just a little before your normal bedtime?'

'It was midnight. Mebbe later. Don't you know anything?'

The question was meant as a piece of rhetorical scorn, but Sixsmith could see the boy downgrading it to simple interrogative and being surprised by the answer.

'Look, what's all this about? The cat? I never saw the fucking cat, OK? I didn't even know it was missing till Mum came home on the Monday and started making a fuss. She was more concerned about the fucking cat than who was going to do the cooking! Christ, it really makes you realize where you come in the pecking order when your own mother's happy to let you starve so she can go out looking for a bloody cat!'

There were all kinds of things in here, Sixsmith felt. Facts, atmospheres, implications. But he didn't have the kind of mind to make instant computations. His synapses were pre-micro-chip stock. You had to wait around for results.

The kitchen door opened.

'Bloody hellfire! What a mess!'

It was Ellison, who regarded the kitchen table with angry amazement.

'I was going to clean it up,' said the boy unconvincingly.

'You were going to make me a sandwich.'

'All right. What do you want?'

The tone was surly still, but Sixsmith detected a genuine desire to please his father.

'I should like beef dripping on a slice of fresh baked bread, but I don't suppose we run to that, so make it cheese and onion on wholemeal, and don't stint the onion. What about you, Sixsmith? At sixty quid a day, do you give yourself a lunch-break?'

'I'll just tighten my belt a while,' said Sixsmith. 'I've got an appointment with your daughter.'

He went out into the hallway. Ellison followed him.

'Third on the left when you reach the landing,' he said. 'If your bloodhound nose misses the scent, just follow your droopy ears.'

89

The gibe set Sixsmith's clockwork mental calculator clicking a couple of notches.

'First thing you said to me was *Hello Sherlock*, Mr Ellison,' he said.

'So?'

'So how'd you know I was a detective?'

'Mebbe my wife told me,' said Ellison.

'I don't think so,' said Sixsmith. 'I mean, communication hasn't exactly been flowing like the crystal stream between you two. Also, she was surprised when she spotted I was no WASP. You weren't. Just amused.'

Ellison didn't answer straightaway, then said speculatively, 'Could be you're not so daft after all.'

'Meaning?'

Ellison said, 'My wife got you out of the Yellow Pages, Mr Sixsmith. Nice ad you've got there. I heard her make the call. I like to know what my family's getting for their money, so I made a couple of calls myself. What did I find? That until two months ago the head of *Sixsmith Investigations Inc.* was a lathe operator at Robco Engineering who took his redundancy money, got himself an office on a six months' lease, and set up as a private eye. This your first case?'

'Second,' said Sixsmith. 'I did a tailing job. Divorce case.'

'How'd that work out?'

'Not so hot. I got pulled in on sus, loitering outside the Four Seasons Restaurant. Well, I couldn't afford to go in there, could I, man?'

Ellison hooted with laughter. The Four Seasons was the area's top restaurant, famous for its food, infamous for its prices.

So, I've reassured him, thought Sixsmith as he went up the stairs. But why should this man, who likes to be sure his family gets the best value for money, need to be reassured that his wife had got herself the most inexperienced and inefficient gumshoe in town?

The landing ran left and right. The noise of the music came from the left. Sixsmith turned right.

There were four doors. One opened on a palatial bathroom, another on the master bedroom, the third on a room which had once been a nursery and was now a store room for all the sad relics of childhood. The fourth revealed another bedroom, probably normally reserved for guests but currently, from the evidence of discarded clothing, being used by Ellison.

The other end of the landing also had four doors. There was another bathroom, a bedroom which was clearly Auberon's, then the girl's room. The door was ajar. Through it he could glimpse the bottom half of a bed with the girl's legs sprawled across it. The boom of the hi-fi and the thickness of the carpet gave him ample cover and he moved swiftly by to the fourth door. This led into another bedroom, but this one had the bed stripped and was devoid of ornament and all other evidence of present use.

'What do you think you're doing here?'

So much for cover! The girl had come up behind him.

'Hi,' he said. 'I was just looking for you.'

'You deaf or something? I'm in here.'

She led him into her pulsating room and said something. He grimaced and cupped his ear with his hand. She rolled her eyes in irritation and switched the hi-fi down.

'Mum says I've to talk to you,' she said.

He sat down in an old basket chair and said, 'You always do what Mum tells you?'

'Look, just get on with it, Sixsmith or whatever your name is.'

'That's my name, honey,' he agreed.

'It'll be your slave name, won't it?' she flashed. 'And don't call me honey.'

'What'll I call you then? Missie Ellison. *Ms* Ellison? Or why don't you call me Joe, so you won't have to soil your tongue with no slave name, and I'll call you Tittie. That's a nice old-fashioned name, now. Short for Titania, is it? Or Letitia?'

'It could be long for Tit,' she answered, studying him slyly to see his reaction.

'Man, from what I've seen, it just wouldn't be long enough,' he replied with a grin.

'You liked that, did you?' she said. 'Gave you a thrill?'

'Listen, girl,' he said seriously. 'I think you've been reading too many books about them poor repressed negroes in Alabam' and such places, who get off on a white woman's ankles, and get burned alive if they're caught looking. You want to give instant thrills, you stick to that brother of yours!'

'Him? God, he's disgusting. He's just obsessed. He once offered me five quid to jerk him off. Five quid! Can you imagine?'

Whether he was being invited to express indignation at the proposal or merely the price wasn't clear. Sixsmith's affections tended to blossom as leisurely as his deductions, but he was beginning to doubt if he could love this family. At the same time he suddenly found himself feeling genuinely concerned at the fate of poor old Darkie.

He cast around for his best line of questioning and into his head popped something that Auberon had said. 'I went *back* to bed.'

He said, 'That weekend, that Friday night, what time did you get to bed?'

She looked at him doubtfully and he chanced his arm and said, 'The first time, I mean.'

'Just after midnight,' she said, as if reassured that he was merely confirming what he already knew.

'And how long was it before . . . ?' he tailed off, crossing his fingers.

'Half an hour. Twenty minutes maybe. It didn't take long!' she said with indignant scorn.

'No,' agreed Sixsmith. 'That evening, what kind of evening had it been? For you I mean?'

Surprisingly he seemed to have hit a good line.

'Oh, it was all right, you know. A bit draggy, really. I mean, you'd have thought we could have gone somewhere a bit lively, a night club maybe, but Mummy likes queening it at the Four Seasons. Me, I'm trying to diet, and they cover everything in cream, so all I got out of it was a bit of salad. But it pleased them, and then there was going to be the party . . . oh Christ, it was so awful! I've never been so humiliated . . .'

To Sixsmith's dismay the podgy face screwed up in grief. Tits he could deal with; tears were beyond him.

'It must have been awful,' he said. 'Really awful.'

'It was, oh, it was!' she agreed tearfully.

But what was? And what had it all to do with the bloody cat?

'To get things quite clear,' he said. 'You were all at the Four Seasons? All four of you?'

'Five,' she said viciously.

Five? For a crazy second he thought she meant they'd taken the cat! Then the old machinery clicked.

'I meant the four of you in the family. Plus, of course . . . what's her second name, by the way?'

'Netzer. Astrid Netzer.'

'Yes. Plus Astrid. You got back here before midnight . . .'

'About half eleven. Daddy said, was I going to open my presents at midnight? and I said, no, I'd leave them till the morning, and Daddy said he'd open a bottle of champagne anyway, and Mummy said she had a bit of a headache so she thought she'd go on up. Off she went. Daddy got the champagne, opened it and filled our glasses. Midnight struck, they all toasted me and wished me happy birthday . . .'

At last! It had been the kid's birthday, seventeenth probably, on the Saturday. Friday night had been family celebration night with the posh dinner out. But the big occasion as far as the girl was concerned was to be her own party on Saturday night.

He began to guess the rest, but pressed for confirmation.

'Who went upstairs first, you or your brother?'

'We went at the same time. He drank his champers straight down and wanted some more. He was a bit tiddly, he gets like that very easily, and Daddy said he'd be better drinking coffee and he got on his high horse and said in that case he was off to bed. I said I'd go up too. I didn't want to risk waking up with a headache and spoiling things. God, it makes me sick just thinking about it. I went to bed not to spoil things. Perhaps if I'd sat up a bit longer . . .'

'You went to bed, leaving your father and Astrid downstairs?'

'Yes. He said he'd finish the bottle and she said she'd clear up. I got undressed and into bed. And then, it hardly seemed any time at all before I heard the yelling.'

'The yelling?'

'Yes. Mummy. God, what a noise! I thought we must be under attack. By the time I got downstairs, she'd quietened down a bit, but that was worse. When she goes all icy and under control, that's far worse than yelling.'

'But you gathered what had happened.'

'Oh yes. Well, it was clear enough. Daddy was busy buttoning up, but that bitch didn't even bother. Mummy had got tired of waiting for Daddy to come to bed and gone downstairs. She looked in the snug . . .'

'The snug. That's the little television room?'

'That's right. The lounge, you see, is right underneath their bedroom, so they'd gone into the snug. And there they were, hard at it . . .'

The girl was once more close to tears. Perhaps, thought Sixsmith, he'd misjudged her. Even spoilt brats had feelings.

'There, there,' he said awkwardly. 'It'll be all right.'

She took a deep breath.

'How can it be all right?' she demanded. 'There was a terrible row and Mummy packed her case, and said she wouldn't be back while that creature was in the house and walked out, and the next day . . . the next day . . .'

Her sobs were almost choking her.

'Yes, honey?' urged Sixsmith.

'The next day I had to cancel my fucking party!'

So what have I got so far? Sixsmith asked himself as he walked up the driveway of the house next to the Ellisons.

A neurotic woman, a frustrated man, a pair of spoilt, self-centred kids and a randy au pair.

And Darkie.

The woman loves Darkie as much as she loves anything, but in her rage at finding Ellison on the job, she sweeps out

without a thought for him. Understandable in the circumstances. But where does that leave the cat?

In a houseful of enemies, that's where. Enemies in many
ways. Well, three ways anyway. He mentally catalogued.

(1) *Enemies by neglect.*

A cat, used to the best of everything from its mistress,
suddenly finds its source of warmth, comfort and gourmet
meals is cut off. Not enough to kill it, though, but maybe
enough to make it take a powder.

(2) *Enemies by accident and irritation.*

In the emotional atmosphere of the house that weekend,
who'd pay any heed to the cat? And if it was too imperative
in its demands for attention, well, he already had the boy's
admission that he wasn't above taking a swing at it with his
boot.

(3) *Enemies by malice aforethought.*

Mrs Ellison must have been the object of considerable
antagonism after she left, and what better way of taking
revenge than striking at the thing she loved? Ellison, tired
of playing second fiddle to a cat and in that excess of
righteous fury known only to those caught in the wrong,
could have done the deed. Or Astrid, told to pack her bags
and still smarting from the stream of nasty things Mrs
Ellison doubtless called her, may have looked for some
particularly bloody parting shot. Even Tittie may have
blamed her mother as much as her father for the cancellation
of her party. Auberon alone seemed to have no motive for
deliberate slaughter, but who knows what goes on in the
mind of a mixed-up adolescent?

Well satisfied that with such a fine analysis, a solution
could not lag far behind, Sixsmith rang the bell of the
Bullivant residence.

Ten minutes later his analysis had been modified to
include two more prime suspects, one of which came very
close to an open confession on the part of the other. The
talkative one was Bullivant himself, a small dark prickly
man, like a blackthorn bush in motion. Sixsmith, unsure of
his reception, had mentioned the cat with some diffidence.
Immediately he was swept round the side of the house into

the rear garden to be shown the variety of anti-personnel devices which Bullivant had erected in his war against Darkie and all other four-legged intruders. These devices ranged from the merely deterrent such as pepper, netting and a tight-mesh wire fence, to the captivating, such as pitfalls and mink-traps.

The final weapon in Bullivant's armoury was unequivocally lethal.

'It's all right. He won't harm you without my say-so,' said Bullivant confidently. 'Will you, Kaiser?'

Sixsmith looked uneasily at his second new suspect, a huge black Dobermann who returned his gaze assessingly.

'You let this thing run loose?' he inquired.

'He has the run of the garden at night, yes. No pests here, I tell you. Saves on his food bill too.'

He laughed as he spoke and patted the dog's head approvingly.

'You mean, he catches . . . things, and eats them?'

'That's it.'

'Including cats?'

'Especially cats!'

Sixsmith looked at the animal with a distaste which was clearly mutual and said, 'What about traces? I mean, if he's eaten something, would you know?'

'Oh, a bit of blood on the grass maybe. Sometimes I hear a bit of squealing in the night,' said Bullivant cheerfully.

'Two weekends ago, did you spot any blood, or hear any squealing?'

'Two weekends ago?' Bullivant's tight little face screwed up like a brussel sprout in the effort of memory.

'You're wondering about that monster of Ellison's, aren't you? No I don't recollect any blood or squealing. But there was something, I remember. Early Saturday morning, or was it Sunday? He woke me up. Doesn't bark much, but I'm a light sleeper. I had a look out. Nothing in the garden, but he seemed to have caught a noise in the woods. Over there.'

He pointed diagonally across his own garden. Sixsmith followed the line of the finger through the dividing fence and across the neighbouring garden, and found himself looking at Ellison standing in his shrubbery, watching them. Their eyes met, then Ellison turned away and walked back towards his house.

'Do you often get disturbances in the woods?'

'All the time,' said Bullivant. 'Kids in the day, God knows what at night. Lot of people are scared to go walking in the woods these days. But not me, not when I've got Kaiser! Which reminds me. It's time for his constitutional now. Come, Kaiser. You can see yourself out, can't you?'

'Sure,' said Sixsmith, watching as Bullivant set off down his garden with the dog at his heels. There was a solid, heavily padlocked metal gate in the wire fence leading into the woods. Bullivant unlocked it and sent the dog out ahead of him.

Turning back, he called, 'Tell Ellison, yes, Kaiser could have had that moggy, it's true. But where's your proof, eh? Where's your proof!'

And with a bark of laughter, he followed the silent dog into the wood.

As he returned to the Ellisons, Sixsmith said to himself, 'Joe boy, you were wrong. Sixty a day is no fair payment for trading with the natives of Brock Wood Lane! They're cannibals, man, real cannibals!

Ellison met him at the front door. He looked very angry.

'Who the hell gave you the right to start bothering my neighbours!'

Bullivant would have been surprised by this protective-ness, Sixsmith guessed. He also guessed Ellison was more concerned that the squalid details of his private life were being bandied about than with his neighbour's privacy.

He was saved the trouble of defending himself by Mrs Ellison's appearance.

'I will remind you that this man is in my employ. Mine is the only authority he needs to question anyone!'

'You think so? This is still my house!'

'Still *half* your house. Even our grossly biased divorce laws allow the woman that right.'

97

Ellison glowered at her, then to Sixsmith's surprise became relatively conciliatory.

'All right, all right. No need to talk like that, not in public. Look, don't you think this has gone far enough? The bloody cat has obviously just taken off. Mebbe it got knocked down, like this fellow said when he first arrived. Well, all right, it's sad and I'm sorry. But either it'll come back or else you can get yourself another. You can get yourself a whole bloody cattery for what you're likely to end up paying Sherlock here!'

Sixsmith couldn't fault the man's logic. He wished he'd made it clear the advance was non-returnable. He made a mental note to get such things written down in future. If there was a future. With only three months of his lease left to run, he was a long way from making a living. Not that there wasn't the work, but half a dozen prospective clients in this liberal, integrated country had shied off when they realized what they'd caught by the toe.

Happily Mrs Ellison was not in the mood for right reason.

She ignored her husband and said, 'Come with me, Mr Sixsmith, and report.'

Meekly he followed her into the house.

They went into the lounge once more.

'Well?' she said.

'It's early days,' he said.

'At sixty pounds an early day, I'm entitled to an hourly update if I so require,' she retorted.

She had a point.

He took a deep breath and said, 'All I've worked out is probably what you could have told me when I first arrived, Mrs Ellison. Which is that, the way things were that weekend, anyone in this house might have harmed Darkie. Or at least encouraged him to leave.'

'Anyone?' she said, giving nothing away.

'Mr Ellison. The kids. Even the au pair. Maybe particularly the au pair.'

He threw this in out of charity. If there was no positive solution, and this seemed the probable outcome, then it would hurt least to have the most distant suspect in terms of space and relationship elected the most likely.

'You know about that?' she said, very chill, very formal.

'I had to know. It was relevant,' he said.

'I suppose so. And you think that that *woman* might have been responsible?'

She made *woman* sound like it had four letters.

'Could be. You probably tore a strip off her, right? She may have resented that so much that . . . well, it depends what sort of girl she was.'

'Wanton,' she said crisply. 'I can find out her home address through the agency.'

He shook his head in disbelief.

'Lady, you don't really want me to go to Germany, do you?' he said.

She thought a moment, then said, 'No, I suppose not. But if that creature did do something to Darkie, then he must be still around somewhere, mustn't he?'

It was a fair deduction. Astrid was hardly going to pass through Customs with a dead cat in her holdall.

Sixsmith nodded.

'Then at least earn your money by finding him so that we can give him a proper burial!'

She left the room swiftly and Sixsmith thought he heard a scuffle of footsteps on the stairs. He wondered if he should have offered his alternative theory, which was that Kaiser had disposed of Darkie. Kaiser, too, was outside the family. On the other hand, she had to live next door to the monster. Both monsters.

He went into the hallway and ran lightly up the stairs. Tittie's room was closed, but the door to her brother's was ajar.

He pushed it open and went in. The boy was lying on the bed.

'Don't you knock before coming through doors?' he demanded.

'Don't you knock before listening at them?' replied Sixsmith.

He sat on the edge of the bed and said, 'When do the bins get picked up round here?'

'What?'

'The dustbins, man. Those big round containers you dump the rubbish in.'

'I don't know. Thursday, I think. Or Friday. That's right, Friday. They come early and make such a fucking din, they wake me up.'

'That's terrible,' said Sixsmith.

So a dustbin disposal was unlikely. You might dump your dead cat there if the bins were going to be picked up very soon, but not when it was almost a week away.

'Do you think Astrid could have killed the cat?' he asked suddenly.

The boy sat up, alarmed.

'I don't know. Why ask me?'

'Because you know the girl. I don't. Listen, son, I know all about what went on that weekend. I'm sorry, believe me. But it happens. An attractive young chick can turn anyone on, so don't blame your dad too much.'

'I don't,' said the boy in a muffled voice, slumping back on the pillows.

'No? Well, OK.'

A thought occurred to Sixsmith. Ellison senior had proved susceptible, true; but the real centre of unsatisfied male desire in this household lay on the bed before him.

'You ever fancy her yourself, Auberon?'

The boy did not reply, but he didn't need to. His face was flushed like a dawn sky.

Sixsmith said, 'And did you ever try your hand?'

'Shut up! Shut up! Just go away and leave me!'

'OK, OK!' said Sixsmith, standing up. 'Sorry I spoke, man. Look, I'm going. Don't let it worry you, though. We all get the cold finger some time, believe me.'

His words of consolation were clearly falling more like hailstones than the soothing rain.

He left.

Tittie's door opened as he went by.

'You still prowling around up here?' she said.

'I've been talking to your brother,' he said. 'About Astrid.'

'What about her?' she demanded.

'Just about the play he made for her.'

'Play? You call it play to wander naked into her room? Child's play, maybe. That's what he is, a child. Imagine thinking just because she let Daddy do it, she'd be happy to accommodate poor little Auberon too!'

She laughed stridently, humourlessly.

Sixsmith said, 'Where do I get the key to the garden gate?'

'Why?'

'I'd like to go into the woods at the bottom of the garden,' said Sixsmith. 'To see if I can spot any fairies.'

'Oh. It's hanging up in the kitchen. But you'll have to ask Daddy.'

'You ask Daddy,' he said. 'Daddy and I ain't exactly speaking.'

She followed him into the kitchen and offered no help as he examined a selection of keys on a row of hooks.

'You don't sound like a West Indian,' she said suddenly. 'Only sometimes.'

'I've been here a long time,' he said. 'More than twice as long as you, which is to say, all my life. This the one?'

She ignored the question and said, 'You're going bald. I didn't know that kind of hair went bald.'

'It don't,' he said. 'We shave it off and sell it to bed manufacturers to stuff mattresses with. What about this one?'

But she wasn't going to answer. She simply stood there with sudden tears in her eyes. She looked about twelve.

Don't start feeling sorry for them, Sixsmith told himself. That's the way you end in chains.

He took the three most likely keys and went into the garden.

The gate was even bigger and solider than Bullivant's. It fitted snugly into an iron mesh fence whose ugly angularity was hidden from the house by a boundary of shrubs and further disguised by clematis, and ivy, and various other climbing species.

The first key fitted and Sixsmith passed through the gate. He saw at once that the woods were far too extensive for one man to have much hope of finding the small patch of disturbed ground under which a cat might be buried, but this didn't bother him. All he really wanted was a quiet stroll and a bit of space for thinking in.

He had paused just through the gateway and he became aware that Ellison's metal fence was not the outermost boundary of his garden. Before the fence, a mixed hedge of beech, hawthorn, blackthorn and bramble must have ringed the property. The fence had been built about three feet inside the hedge and since then the unchecked growth of the vegetation had formed a narrow tunnel between the metal and the vegetable barriers.

It was a noise somewhere along this tunnel that attracted Sixsmith's attention, a snuffling, scraping noise. He thought of investigating, then heard another noise which at the same time solved the problem and made him glad he'd stayed put.

'Kaiser! Kaiser! Where are you, damn you!'

It was Bullivant's voice and a moment later the man himself appeared.

'Oh, it's you,' he said ungraciously. 'You haven't seen that blasted dog, have you?'

'I think it's up there,' said Sixsmith, pointing.

Bullivant stooped down and began to make his way along the tunnel. Sixsmith hesitated, then the clockwork of his mind clicked with unwonted speed, and he turned and followed.

They found Kaiser about twenty yards in, scrabbling away with his front paws at a patch of ground thickly covered in dead leaves. But where the dog had shifted the leaves, it was clear the revealed earth had been recently disturbed.

'Kaiser, what the hell are you playing at? *Still*, boy. *Still!*'

The dog growled in its throat, but obeyed.

'Must be a bone. Or maybe a rabbit burrow,' said Bullivant.

Sixsmith shook his head sadly.

'Neither,' he said. 'I reckon it's a cat.'

'A cat?'

For a moment Bullivant was puzzled, then suddenly he laughed.

'Oh, you mean *that* cat? What's this, then? Dirty work at the crossroads? Someone in there dislike it as much as me, did they?'

'Why don't you shut up?' said Sixsmith. 'If you stop here, I'll go and get a spade.'

'Why bother?' said the man. 'Kaiser'll have it up in no time.'

'Look, man,' said Sixsmith. 'You get a grip on that fucking beast of yours, right? It couldn't catch the cat alive, I see no reason why it should get to maul him dead. Also it's going to be painful enough for Mrs Ellison as things are without finding Fido here chewing at the remains.'

Bullivant was clearly not happy at Sixsmith's assumption of command, but he contented himself with saying, 'Could be the poor moggy's been mauled around already!' and gripped Kaiser's collar.

It was Sixsmith's hope that he could get back to the house and find a spade without being spotted, but he was out of luck.

Ellison was in the garden once more approaching the open gate. Behind him was Tittie.

'What the hell are you up to, Sixsmith? You've no right to go pushing your way round this house as though you own it!'

'Sorry,' said Sixsmith. 'But I think I've found the cat. I'll need a spade.'

'Oh Christ. Where?'

'In that sort of tunnel between the fence and the hedge. Mr Bullivant's there with his dog.'

Ellison looked towards Tittie, his face pale with an emotion which could have been anything from shock, through pity, to guilt. The girl didn't look much better.

And now to make things worse, Mrs Ellison, seeing them from the kitchen window, came running down the garden, followed by Auberon.

'You've found something, haven't you?' she cried.

103

'No,' said Ellison savagely. 'You stay here! Auberon, look after your mother.'

He turned and headed for the gate with Tittie close behind.

Auberon put a hand on his mother's arm, but she shook it off.

'Wait!' she cried. 'Wait!'

And she too was gone.

'Where will I find a spade?' Sixsmith said to the boy, who looked as though he was feeling sea-sick.

'In there,' he choked, pointing towards a garden shed.

Then he too went running after the others.

The shed was locked. None of the keys Sixsmith had with him opened it, so he went back to the kitchen in search of the right one. He could hear the front doorbell ringing, but he had no time for that.

He tried his new selection, found one that fitted and opened the shed.

From the comprehensive supply of tools, he selected a spade and hurried back through the door, almost crashing into the bosom of a uniformed policeman.

'Hello,' said the officer.

Sixsmith paused and studied the man.

He was a young constable. In his hand he carried a plastic carrier bag.

'You the owner?' asked the constable doubtfully, adding, 'Sir?' just to be on the safe side.

'No,' said Sixsmith. 'I just work here.'

'Ah,' said the youth, relieved. 'Gardener, eh? Look, is there anyone around? I've been ringing the bell.'

'What's it about?' asked Sixsmith.

The constable looked inclined to tell him it was none of his business, but then changed his mind. The reason why became quickly apparent. He wanted information.

'The lady, Mrs Ellison, is she all right?' he asked, with an intonation which made it clear it was mental health he was interested in.

'A bit highly strung,' said Sixsmith. 'Why?'

'It's these,' said the constable, opening the bag.

104

It was full of bits of female clothing.

'They've been found all over. There was a laundry mark on some of them, that's how we've got on to Mrs Ellison. Then someone remembered she'd been causing a stink lately about a lost cat, you know, going on like it had been kidnapped or murdered.'

Suddenly Sixsmith saw a chance to be out of the way when this miserable business came to its sad and grisly climax.

'Here,' he said thrusting the spade into the young man's hand. 'They're all out there. Through the gate, turn left straight away. There's a sort of a tunnel. The whole family's there.'

'Eh? What're they doing? And what's this for?' demanded the constable, examining the spade dubiously.

'They've gone to dig up a body,' said Sixsmith. 'That's called a spade. It's for digging. You could do yourself a bit of good, maybe.' He didn't wait for a response but headed for the house. He reckoned his expenses covered at least one stiff drink and he went into the lounge, poured himself a large whisky and slumped into one of the deep armchairs to enjoy a moment of peace before the Ellisons returned and the recriminations began.

As he took a long pull at his drink, he heard a noise from the hallway. A sort of click. The letter-box perhaps, but it lacked the metallic sharpness of a letter-box. It was more like the . . .

There was another click, this one in his mind. He sat up and stared at the open door.

It caused him small surprise but the beginning of infinite horror when a small black cat, with a white patch over its left eye and ear, came round the corner, miaowed a greeting, then jumped on to his lap and began purring in clear anticipation of being made much of.

Now his mind was clicking and whirring like a clock-maker's repair room.

'Oh Jesus!' he said aghast. 'Oh Jesus, Jesus, Jesus!'

The cat purred on.

*

The telephone rang on Joe Sixsmith's leather-topped desk.

He picked it up.

'Sixsmith,' he said crisply.

'Hello. Is that the Mr Sixsmith who solved the Astrid Netzer case?'

'The very same.'

'Good, that's fine. Look, Mr Sixsmith, I'd like to hire you to do a job . . .'

'Hold it,' said Sixsmith, riffling through his desk diary. 'I can't talk now, I'm on my way out. Anyway, I like to see my clients before I take a job. Wednesday morning, eight-thirty, I can fit you in. That suit?'

'Not till Wednesday? I hoped . . .'

'Sorry. When you get the best, you get the busiest. Shall I put you in?'

'Yes, I suppose so.'

The details noted, Sixsmith replaced the receiver, connected his answering machine and stretched luxuriously.

The past three months had been good to him. The case had still to come to trial and the police where still uncertain who was to be charged with what, but that didn't matter to the media. There'd been a crime of passion. A dead *au pair* always made for good headlines, but this time they'd been handed a new folk-hero on a plate, a man for all political seasons.

What better symbol of the times could there be than a balding, redundant, West Indian lathe-operator who'd made good?

Joe Sixsmith glanced at his watch. It was time to go. He was lunching with a client and had a reputation for punctuality to keep up.

As he stood up, there was a protesting noise from the bottom drawer of his desk. He pulled it open and a small black cat with a white patch over its left eye and ear yawned up at him.

Mrs Ellison was resting her shattered nerves in a Swiss sanatorium and Sixsmith had agreed to look after the cat. He charged no fee but had made one condition, a simple matter of nomenclature.

'Sorry, Whitey,' he said. 'They don't allow no live animals where I'm going, but I'll bring you back a slice of rare beef, shall I?'

The cat purred its agreement. It had a loud rasping purr when it was happy. It sometimes reminded Joe Sixsmith of his old lathe.

He smiled at the memory, checked to see that his well-filled wallet was bulging in his inside pocket like a shoulder-holster, and went out to walk down the mean streets that led to the Four Seasons Restaurant.

THE BULL RING

'You horrible man!' shrieked the canary. 'You useless fucking lump of dogshit! You're not down among the turnips now trying to stick your pathetic little prick up a sheep's bum! That's a Boche there, that's a nasty fucking Hun, and that's your bayonet! You're trying to kill him not tickle him to death! *In*! *Rip*! *Twist*! *Out*! I want to see his guts trailing round his ankles! I want to see Hun shit squirting in all directions! *Out*! *Out*! Stand on him! Use those great plates of meat! Jesus Christ! I've seen some useless fucking specimens in my time, but you're the worst yet, you're the scrapings off the bottom of the barrel!'

By looking over the canary's head, which was not difficult as he was a good twelve inches taller, Harry could see across the heat-trembling sand dunes and across the sparkling estuary, to where the little sea-side resort of Le Touquet Paris-Plage nestled in the sun. Whitewashed walls, red roofs, women at their baking, children at their play—it was less than a couple of miles and more than a couple of centuries away.

'Bloody hell,' he gasped suddenly and doubled up in agony. It took several seconds for the pain to ease enough for him to realize the canary had struck him between the legs with the short wooden baton he carried.

'You listening to me, soldier? You paying attention now, are you?' yelled the man. 'You won't get away from me by daydreaming, I promise you. I'll follow you in your fucking dreams till you beg to wake up, and I'll still be there! Stand up straight when an NCO addresses you, you long bloody clothes-pole, you!'

Painfully Harry straightened up. The canary came close and stood on tiptoe to bring his face as nearly level with Harry's as possible.

'Wouldn't you like to kill me now, sheep-shagger? Wouldn't you like to stick your bayonet in *my* belly and rip and twist? But you don't have the nerve, do you, you long streak of owl-shit? You're as yellow as my brassard, Bowden, and that's the way you'd like to stay, isn't it? But never you fret, lad, I'll make you or I'll fucking break you! *On guard! Advance! Run! Run! Run!* Pretend it's me, Bowden, pretend it's me! *In! Rip! Twist! Out!*'

Harry did his best, but his heart wasn't in it. He stumbled from one line of dangling figures to the next, thrusting and twisting, thrusting and twisting, but it seemed such a pointless exercise, like running across the five-acre at home and hitting the old scarecrow with his pitchfork! The figures were as real as they could make them. Suspended in rows of six from a series of cross-bars, with their legs trailing like a cripple's on the golden sand, the grotesque effigies were clad in German grey with their tunics stuffed solid with straw to admit the passage of steel and their trousers packed with sand to give weight and resistance. But to Harry they were nothing but scarecrows, and this whole business of running and screaming and thrusting was just a lunatic part of a vile, incomprehensible nightmare from which there seemed to be no waking.

He had volunteered three months earlier on his eighteenth birthday in February, 1916. Everyone said that soon they'd be bringing in conscription, so he'd decided he might as well sign up of his own accord, particularly as everyone said that volunteers were bound to get better treated than pressed men. It had seemed a big adventure at the time, going with his mate, Bert Pogmore, to the recruiting station in Nottingham to sign on. And that's how it had continued to feel for a while. The initial training was tough, but he and Bert were used to getting up early and working hard all day. Also the regimental depot was not above five miles from the village where they were born, so there'd been plenty of opportunity to show off in their new uniforms. And when word came that they were going overseas, they'd been fêted like heroes by their fellow villagers.

It was after that that the nightmare began. They'd landed at a place called Boulogne. His first view of French houses and French people had been a bit of a disappointment. They looked different, but not so different you could write a long letter home about it. But the way they yapped on like Old George, the village idiot, as if their rapid mutterings made good English sense, *that* was fascinating to hear.

Soon after arrival, the newcomers had done a big ceremonial march through the town, just to show these Frenchies they were in good hands, and there'd been a great deal of cheering, and waving of Union Jacks and Tricolours side by side, and that night he'd had his first taste of plinkety-plonk which was a bit sour but it made you just as cheerful as Burton ale, so that was all right.

The next day they'd been put on a train. Harry wasn't much used to trains, but in England they'd always had cushioned seats, not hard benches like this one, and they went a sodding sight faster too! It must have taken over two hours to go not much above fifteen miles.

But when they reached their destination, they soon had cause to wish that it had taken them a good deal longer.

They were at a small town called Étaples, or rather in a camp close by. The town itself was out of bounds to all except the permanent staff of the camp, so it remained as mysterious to Harry and his comrades as Timbuctoo. But the camp they were in had no mysteries. All its horrors were on open show.

The nearest Harry could get to it in his own experience was the Great County Show he'd gone to in 1913. There too there'd been acres of ground covered with marquees and huts, with the earth between all rutted by the passage of cattle and agricultural machinery. But that experience had been exciting and interesting and full of delight, and even when it started raining and he'd got soaked and his boots were covered with mud and his nostrils full of the scent of wet canvas and crushed grass, he'd still enjoyed it.

But this place was not for enjoyment. It reminded him also of what they called a shanty town in a film he'd seen at the new Picture Palace in Nottingham. There was the same air of wildness and strangeness, with supply wagons and gun limbers being dragged by teams of horses along the primitive streets, with arguments breaking out, and accidents, and the military police rushing in to sort things out. The difference was that in the shanty town there'd been a saloon, with drinks on sale, and girls dancing, and men enjoying themselves.

Here there was none of these things. Here there were primitive sleeping conditions, constant parades, gruelling route marches in full pack, so that even the promised relief of the Church Army rest hut or Expeditionary Force Canteen was often out of reach of the exhausted men.

But still the worst was to come, for after a couple of days of being issued with equipment, harangued, bullied, threatened, marched and inspected, they were introduced to the Bull Ring.

The Bull Ring was the name given to Number 2 Training Camp. The name was not ill chosen, for here men were pricked and pushed, abused and assaulted, driven and degraded, till something in them sank to its knees and died.

The Bull Ring was a complex of training grounds set among the sand dunes with a huge levelled parade ground at its core. There were rifle ranges, bomb-throwing ranges and machine-gun ranges; there were bayonet courses and gas-training courses; there were trenches to crawl along, barbed wire embuscades to crawl through, and mines to crawl down. In short, there was here a miniature of the war which waited for them not many miles to the east.

And for every man being trained, there seemed to be at least one canary.

The canaries were the instructors, so called because of the bright yellow armbands they wore to make themselves easily identifiable. Not that they needed such aids to identification. Wherever there was a man screaming filthy abuse, perpetually livid with rage, and delighting in driving his fellow human beings to the point of collapse and despair, that was a canary.

Perhaps there were some who were not like this, but there were so many who were that those who still had a residual humanity went unnoticed.

And for poor Harry Bowden there was only one. Corporal Pierce.

Corporal Pierce seemed to have been drawn irresistibly towards Harry from the start. Perhaps it was the attraction of opposites. Harry was broad-shouldered, over six foot tall, fresh-faced, fair-haired and of an open sunny disposition. Pierce was dark and skinny, foul-mouthed and evil-tempered, and he didn't stand much above five feet in his socks. He was small enough almost to have got into one of the so-called bantam regiments, and indeed Banty Pierce was the name by which he was known to his few friends and many enemies alike.

But if it was an attraction of opposites, then it was an attraction expressed as pure hate.

Whatever activity Harry was allotted, Pierce materialized at his side within ten minutes. It was Pierce who screamed in his ear till he missed the target completely on the rifle range. It was Pierce who made him stand and watch the flight of the Mills bomb he had thrown a good three seconds after everybody else had hit the bottom of the trench. It was Pierce who snapped at his heels on the drill ground till he forgot which was left and which was right.

'That Banty, I think he fancies you, Harry,' joked Bert Pogmore as they sat together in the dining hut one day. Harry didn't reply. He was out of breath, having doubled all the way from the bomb range. As usual, Pierce had made sure he was last to leave which meant that the dining hut was already crammed when he got there. Fortunately Pogmore and a few more of his intake had managed by brute force to keep him a place on one of the hard wooden benches.

'That Banty, he needs a bloody good kicking,' said a man called Tommy Carruthers. There was a chorus of agreement but they all knew it was an empty threat. Canaries flocked together in camp and did their socializing across the river in the forbidden township of Étaples. And even if the chance had offered itself, fear of the consequences was a strong inhibiting factor in most of the men.

'I can't figure it out, Bert,' said Harry in honest bewilderment. 'I never harmed him, did I? Christ, I never set eyes on the little sod till I got here! Why's he keep on at me?'

'Fuck knows,' said Pogmore. 'Look out, here comes the swill.'

Swill wasn't an inexact term for the food which was ladled out by orderlies from big churns. The orderlies, dressed in filth-encrusted aprons which were their only concession to hygiene, were more concerned with speed than accuracy, and the food frequently splashed over the edge of plate or bowl. The table top, casually wiped down once a day, had its coarse grain permanently packed with old dried food, whose stale smell mingled with the odour of sweaty bodies to produce a stench almost as visible as the steam from the urns. And unless you were fortunate enough to get in for the first sitting, you were likely to find yourself confronted by a table awash with fresh leavings from those who preceded you.

'For fuck's sake!' yelled Pogmore as an orderly deposited a ladleful of stew with such force that it splashed the soldier's face.

'What you moaning at, mate? You'll be praying for this when you're up the Line!' mocked the orderly.

'If I had my way I'd send you and all these other fucking base-wallahs up the line tomorrow!' yelled Pogmore.

But the orderly was already out of earshot and in any case quite impervious to these outbursts of abuse which were a price he gladly paid to remain so far removed from the fatal East.

'It's bloody disgusting, this,' complained Tommy Carruthers. 'They take better care of animals back home.'

'That's what they want to make us,' said Pogmore. 'Animals. They want to turn us into beasts.'

'They'll not make a beast out of me,' said Harry. 'They'll not!'

That afternoon they were on the machine-gun range. Each platoon had its specialist Lewis-gun section, but everyone had to be proficient in the weapon in case of need. As usual, Pierce was soon snapping at Harry's heels but midway through the session even his malice was diverted when there was a tremendous scream from the next position.

Pierce shot off and after a while Harry rose and went after him.

He found a group of men standing around Bert Pogmore who was sitting on the ground looking in pale amazement at his right hand. Dangling from it by a thread of skin and tendon was his thumb. Blood pulsed regularly from the open wound in which the socket of his thumb joint was clearly visible.

'He left it in the way of the cocking-handle,' said a canary. 'Stupid bastard! If they've been told once, they've been told a thousand times!'

Someone had sent for a stretcher but when it came, Pogmore refused to get on and with a canary in attendance, set off to walk to the medical hut.

Without thinking, Harry began to follow but Pierce screamed at him, 'Where the fuck do you think you're going, Bowden? Seen a bit of blood, have we? That's nothing to what's waiting you out there. Nothing! Let's get back to work. And don't be getting any ideas, any of you! Just because you've seen your mate get a Blighty, don't think you'll follow suit. Next thumb that gets lost in this lot is a self-inflicted wound and that's a topping offence. So watch it!'

This aspect of the accident hadn't ocurred to the new-comers to France, but they soon found it dominated the reaction of those around them who were here on so-called refresher courses.

'Lucky sod,' was the general opinion.

'Lucky? How the fuck is it lucky to lose your thumb?' demanded Tommy Carruthers.

'I'll tell you how. He'll be back in Blighty in a couple of days, back home soon after that. He'll get a bit of a pension too, likely. And it don't matter if this bleeding war goes on for a hundred years, they'll not send for him again. That's what I call lucky. I'd give a thumb for that? What's a fucking thumb anyway?'

'It's a lot if you want to hold a plough, or harness a team, or swing a cricket bat,' said Harry slowly, looking at his right hand and trying to imagine it thumbless.

114

'Bollocks! You soon get used to it. There's a mate of mine, lost half a foot at Loos. Now he's hopping around at home, flogging scrap metal down in Bromley, making a fucking fortune. He's probably sniffing around my old lady too, manky bastard!'

There was a general laugh which Harry alone did not join in.

How could anyone be envious of a maimed man? he wondered. How could anyone be willing to swop part of himself for safety.

Then he thought of home and the village and his work on the farm, and the longing swept over him like sexual desire, and he looked at his thumb and half understood.

The sight of Pogmore's blood seemed to have driven Pierce into a new frenzy of hatred for Harry Bowden. He pursued and screamed and assaulted and abused till he succeeded in his early threat of entering Harry's dreams, permitting him no peace even beneath the rough blankets on the scratchy palliasse which fatigue usually turned into a feather bed.

Gas-training was the worst of all. This consisted of passing through a covered trench filled with gas, wearing a respirator. The respirator was a chemically treated grey flannel helmet with mica eyepieces made airtight by being buttoned down beneath the wearer's tunic. Harry, who hated any sort of confinement, found simply wearing this was an agony, and wearing it in the blind confines of the covered trench was almost more than he could bear.

Pierce quickly spotted this and found excuses to send him back through the trench again and again. After the third time, perhaps aware that this excess of zeal was attracting the attention even of his fellow canaries, he told Harry to take his respirator off.

Harry drew in the fresh air, strong with the taste of the sea, and rubbed his stinging eyes, his face alight with relief.

'Thanks, Corp,' he said in instinctive gratitude.

'Thanks? You're thanking *me*, you great useless moron?' screamed Pierce. 'You've got nothing to thank me for, turnip-head. You're useless! I've not been able to get a single thing through that thick skull of yours! You're useless, useless, useless! And when you get out there, they'll kill you straightaway, you'll be the very fucking first, mark my word, you're so fucking useless. So *don't thank me*!'

Harry stood there, dazed by the onslaught. He couldn't understand it. Did the man really believe he was trying to help him? Was there some flaw in himself which made him different from all these other men? It must be so, else why should Pierce have such contempt for him?

He said something of this to Tommy Carruthers, who said, 'Pay him no heed, Harry. You're a good lad. Just because you put up with what most wouldn't doesn't mean you'll not do your duty when time comes.'

The implication that there was indeed a weakness in him did not escape Harry.

But I'll not be made an animal! he told himself. *Surely there's nowt wrong with that?*

Then all consideration of his own spiritual state vanished with the news that Bert Pogmore's wound had got infected and he was seriously ill with septicæmia.

They were close to the end of their Bull Ring training now. At first rumour, and finally written orders, confirmed that they were going up to the Front, entraining for a town called Albert a few miles north of a river called the Somme. The general opinion was that this was close to being a cushy number. There'd not been much in the way of serious fighting along that bit of the Line for nearly two years, and the positions there were well dug in and properly organized.

'Just as well for you, Bowden,' said Corporal Pierce. 'You might live for as long as twenty-four hours in a cushy billet like that. But they'll get you in the end because you're soft and useless.'

'Why? said Harry. 'Why do you treat me like this?'

It was unpremeditated, a plea from the heart.

It was the last day of training. They were on the bayonet course. The grotesque rows of grey-clad, bucket-helmeted marionettes hung slackly at fifty-yard intervals. But today they were not attacking dummies. Today they were doing

116

individual hand-to-hand bayonet fighting each man taking his turn with a canary.

Naturally Pierce had sought out Harry.

The corporal did not reply but hefted his rifle and said, 'On guard!'

Instinctively Harry came into the position, left leg forward, right leg braced, rifle butt locked against his hip by his right hand while his left held the barrel and its razor-sharp bayonet steady, pointing slightly upwards at waist level.

'Attack!' said Pierce who had adopted the same stance.

Three times Harry attacked. Three times Pierce parried his thrust easily and countered with what would have been a killing riposte. Each time he said, 'You're useless, see? A big wet lass. No balls! No guts! Nothing!'

The fourth time, Pierce's parry was weak and Harry counter-parried. Steel clashed sparks. The corporal's blade fell away exposing his unprotected front. Harry thrust forward. His point touched the corporal's shirt front just above the bright buckle of his belt. Their eyes met and locked.

'A useless wet nothing,' said Pierce softly.

Harry's muscles tensed. He felt Pierce lean slightly against the bayonet point. For a moment neither moved then Harry relaxed and let his rifle slip down till the bayonet touched the yellow sand.

Pierce said, 'I've failed with you, lad. Failed abso-fucking-lutely. Make 'em or break 'em. I've done neither. You're my failure. You're your own failure. You're everyone's fucking failure!'

He turned away. Harry watched him go, uncertain whether to feel triumph or despair.

That night he went to the medical huts to find out how Bert was.

A bored orderly consulted a list.

'Pogmore?' he said. 'Dead.'

'Dead?' said Harry incredulously.

'That's what I said. Blood-poisoning. Anything else, mate? Then sod off, will you.'

Harry turned and walked away.

For the next couple of hours he simply walked around the camp, avoiding those places where he might be engaged in conversation. For the first time in his life he found he needed a drink for some reason other than thirst or conviviality. There was nowhere officially to buy drink in the camp, but there was always a supply if you wanted it. What Harry got was not the usual watery beer or plonk but a couple of bottles of fiery apple brandy.

It was a warm summer's night in early June and even at this late hour there was still plenty of light. He made his way out of the main camp area in search of something approaching solitude and after a while found himself on the edge of the Bull Ring. Here among the dunes a man could relax and look at the enormous sky and let the friendly spirit burn all this pain out of his soul. Except that, despite consuming half a bottle, he still felt completely sober.

'What the fuck are you doing here, Bowden?' demanded a familiar voice.

Harry looked up. Even recumbent, he didn't have far to look to see Banty Pierce. Awkwardly he began to scramble to his feet.

'Sit down for fuck's sake or someone'll see you,' said Pierce.

He squatted down alongside Harry. He too was carrying a long-necked brandy bottle and it was almost empty.

'I often come out here,' he said. 'Only fucking place where a man can get a bit of peace in this stinking hole.'

Harry looked at him in amazement. The little corporal's voice was suddenly pitched at a level and in a tone which made it almost unrecognizable. It sounded . . . Harry sought for the word . . . *ordinary*! Ordinary and conversational, like the way a fellow in a pub might address an acquaintance.

And slightly slurred too, like a fellow in a pub.

It occurred to Harry that Pierce was drunk, much more so than himself. He felt sudden envy and took a long suck at his bottle.

'That mate of yours, the one with the thumb, or rather without the thumb,' said Pierce. 'He's dead, did you know that?'

Harry nodded.

'Yeah, of course, you did. That'll be why you're here likely, getting pissed. It's an expensive habit, getting pissed when your mates die. You'll find that out if you live long enough, which isn't fucking likely!'

He laughed raucously in a sudden return to his usual contemptuous manner, took a long last drink and hurled the empty bottle away.

Harry spoke for the first time.

'What do you get drunk for, Corporal?' he asked.

'Me?' Pierce glowered at him as if deciding whether to take offence at the question. 'Me? Not for some fucking stupid bastard who doesn't know enough to keep his thumb out of the way of a cocking-handle, that's for sure! I get drunk because . . .'

He made an expansive gesture with his left hand.

'. . . because I like to get fucking drunk, that's why! You using that bottle or just keeping it warm for a friend?'

'Help yourself,' said Harry, passing the brandy.

Once more, Pierce drank deep. Looking at the level in the bottle, Harry saw his own escape route considerably endangered. For a while he thought that the draught had finished the corporal off, so still and silent did the little man sit, his head slumped forward.

But when Harry tried to take the bottle from him he sat up at once and swore fiercely and drank again.

'Fair do's, Corp,' protested Harry.

'Fair do's! What the fuck do you know about fair do's? There's no fair do's out there, Bowden, you'll find that out too fucking soon!'

Harry started to struggle to his feet, but Pierce's hand shot out and seized his arm and held him fast.

'You think I've been hard on you, don't you, Bowden?' said the canary. 'You think you've been hard done to! Well, I'll tell you something, I haven't been hard enough! I see you come here, and what do I see? A big good-looking lad with a smile on his face and nothing in his head, and they've put a uniform on his back and called him a soldier. Soldier! Dead fucking soldier! Like this one!'

He drained the bottle and hurled it into the fast falling darkness. His grip did not relax, and now his newly freed hand came round and took Harry by the other arm and turned him so that he was facing the little corporal.

'That's all I see. Big handsome chap, but soft, soft, dead soon. Save him, toughen him up, help him so he'll come back, but they never come back, Harry, never come back, you'll be the same, just the same, my failure, I've failed with you, failed, failed, failed . . . Harry . . .'

Inexorably, by force of will as well as by sheer power of muscle, Harry felt himself being drawn towards the canary. With horror, he saw the man's face, stained with tears, swim closer and closer till he could smell the spirit-tainted breath as he repeated 'failed . . . failed . . . failed . . .' Now the night, so light not long before, was dark with a blackness which seemed to ooze between them like an oily liquid, so he could not see Pierce's face, just hear his voice as he murmured. 'You thought I did it out of hate for you, Harry . . . not hate, lad . . . not hate . . . love . . . love . . . love.'

The next morning Harry was up even earlier than their early entrainment required.

All his gear was packed and stacked ready for putting on.

'Tommy,' he said to Carruthers. 'Would you watch that lot for me?'

'Sure. But we'll be off soon. Where're you going anyway?'

'Oh, just taking a last look around.'

Carruthers laughed in amazement.

'Blimey, Harry. I'm beginning to think Banty Pierce was right about you! A last look at *what*, for fuck's sake?'

But Harry had already gone.

He made his way to the sand dunes of the Bull Ring and climbed up a dune till he could see the sea. Across there lay England, an England which Bert Pogmore would never again see. He wondered indifferently if he himself would.

If Corporal Pierce was right, his chances were very slim.

And what, he wondered, of Corporal Pierce's own chances?

He turned so he could look down upon the bayonet-

120

course. The first row of dummies dangled like corpses after a dawn hanging. He studied them carefully. To his knowing eye the third from the left hung a little heavier, looked a little bulkier than the others, but that was probably delusion. In any case, he doubted if anyone else would notice.

Despite the earliness of the hour, the sun was already hot. What better for waking a man than the heat of the morning sun? Though whether its reviving touch could easily overcome the torpefying effects of a couple of pints of brandy he did not know. He doubted it.

Cold steel was another matter.

Soon the first batch of bewildered trainees, driven by their attendant flock of canaries, would be here. Soon they would be urged to advance, to charge full pelt with screams of exultant hate. Perhaps the screams would awake Banty Pierce. Perhaps he would add his own unheard scream of pure terror to the soaring choir.

Perhaps there would be a moment between the rip and the twist when he would know that he had not failed after all.

Harry Bowden turned away and strode rapidly back to his billet where men were already helping each other, with bitter joke and blasphemous complaint, to lift their heavy packs on to their shoulders prior to marching to the line of horse-trucks which formed the train waiting to take them on their slow and winding journey to the quiet waters of the Somme.

AUTEUR THEORY

Nothing in this story is what it seems.
You should remember that.

I am standing, sunlit and windswept, in the middle of the lawn of an eighteenth-century country house. To my left is a fat middle-aged woman wearing a twin-set, pearls, and an expression of solemn piety. To my right is a fat middle-aged man wearing an old black suit and a white shirt which must be of some very rough material as his hand is constantly inside it, scratching. At our feet is a hole. Beyond it, is a truck with a crane mounted on the back from which depends the eight-foot-tall bronze statue of a nude woman.

In the hole lies a scatter of human bones.

'You are in charge here?' the woman says to me.

'No, ma'am. Mr Dalziel here, Detective-Superintendent Dalziel's, in charge.'

She looks in disbelief at the fat man who belches and says, 'Who are you?'

'I am Miss Disney, deputy principal,' she snorts indignantly.

'Oh aye?' says Dalziel. 'You're the one that passed out, right?'

'I *swooned*.'

'Is that right? Well, Sergeant Pascoe here will take your statement just now. Hold on. Are you the one that shouted, "It's Miss Girling" before you went down?'

'I may have said . . .'

'What made you say that?'

'Association of ideas, Superintendent. This statue is—or rather was—a memorial to our late Principal. The bones cannot of course have anything to do with her.'

'Why's that?'

'Miss Girling died abroad, sir,' I interpose. 'Four years ago. Buried there. An accident. Hence the memorial.'

'Is that right? Smart lad, my sergeant, Miss Disney. Joins up his letters when he writes. Is there owt more?'

'Superintendent,' said Miss Disney, her bosom swelling. 'When are these bones going to be removed. These premises are occupied by sensitive young people . . .'

'I'll watch out for them,' says Dalziel. 'Not many left these days, not like when we were young, eh, love? Why don't you run across to the kitchen now and make us a cup of tea? We'll be over in a second.'

Disney retreats in majestic indignation.

'What makes her tick, do you reckon?' wonders Dalziel.

'Sexuality repressed, maternalism diverted, ambition thwarted, I'd say at a guess.'

'Christ, you should get on well here, Sergeant. You speak the lingo. Start sniffing around, see what the gossip is. I'm sure you can worm your way into the inner circle.'

'Yes, sir,' I say hesitantly. 'In fact there is someone on the staff here I was at university with. I saw her name on the staff list . . .'

'*Her?*'

'It was a *mixed* university, sir. They're catching on fast.'

'Piss off, Pascoe. You take the young stuff, I'll go and charm the oldies.'

'Yes, sir. By the way, this statue . . .'

'What about it?'

'Seems a strange kind of memorial to the Principal of a Teachers Training College?'

Dalziel looks up at the pendant nude.

'Don't see why. Perhaps this Miss Girling had big bronze knockers too!'

'Cut!' shouted Andy Adamson. 'We'll take lunch.'

He came across to us, frowning. The bright sunlight dimmed from the arc-lights, the wind died away from the wind machine and we were back to a dull still spring day. A microphone boom swung over our heads and hit the 'bronze' statue, denting the polystyrene.

'Jesus Christ, watch it! That costs money!'

'Sorry, Andy.'

Adamson halted in front of us, but didn't speak, though I could hear his white teeth clicking away in the explosion of black wire he called a beard.

'Was that OK, Andy?' asked Griffin, as always eager for praise.

'You were fine, Gordon,' said Adamson. 'Sam, can I have a word? Come and have a sandwich with me, if you've got no plans.'

'What's there to plan in a dump like this?'

He led me round the far side of the old house to the tatty old trailer he always lived in on location. He was probably wise. It was at least as comfortable as the room I'd been allotted in one of the campus halls of residence.

He had things well organized, you had to give him that. A nice little girl with orange hair and a cute behind arrived simultaneously with a pile of sandwiches and a pot of coffee. I'd have preferred Scotch, or beer at least, but I wasn't making a fuss.

I smiled sweetly and said, 'Thanks, darling.'

She didn't even look at me. So much for stardom.

Adamson said, 'It's a load of shit, Sam.'

'Is it? The script, you mean? Or just the sandwiches?'

'You know what I mean. We've been here just three days and already we're behind schedule. What's the reason? It's you, Sam. The way you're handling this part. *That's* the load of shit.'

'Could you qualify that?' I asked. '*Dog*, do you mean? Or *horse*? Surely not *pig*? I would be hurt by *pig*!'

'I'd like to believe that, Sam, but I don't. I get the impression you're past being hurt by anything. You've got to be vulnerable, all right? This is your love story as much as anything.'

'Is that what it is? I didn't realize it was one of the great romantic parts. Sergeant Heathcliff, that's what I'll be from now on. Promising young stage actor responds to brilliant screen direction! I can see the headlines. Come to think of it, I seem to recall I once *did* see them!'

Suddenly Adamson was very angry.

'That was a long time ago, Sam,' he grated. 'You're

beginning to look your age on the screen as well as off it. What's promise at twenty is infantilism at forty. And there's no way back. All that crap you shout about going back to the legitimate theatre after your next movie! Christ, you wouldn't last a week before you get too pissed off or just too pissed to turn up.'

This stung and I wasn't quick enough to hide it, so I made a big production of it instead.

'Gee, Andy, I'm really sorry . . . I didn't realize . . . just one more chance . . . please!'

He said in disgust, 'Just fuck off out of here, will you, Sam?'

Suddenly it was my turn to be angry. I'd promised myself I wouldn't, but when you've broken promises to as many people as I have, it seems silly to miss yourself out.

I said, 'Listen, Andy. You'd be a lot more convincing as the big, tough, hard-talking director if you dished out the crap a bit more evenly.'

'What's that mean?' he said dangerously.

'It means Wanda, as you well know, your little child-bride. I may not match up to your Himalayan standards, but that girl sticks out like a third tit on a fan-dancer. I need a big hit, yes, don't we all? But I'm not going to fucking get it teamed up with a refugee from a third-rate rock group.'

'Talking about anyone I know, Sam?' said a woman's voice.

I turned. The door had opened. Standing on the trailer steps was Wanda Sigal—now Wanda Adamson—her face pale with fury. Behind her, with a restraining hand on her arm and a worried look on his face, was Mickey Defoe, the film's producer.

'I doubt it, Wanda. I very much doubt it,' I said, pushing by her down the steps. She went into the trailer, slamming the door so hard, the whole thing rocked.

Defoe came after me.

'Sam, what the hell's going on?'

'Teething troubles,' I said over my shoulder. 'When you deal with infants, that's what you get, isn't it?'

'It's not serious, is it?'

125

'Oh no. It usually works itself out in a couple of years, I believe, Mickey. A couple of years should see everything fine!'

I am in Ellie Soper's college flat. She is wearing a dressing-gown.

She says, 'You might as well have a drink, now you're here.'

I say, 'I'm sorry. I didn't realize there was a college curfew.'

She says, 'I just felt flaked out. The intellectual life can be very exhausting too, remember?'

'No, I don't remember that. I seem to remember falling into bed around two a.m. most nights.'

'I don't remember that.'

She hands me a drink. She doesn't take one herself.

'I'm sorry I was rude when we met before,' she says. 'It was a shock.'

'Also it wouldn't help your image with the students,' I say. 'Swinging sociology lecturer in cahoots with cops!'

'You still see things very simply, Peter. Is that why you joined the police?'

'Now who's being simple.'

I finish my drink and stand up.

'I'd better be going,' I say.

'But you haven't questioned me!'

'Tomorrow. Tonight was social.'

I move to the door. She follows me.

'Social, you say?'

'Yes.'

'In that case, you may kiss me good night, Sergeant.'

She offers her cheek coquettishly. I seize her by the shoulders, pull her towards me and kiss her passionately.

'Jesus Christ!'

'Cut!' yelled Adamson. 'Sam, what the hell's wrong now?'

'Ask this cow,' I snarled. 'She's been chewing garlic!'

'I like garlic,' sneered Wanda. 'It's good for keeping off vampires and creepy-crawlies of all kinds.'

Adamson approached and sniffed.

'For Christ's sake, Wanda, go and rinse your mouth out.'

She saw that she'd really angered him and left without demur. Adamson doted on her, but when it came to mucking up his shooting schedule, he was unforgiving. If I thought that for once I was getting off blameless I was wrong.

'As for you, Sam, you're supposed to be an actor. That means you act! All right? If the script says *smile* and there's a wasp crawling up your trouser leg, you still smile!'

'Yes, of course, Andy,' I said. 'I should have realized Wanda was just trying to cover up her halitosis. Jolly decent of her, really.'

One of the lighting men tittered and Adamson glared at him.

Jake Allen, the cameraman, said, 'Are we doing the whole scene again, Andy?'

Adamson hesitated. He'd planned the scene as a single take. Some directors shoot film like they've got shares in Kodak. Adamson shot it like it was strictly rationed and he wanted to put editors out of business. This was a tight budget movie in terms both of money and time. Defoe had got the college premises cheap for the three-and-a-half weeks of the Easter vacation. It had seemed like a good idea at the time, but Adamson had found all kinds of faults with the interiors. The rooms were too small for a man who liked to work his cameras, and their sound properties were odd, so with a couple of them, including Ellie Soper's flat, he'd ended up building a set in the college drama hall. He'd treated the weather with similar distrust. Spring weather was likely to be windy and sunny, so he created wind and sunshine in every outdoor shot against the moment when this spell of dull calm weather would come to an end.

'I don't know why I bothered to rent this place!' moaned Mickey Defoe. 'We should have stayed in a studio.'

And it was undeniable that sod's law seemed to be operating. When you're on a tight schedule, things don't go smoothly.

Perhaps a lot of it was down to me, but not this present cock-up. That was all Miss Wanda's.

Adamson made up his mind.

'No,' he said. 'We'll mix to a big close-up of the kiss, then follow on with the rest of the scene. OK?'

Wanda returned and made a big production of breathing on us both for inspection. The garlic was still there, but distant now. I looked at Adamson and nodded.

'Right, studio,' he called. 'Positions. And roll 'em!'

I kiss Ellie passionately, then we break apart.

'Well, Sergeant!' she says. 'What's the meaning of this?'

I reach forward and tug the belt of her dressing-gown. It falls open revealing her naked body beneath.

'You're under arrest,' I say.

I pick her up in my arms and walk towards the bedroom door. She coils herself around me. We pass through the door and I heel it shut behind me.

We were in a dark world of metal scaffolding and wooden props leaning against a solid brick wall.

I set Wanda down and she said, 'Jesus! I'll be black and blue where you got hold of me. This the first time you've had hold of a naked woman, or what? It'd figure.'

I reached out and tweaked a nipple.

'Wanda, baby, with the weight you're putting on, you're surely too much woman for poor little me.'

Angrily she pulled her dressing-gown around her and with a look of sheer hatred pushed past me to return to the set.

That night I had a drink with Gordon Griffin in the college bar. The steward and his wife were mightily unimpressed by the showbiz stars they were serving. Or perhaps in my case they simply didn't recognize me. I was still an athletic thirty-year-old on the screen, but out of the lights and the make-up, I was looking my age plus a bit extra these days.

Gordon and I went back a long way, both professionally and personally. We'd met in one of my earliest films. It was odd: Gordon was much the same age as me, but he was already playing chunky middle-aged character parts in his mid-twenties. We'd laughed at the incongruity then. Now the incongruous thing was that I looked like playing handsome young heroes till I drew my pension. This I didn't find so funny.

Our personal connection was that we'd shared a wife. His first, and indeed only, wife had divorced him to become my second. You may remember the fun the papers had at the time, mainly because of the accusations my first wife, Sandra, hurled around. I'd met her at drama school and we'd married young. Nothing in her low-key career ever matched up to the talent for tragic drama she displayed during our divorce. She'd read (unsuccessfully) for the part of Lady Byron in a short-lived West End play the previous year and this was the role she chose for herself. Insinuations of violent, brutal and perverted behaviour abounded. She even suggested that I needed to undergo psychiatric treatment, and only my lawyer's threat of suing her for every one of the innumerable pennies she managed to screw out of me shut her mouth subsequently.

Annie Griffin's parting from Gordon was much quieter. There was some natural coldness between Gordon and me for a little while, but the cause of this had disappeared with my divorce from Annie three years later, and we'd worked together on a couple of occasions since.

Now he said, 'Are we going to finish this picture, Sam?'

'Give me one good reason why not.'

'I'll give you two. You and Wanda. What've you got against the girl, anyway?'

'Absolutely nothing, Gord. Nature supplies her own objections. I know that in these uncritical days mere acting ability counts for very little, but, tell me true, does she even look or sound right for the part?'

Gordon smiled and said, 'Hell, she may not have been my choice, but I'm no great shakes at casting. I'd have offered Scarlett O'Hara to Mae West!'

'Yeah, sure. Then whose choice was she and why?'

He waved his glass at the steward to warn him it was time to make another. The steward looked away and yawned.

129

'That's obvious and it's also unfair. She was Andy's choice because she's Andy's wife. But that doesn't make her the *wrong* choice. Hell, if you ask yourself whose choice you were, and why, what's the answer?'

I thought about this.

'I should like to think that I was everyone's choice, because I'm a fine acting talent and could bring real conviction and power to the part,' I intoned magniloquently.

'Sure,' he laughed. 'That's true. But it's also true that you were Mickey Defoe's choice because the old husky voice and the big brown eyes can still get the ladies squirming in their stalls, and also because you haven't made a film for nearly two years, and the last couple you made were real bummers, so low-Budget Mickey could afford you!'

I won't say I didn't mind this from Gordon, but I minded it less than I would have done from a lot of other people.

'OK,' I said. 'Admitting that there may be just a smidgeon of truth in what you say, the fact remains that I'm in the picture because of the effect I have on the sex organs of a mass public, whereas Wanda's in it because of her effect on the sex organ of one ageing director. I rest my case.'

'Yeah, you're pretty good at cases, Sam. You've had the practice,' he said bitterly.

I understood at once what he was getting at. Many years ago one of my films had folded up because of a disagreement between myself and the female lead. By chance it had been Annie, his ex. Or not by chance. Some Hollywood producer had thought it smart to co-star us, though she was hardly a name in her own right. Our already creaking marriage had burst right open under the strain of a passionate screen love-affair. In a scene when she was supposed to slap my face, she'd really let go and almost took my head off. Instinctively I'd retaliated with a left hook which laid her cold. The director had remonstrated with me. I reckoned he was probably sticking it to Annie on the sly, so I gave him one too and walked off the set. That was the end of the film, of course, and somehow I got all the blame. The lawyers had a field day in the wreckage. It cost me a not-so-small fortune, but I survived with the bonus of an extra gloss on my hell-raising reputation, which is always good box-office. But, as I'd eventually discovered, a man may walk on water but he'll sink in crap, and a succession of lousy films plus too much booze had brought me back to Mickey Defoe.

I said, 'Don't worry, Gordon. This one will get finished, I promise you. For one thing, Wanda's not my wife, thank God!'

I thought of my Estelle, young, beautiful, a mother, and above all, not an actress and I thanked my lucky stars. I didn't try to explain this to Griffin. I guessed he had as much need for success as I had. At least my name was still known, but he'd dropped out of sight for the past couple of years, doing God knows what, and he needed a success to remind people he was still alive. Well, he'd probably got the part for it. In fact, Dalziel was just a bit too meaty for my taste. I'd no desire to find myself playing second fiddle to Gord in the reviews!

I tried to lighten the atmosphere by saying, 'I've heard nothing of Annie for a long while now. She must be quieting down.'

Annie's career had nose-dived after our split and eventually she'd followed it into a deep pool of booze from which she emerged from time to time to perform antics which were often pretty comic—from a safe distance. She'd been crazy enough to marry the director, thus saving me the permanent halter of alimony. He'd tried to build a big movie around her, got into all kinds of trouble, and when inevitably the whole project collapsed leaving him penniless, he'd gone for a long walk in the Pacific. Christ, who writes these scripts? You've got to laugh if you don't want to cry.

Gordon wasn't laughing much. He said to me in a rather flat voice, 'You never hear anything, then?'

'Not even a begging letter for a couple of years. Probably the calm before the storm, knowing Annie.'

'Probably,' he said. He finished his drink and left with a rather short good night. The poor bastard was still worrying about his future, I guessed. Weren't we all? At least I knew what mine was going to be. I conjured up a picture of my

lovely Estelle with little Fiona on her knee, and suddenly
the days that stretched ahead seemed endless.

I'm sitting in my room at the college. The door burst open
and Ellie rushes in.

'That fat bastard!'

'Mr Dalziel, you mean?'

'You recognize the description! Christ, it's like having
Attila the Hun on campus! Do you know, he's helped himself
to all the students' confidential files?'

I laugh and say, 'I thought in the modern education
system students didn't have confidential files. What happened to open access?'

'You know, Peter, I sometimes think you're as bad as he
is. At least there's no mistaking him!'

I say, 'He's investigating a murder, Ellie. *We're* investigating a murder. You know it's been confirmed those *were*
Girling's bones? Put that alongside that dead girl in the
sand-dunes and you've got something a lot more serious
than some kids' sensibilities.'

Suddenly she drops down on her knees in front of me and
looks at me very seriously.

'Peter, you haven't changed, have you? Not that much,
anyway. I mean, I don't want to feel I may be getting
involved with a . . .'

'With a fascist pig?' I laugh. 'And what's this about *may
be getting involved*? There was no *maybe* about the other
night.'

'What? Oh, *that*. That's nothing. I do this . . .'

She leans forward between my legs and puts her hand on
my inner thigh.

'. . . and up you come. I stop it, and down you go. Simple
reflexes. That's not what I'm talking about. It's about us,
the kind of people we are, how we think. Peter, they're
saying you think that Sam Fallowfield may have killed
Anita. Is that true?'

'How the hell do I know what they're saying?' I ask.
'They hide in corners when the dreaded fuzz approaches.'

'I mean, is it true that's what you believe? Because, if you

132

can believe something as stupid as that, then there can't be any hope for us.'

'I'm not in the hope business, Ellie,' I say steadily. 'I'm in the justice business.'

She stands up and shakes her head.

'Well, at least we know where we stand,' she says.

She leaves the room.

I lean back in my chair and say, 'Oh shit!'

'Cut,' said Adamson. 'Well, that wasn't so bad. Well done, honey.'

He really does think she's great! I told myself, still amazed every time I made this discovery. I rated Adamson as a good workaday director, able to produce solid, box-office films. It was dismaying to see what a blind spot he had for Wanda. She knew her lines and that was about the most you could say. She needed direction more than any actor I'd ever seen and all she got from Adamson was complacent approval. Yet he was sharp enough to notice any deficiencies in my performance!

Wanda smiled rather wanly at his praise. She was not so stupid she didn't know there was something lacking, but she was too inexperienced to know how to set about improving matters. Well, she'd get no help from me. Since the garlic business we'd been icily polite. Today I'd been rather surprised as she knelt between my legs and caressed my thigh to feel a faint frisson of sexual excitement, but I made damn sure she didn't catch on. I could imagine the fun she'd have if she found me susceptible to that kind of provocation.

That night I had dinner with Mickey Defoe. He was in close confabulation with Dick Morland, the head scriptwriter, when I came to his table.

'Don't tell me, you're writing me out,' I said.

'No, just trimming a bit of fat,' said Mickey.

'The author's here, did you know?' said Morland to Defoe. 'Should I OK this with him?'

'No way,' said Defoe tetchily. 'Listen, he's got no rights, that guy. He signed them all away for more bread than he's ever seen in one bunch in his life. I wish to fuck he'd stay away and spend it and not hang around here like the ghost at the feast.'

I'd seen the novelist a couple of times, a gaunt bearded figure, always skulking furtively in the background. I was willing to be friendly till Morland told me one of his main gripes was that I was far too old and temperamentally unsuited for the part of Pascoe. After that I kept out of his way.

'One thing,' I said. 'Why's Gord Griffin got all the best lines? I'm feeling a bit like his straight man.'

'Yeah, but you get all the steamy sex plus the big action climax,' said Defoe. 'It'll be you they remember, believe me. If they remember anything.'

I didn't like the sound of that. Morland left and I started on my soup and waited for Defoe to start on me.

Mickey and I went back even further than me and Griffin. He was a Canadian who'd learnt the film business from the bottom up in California in the 'forties and 'fifties. He'd transferred his action centre to the UK not, as he now liked people to believe, because he'd refused to cooperate with the McCarthy Hollywood witch-hunt, but because his sharp nose had somehow scented the London-centred Swinging Sixties while Carnaby Street was still just a Soho alleyway. He spotted me at the Old Vic playing Hotspur in my genuine Geordie accent and signed me up for my first film part in the title role of *Roderick Random* which is still a popular historical romp on the telly. I saw it only last week and sat amazed at the incredibly vital younger stranger who was usurping my name.

Mickey had got me tied up for one more film, an Indian Mutiny melodrama, before I moved off to Hollywood and out of his price league on a wave of young Olivier notices.

Since then I'd been everywhere, and done everything except what I was always promising interviewers, return to the stage. In fact I'd done a couple of short tours in a Shakespeare's-greatest-hits compendium, but these had been more in the nature of celebrity appearances than real acting. As one critic had unkindly put it, 'Sam Stuart's royal progress round the country continues to pull in the provincials. One recalls his illustrious namesake, King James the First, who declared as he travelled south to claim the English crown, that if he'd shown the people his bare behind they would still have cheered!'

Things had changed since those days, and I had changed with them in one way, though of course in another I had not been permitted to change at all. Change is a property of reality and an actor is only intermittently a real person while a film actor is not even flesh and blood. If anyone asked who I was, the best I could do would be to run them my films and say, 'I'm in there somewhere.' An actor's only form of definition in the real world is how much he can charge.

And now Mickey Defoe could afford me again.

Over a bowl of cold soup, he said, 'You seen the rushes, Sam?'

'Some. They're OK.'

'That's about all, though. OK.'

'It's a low budget thriller, Mickey. That guy with the beard might think his book was great literature but it wasn't even a bestseller. There aren't any Oscars in this for anyone.'

'Why the hell not? Even a nomination would help. We've got a good enough team, right?'

I shrugged and said, 'There's something about producer's purses and sow's ears.'

'Meaning Wanda?'

I said, 'Look, Mickey, a year ago she was bouncing up and down with purple hair and clown's make-up in front of one of the worst bands ever to squeeze into the Top Fifty on a bad week. Then Andy gets the hots for her and, being an old-fashioned kind of idiot, feels he's got to marry her in order to have his wicked way.'

'That's pretty rich coming from a guy with your track record, Sam.'

I laughed and said, 'But I never married out of my weight. Anyway, Andy's been lugging her around ever since, having his ear bent every time he's on the job by that squeaky little voice reminding him he promised to get her into movies. At last he's done it, God help us. Trouble is, you can take a horse to water, but only God can stop it crapping.'

'You're full of wise little saws today, Sam,' said Defoe. 'Listen, you knew about Wanda when I signed you up, right?'

'Wrong,' I said. 'I knew about "this exciting new talent" who was going to sell the movie to a "big young audience" to occupy the seats not packed by the big old audience I'm going to sell it to. Instead, what do I find I'm landed with? A no-hoper who's justifiably unknown even in the circles she allegedly shone in. I met this kid the other day who's really into rock. I said to him, "Wanda Sigal?" and he said, "No, thanks, I don't smoke." True story. Well, almost.'

He soaked up the lees of his soup with a bread roll and said, 'I'm sorry you two don't hit it off, Sam. I don't think she's so bad though. There's something there if you'll only help it come out. Listen, you've seen the early rushes. The camera likes her, you've got to admit that. Just like it likes you, Sam.'

I didn't like to qualify my objections to Wanda but I had to admit this was true. She couldn't act and she was wrong for the part, but the camera certainly liked her.

'I'll level with you, Sam,' said Mickey, sensing my reluctant agreement. 'You're not the only one who's had a bad run lately. I need this one real bad, you're with me? I'm hocked up to the eyes, Sam.'

'You mean you've got your *own* money tied up here?' I said in amazement. Like all wise old producers, Mickey Defoe usually kept his commercial and private assets separated by at least a mile of impenetrable legal clauses.

'Yeah. Everything I've got. Plus a helluva lot I ain't! This needs to be a real earner for me, Sam. You too, from what I hear.'

'What the hell does that mean?' I flashed.

'Nothing. Only that you've got a family now. You showed me the photos, remember? Cute kid, that Fiona. But it's a real responsibility, Sam, bringing up a family. You won't be able to throw good money after bad the way you used to. And OK, so you've got your front money in the bank, but this time you'll want your percentage to be more than a percentage of sweet f.a.'

He was right, of course. Becoming a father at last had changed things. My first three wives had had several things in common, namely they were British actresses, second-rate, greedy, malicious, and by either God's or their own design, infertile. My fourth and, I intended, final wife, Estelle, was a darling American girl, sweet-natured, domesticated, nothing to do with acting, and the loving mother of my year-old baby.

I said, 'What is it you're saying to me, Mickey?'

He sighed and said, 'Give it a go, will you, Sam? For your own sake. OK, and for my sake too, a bit. I swear I've started waking in the night and thinking of ways to get the cancellation insurance. Like torching the set, only that'd mean setting fire to this whole frigging college! So it'd have to mean shooting one of my stars, Sam. Don't make me have to choose which! I'm not asking much. Just help the kid along. Carry her if you have to. Try to make her look good. Look, I'm not saying you're not doing your job as things are. You are! The trouble is you're strolling along. You're making it look easy and you're making her look bad. Sam, we don't want either. You can't afford to stroll through another bummer, and I can't afford that Wanda doesn't make an impression. Think about it, Sam.'

'I'll think about it.'

A telephone rings. Ellie sits up in bed, yawning. I turn over and deliberately give the sheet a tug so that it pulls off her naked body. Annoyed, she snatches at it and I turn back so that she punches my shoulder. I open my eyes.

'What's up?'

'Telephone.'

'It's your telephone.'

I roll over again. She gets out of bed. I hook her foot with mine under the sheet so that she stumbles slightly. She glances back at me in annoyance as she staggers naked to the phone.

'Yes,' she says into the receiver. 'Yes! No need to shout. This is a telephone not a bloody megaphone.'

She comes back to me and shakes me.

'It's . . .'

I sit up before she can finish and say, 'What?'

Angrily she says, 'It's that fat bastard you work for.'

I rise, pushing her out of the way and go to the phone.

'Yes. Yes. All right, sir. Right away.'

I put the phone down and start getting dressed.

'What's up?'

'What's up?' I say, elbowing her aside so she sits heavily on the bed, eyes opening wide in surprise at my unexpected assault. 'Those precious, mature and responsible students you're so proud of, they've only broken into our police incident room and occupied it! That's all!'

'Cut!'

Wanda stood up. Up to now, nudity or semi-nudity, despite her apparent brashness, had always made her nervous and self-conscious. This time, under my concealed assault, she'd forgotten all about it and her anger was still blazing. But before she could speak, Adamson was with us, teeth twinkling through his beard as he smiled broadly. 'That was great, darling. That was really something. What do you say, Sam?'

'She did OK,' I answered non-committally.

He grimaced at my lack of enthusiasm, then turned back to Wanda, his face alight with pride. As he led her away, she glanced towards me, anger giving way to puzzlement. I pursed my lips at her in the parody of a kiss.

This was the pattern of the next few days. Whenever Wanda and I were acting together, I pushed, prodded and provoked her into something like a performance. At first there was resistance, then bewilderment, but finally I felt her, like a nervous dancer, begin to relax and respond to her partner's lead. An unexpected spin-off of this improvement in our screen relationship was that the film's centre of gravity started shifting. From being a murder mystery with a romantic underplot, it was becoming a modern romance with a mystery background. Morland was kept busy on re-writes and Defoe and Adamson were kept even busier avoiding the abusive protests of the bearded novelist who

138

seemed to have set up camp in the college grounds. Why a man should get so upset about a second-rate detective story I can't imagine. You'd have thought it was *War and Peace* or *Pride and Prejudice* or something!

I was sitting in my room one night, learning some of the new lines I'd been given. It was a fag, but I was beginning to think there might even be something in this film for my reputation as well as my pocket. There was a knock at the door.

'It's open,' I yelled.

The door swung open. Wanda stood there.

'Can I come in?' she asked hesitatingly.

'It's *your* reputation, dearie,' I said.

'Then I'll plead insanity,' she snapped with a return to her old manner.

'OK,' I said placatingly. 'Look, come in, have a seat. I was just going to pour myself a cup of tea. Want one?'

'Tea?' she said incredulously.

'Aw shit,' I said, picking up the teapot. 'You're on to me! After all that cold tea I've drunk pretending it was whisky, the only way I can take my Scotch these days is out of a teapot. Milk?'

'A touch,' she said, sitting down uneasily. 'Listen, there's something I want to ask, like, what's going on? To start with, you were always blocking me out, putting me down. These past few days you've been pushing me around, trying to make me look good. Why the change? You got religion, or what?'

'You mean you've actually noticed?' I mocked. 'Wonders will never cease. But don't get over-excited, darling. My motive is purely non-altruistic. It's down to the folding stuff, I fear. To be quite frank, we great stars can only afford so many flops and I'm running out of credit. This has got to be a half-way decent movie if I'm to remain a marketable commodity. But I deny blocking you out. Indeed, all I had to do to demonstrate your natural awfulness was stand aside to give the world a clear view.'

Surprisingly, this did not anger her.

Instead she nodded, looking almost relieved.

139

'Money. That figures. OK, smart-ass, you're right. I'm new to this game and I'm pretty useless at it. It's a lot different from jumping up and down and squawling at a bunch of hop-heads. But I learn quickly. All I want to say is, from now on, there's no need to prod and punch. Just *tell* me, OK? We'll rehearse it till you give me the green light, then we'll do it. OK?'

I sipped my tea slowly. I was a little taken aback. It's inconvenient when people don't stick to their scripts, like as if Garbo should say, 'I fancy a bit of company!'

I said, 'Look, Wanda, all right, I've been doing my best for you these past few days, but Andy's the director. He looks after rehearsals, he calls the shots. I mean, how come he hasn't been coaching you, anyway? Christ, he's pretty good at his job, and you *are* married to him, remember?'

This was something which had puzzled me recently; if I could get a better performance out of Wanda just by manipulating her on the set, why wasn't Adamson doing the same from his vastly superior vantage-point?

Wanda looked as if she wasn't going to answer, then she said flatly, 'Andy loves me. He thinks I'm poetry in motion. That's nice, believe me. But he reckons all I've got to do is appear on the screen and everyone else will feel the same way. I've asked him for advice and you know what he says? *Be yourself, baby.* That's it! What I need to put me right is a hard-nosed shit who reckons the better I do, the richer he'll get.'

'I accept the invitation,' I said. 'You eaten yet? Go get your grub, then be back here with your script in an hour. Don't slam the door as you leave!'

She stood up. She hadn't touched her tea.

As she opened the door I said, 'Mind you, baby, I'm going to miss punching and prodding you.'

'Piss off!' she said.

But she didn't slam the door.

During the next week, Wanda and I did a lot of rehearsing together in our spare time. I said we should mention it to Andy but she shrugged and said 'Let's see if he notices, right?' so I suppose she didn't say anything. There was no difficulty for her in getting away. Doting husband Adamson might be, but he was also (his wife's acting ability apart) a thoroughgoing professional, and you don't get a full-length feature shot in three-and-a-half weeks by working a nine-to-five day. He worked hard and so did Wanda, coming to my room at every opportunity to be coached in her next scenes. People must have noticed. Gordon Griffin certainly did. He said one day, 'You and Wanda still just good enemies, then?'

He said it with an insinuating sneer which was not typical of the guy. He'd always resented my success with women as if every conquest reminded him of my affair with Annie, but he'd never come at me like this before. Then it occurred to me that it wasn't simply that he thought I was screwing Wanda. What was really bugging him was that we were now acting so well together! Not a day passed without some new slant of the script to show off our burgeoning partnership. And as the Ellie/Pascoe romance grew in importance, the part of Dalziel diminished from a major character role to not much more than a comic cameo. This was yet another source of loud complaint from the bearded novelist who was kept at such a distance that he needed to be loud in order to be heard.

I said, 'Shove it, Gord.'

I wasn't going to waste time explaining the truth, which was that the relationship between Wanda and me was purely professional. At a personal level, we were still kicking away at each other's shins. But even an exchange of abuse is an exchange of information, and I suppose we both learned things about the other. I learned that she was from a working-class background in the Midlands, that she'd started work in a factory at sixteen, that her real name was Brenda Fenby, that she'd gone punk because she was skinny and shy and ugly and the fluorescent hair and crazy clothes concealed all this, that she started singing because she was too terrified not to accept a dare, that ... well, I suppose we'd got a little way past an exchange of abuse by the time I learned all this. What she learned about me, Christ knows.

I'd never really talked about myself except in a formalized media-interview aren't-I-the-interesting-one? kind of way. Now I talked as we drank tea—never anything stronger—in breaks from our rehearsals, and I never realized how much I was telling her about myself till she surprised me later by how much she knew!

For all that, I still believed our relationship was professional. If so, it was professionalism itself that ruined things.

We were rehearsing an important scene in which I come back to my room to find my briefcase open and Ellie on the phone. I accuse her of reading my latest report and trying to warn the chief suspect. We start struggling for the phone and end up on the floor where we make love, leaving me uncertain as to how much her motive in this has been simply to cause delay.

It was a good dramatic scene, arising naturally out of the script's new direction, though it had precious little to do with the plot of the novel. Indeed, things had developed so that we were working towards two possible endings, in one of which Pascoe tells Dalziel to stuff the police force and rides off into the sunset with Ellie, while in the other his career wins, he solves the case (it was the art lecturer and the president of the students' union who done it) and he and Ellie part for ever. The second was closest to the original, but the first was dramatically very attractive even though it would probably send the bearded novelist running amok with his felt-tipped pen!

But good though the scene we were rehearsing was, we didn't seem to be able to get it right.

'Not to worry,' I said to Wanda. 'In any scene that involves you undressing, the audience will be too occupied trying to get a flash of your tits to worry about fine acting.'

'That's it!' she said. 'That's the trouble! We're rolling around with our clothes on!'

We'd gone as far as me taking my jacket off and Wanda pulling up her skirt over her knees, which wasn't very far, before we fell on to the floor. And that, I thought was quite enough.

142

'Hang about,' I said uneasily. 'This is just a rehearsal, and we're on our own up here . . .'

'Is that what bothers you?' she cried. 'Jesus! It's all right to flash the honourable member in front of a gang of giggling technicians, but not just in front of me! For Chrissake, I promise not to laugh. Come on!'

'OK,' I said reluctantly. 'OK.'

I come into my room. The first thing I see is my briefcase open on the table with papers scattered around.

Then I spot Ellie. She is standing frozen with the telephone in her hand. I stand frozen also and look at her.

Suddenly she slams the phone down. The noise breaks the spell.

'What're you doing?'

'Nothing. Just borrowing your phone.'

I advance and look at my notes and reports.

Then it dawns on me.

'This means something to you it doesn't to me,' I say.

'Don't be absurd. I was just curious . . .'

'It means something! Ellie, who were you phoning?'

I advance on her. She stands firm, saying nothing. I pick up the phone.

'Then let's organize a little test, shall we? You've probably been a big help to us, love. Let's see who starts running!'

I begin to dial. She grabs at the phone. I push her away. She flings herself at me, clawing at my face. I release the phone to defend myself. We wrestle each other to the floor. Gradually, inevitably, our aggression becomes sexual. We tear off enough of each other's clothes to bring ourselves into contact. Almost immediately I enter her and our cries of orgasmic delight are mutual and instantaneous.

'Cut,' whispered Wanda in my ear.

'Oh Jesus, Wanda. I didn't plan this . . .'

'You dare apologize and I'll pull your balls off!'

'No I'm not apologizing; I'm . . .'

To be honest I'd no idea what I was doing! I was saved from further errors of explanation by Wanda saying, 'Christ!

143

Look at the time. Andy'll be back shortly. I'd better run.'

She wriggled out from under me and got dressed swiftly. I watched in silence.

'Sam, I'll see you tomorrow, OK? Thanks for . . . everything.' She grinned widely. 'One thing, though: when we do this scene on the set, don't get carried away!'

Then she was gone.

I sat up late that night with a bottle of Scotch. This was the first time I'd strayed off the straight and narrow since the birth of Fiona. Even before that in the eighteen months of my marriage to Estelle I'd never done anything that had the faintest chance of getting back to her. There was no reason why this should either, but I had bad vibrations.

In the morning things seemed clearer. To these modern kids, a quick screw was little more than trying a new drink. They had none of the sexual hang-ups of my generation. As for me, it ill became a fading superstar with four marriages and any number of brief encounters behind him to agonize over something so inconsequential as banging his leading lady. Hell, back in Hollywood it was almost written into the contract!

With such comforting thoughts I went work and soon discovered how inconsequential it wasn't to everyone else. I guess that most of the cast and crew had already been assuming, like Gordon, that there was more than mere rehearsal going on behind the door of my room. The difference now was Wanda's manner. Though we'd been working together much better, hitherto we'd kept our public relationship pretty cool and formal. Now she greeted me with a big *hello!* laughed at my jokes, consulted my opinion, and deferred to my judgment, in a way which had eyebrows raising like hats at a passing cortège. I tried to distance her with a couple of cutting remarks, But she just laughed the more as if I were the funniest thing since Groucho Marx.

I caught Andy Adamson looking at me very thoughtfully once or twice. Fortunately his mind was preoccupied by other things that day. We were into the final week of shooting and decision time was here. How was the film going to end? You don't need to shoot a film chronologically, of course.

Costume, set, and simple convenience dictate the shooting script order. Now was the time to finish the film in story terms to leave a couple of days to go back and tidy up the beginning so that it fitted whatever ending was chosen.

It had sometimes occurred to me how much more convenient life would be with such an arrangement!

A conference was called that evening. I had a sick feeling that Adamson had summoned it to make a public accusation that I was screwing his wife, and I was mightily relieved to find him deep in discussion of the film with Mickey Defoe, Dick Morland the scriptwriter, Jake Allen the head cameraman, and Gordon Griffin. Wanda was nowhere in sight.

'Sam. Good,' said Adamson. 'Let's run the rushes and all have our say. Dick's come up with an interesting idea and I'd like to toss it around.'

The idea, I suspect, was Adamson's own. Screenwriters rarely initiate. Their skill is basically canine: they sniff around till they work out what master wants.

What's certainly true, though, is that a film has a life of its own, and that's what wins Oscars. You can get together the best director, cast, crew and script money can buy, and still come up with a bummer. No one can forecast the organic growth of a movie in its shooting. And occasionally you get one that starts as a carrot and ends as an orchid.

Something of this process had happened here.

Somewhere along the line, the simple, straightforward detective thriller had changed course. I'd seen the individual rushes of my own scenes, but now we were shown the whole of the story-so-far spliced together in a rough cut. The effect was staggering. For a start, Adamson's use of artificial sunlight and wind with dull March sky in the background gave the strange impression that everything was happening in the eye of some grim tropical storm. Jake's wizardry with the camera had conjured a sense of Gothic menace out of the rather dull eighteenth-century house at the centre of the campus. And the comic element, so important in the initial script, had been left on the cutting-room floor. But the most important shift of emphasis lay in the affair between Ellie and Pascoe. I knew the script had been adjusted to bring

145

this to the fore, but in this version it came across as a huge and potentially destructive obsessive passion. Even the awkwardness of Wanda's acting in some of the early scenes, plus the casualness of mine, came across as a kind of sexual uncertainty which slowly vanished as we entered each other's soul and body. The rough-cut ended leaving me feeling that the story was fast approaching some tremendous climax. But what was it to be?

The alternative endings we'd already been considering were concerned with Pascoe making a choice between Ellie and his career. The new idea now put forward by Morland, at Adamson's prompting, was that Ellie should herself turn out to be the killer!

'But there's nothing in the narrative which makes that possible!' protested Griffin.

Morland looked at him pityingly.

'Exactly,' he said. 'That's what'll make it all that much more of a shock!'

Gordon looked unconvinced. He was right, of course, but I saw it would be easy enough to bend things a little to make Ellie's guilt fairly credible. What was really bugging Gord was the way in which his role as the larger-than-life, irrepressibly vulgar Superintendent Dalziel had been reduced to next to nothing. He opened his mouth to speak again, then shut it tight, working out, I guessed, that he would be in a minority of one.

I was beginning to catch the infectious excitement of the rest of those present. Mickey Defoe was talking now.

'We've got to get it just right,' he said. 'I mean, we could have here just the kind of thing the European critics like. Small budget film which transcends its limitations, right? Great art and fine entertainment reconciled, and neither dependent on a cast of thousands and a budget of millions!'

We all laughed at his parody of a review in the more pretentious journals, but we all knew what he meant.

'And the Yanks love something like this coming out of England, as long as it doesn't happen too often!' added Adamson. 'There's nothing like a bit of breast-beating. *Why can't we do this? Small is beautiful!* That sort of thing.'

'OK,' said Jake Allen, who like most cameramen not-too-secretly believed that movies were lovely camera-work usually spoilt by directors, actors and writers. 'Let's talk turkey. What's to be done. There's only a couple of days left.'

'And, before anyone asks, there's no money to extend into a studio. What we've got by Friday is what we've got,' said Defoe firmly.

Morland looked at Adamson and I guessed that he was wanting his cue for part two of 'his' idea.

Something must have moved behind the beard.

'Here's what I think,' Morland said. 'Pascoe, faced by the choice between taking Ellie in, or saying nothing and letting her get away with it, which of course faces him with another choice in his own personal relationship with her, takes the only way out. He kills her.'

There was silence, then a storm of protest in which I joined. Morland knowing that Adamson, though still silent, was behind him, stood firm.

'It's the natural outcome,' he said. 'You've seen the rushes. He's a man obsessed by two things, justice and sexual passion for this woman. His two obsessions clash. There is only one way in which he can respond to them both and remain true to himself.'

'He could commit suicide,' said Griffin sourly.

'Always a weak ending,' said Morland promptly. 'Could Heathcliff commit suicide? No way. That's what we've got here really. Sergeant Heathcliff! No, I'm not joking, not altogether. Some of those outdoor shots of you, Sam, there's that same brooding intensity like Olivier way back when.'

Sergeant Heathcliff! This echo of my own mocking response to Adamson's complaints about my performance early in the shooting now rang like a bell of good omen. Adamson looked at me as if he too were remembering and smiled gently as I nodded my agreement.

Only Mickey Defoe had anything like the clout necessary to stand up to this uncompromising assertion, and I suspect his mind was already echoing with the gentle tinkle of box-office returns slowly swelling to a Niagara roar.

147

'Everyone happy?' said Adamson.

Gordon Griffin wasn't, but he didn't speak. I expect he was weighing large personal success in an ordinary film against a small association with a big earner. It was a sum he had no influence over, no matter how he personally worked it out.

'Then that's how we play it. There's not much time. Let's turn this into a great movie.'

I went away excited at the thought that this could mean a brake on my skidding career and relieved that Adamson had shown no awareness of what had happened between Wanda and me.

When I got back to my room and found her waiting there, my first reaction was to get rid of her as soon as possible. I didn't want to be too rough and provoke a scene, but my efforts at easing her out by yawning, and saying how tired I was, and what a long hard day it had been, went unnoticed.

'Sam,' she said, 'what's going on? With the film, I mean?'

'You should've come to the meeting.'

'Andy explained it all to me beforehand and said it would be OK for me not to go.'

Adamson was no fool! When you want your own way, don't let your wife in on the act. I learned that years ago. God bless Estelle who had no views of acting, and not many on anything else either!

'If Andy explained it . . .' I said.

'Yeah, but I need someone to explain his explanation. Look. I've read the script and I've learned my part. I even read the novel it comes from.'

She said this proudly as if expecting applause. I guessed that novel-reading didn't figure large in Wanda's recreational activities.

'Now, the script wasn't all like the book, but there was a lot of it like in the book. I mean, the Principal got murdered and buried under her own statue, right? Then that student got murdered. And the biology teacher had been screwing her, and he killed himself too, and it all turned out it was down to the art teacher who'd done the statue and the president of the students' union, right? And you and me had a bit of a fling. Well, all that's changed hasn't it? I mean, it's been changing gradually, and that was funny enough. But suddenly Andy says it's got to turn out that I'm the killer and then you kill me! Well, it's crazy! I just can't see it!'

I could tell she was genuinely upset. It took a little time for it to dawn on me that what was bothering her was that having at last begun to feel comfortable inside Ellie's skin, she found it impossible now to think of herself as a murderess.

I looked at her with a new respect. It was a naive reaction, of course, the reaction of a tyro. But it was a real actor's reaction.

I tried to explain this to her, praising her for her identification with the part, but adding that the next and necessary stage was for her to be in control of the character, not the character of her.

I'm not sure if I got through to her, but my efforts to ease her out of the room were abandoned very soon, and it seemed natural and inevitable that we should pass from an exploration of minds to an exploration of bodies.

Afterwards I felt guilty, of course. I mean, if Wanda had been ready to take our relationship seriously on the basis of one coupling, she'd be taking it twice as seriously now.

I tried to minimize the damage by saying, 'Wanda, for everyone's sake, don't say a thing about . . . *this* to anyone. Especially not to Andy.'

She looked at me in doubtful puzzlement and I heard myself adding, 'Not till the film's finished. We can't risk ruining your first movie, can we?'

I saw that I'd hit the right button and sighed with inward relief. Later? Well, later could look after itself. I was planning to take Fiona and Estelle on a trip to the States to show off the kid to her folks. Estelle deserved it. She'd been looking a bit strained and pale lately. Once I'd got her in the States, we'd be safe. I'd always warned her that the gossip writers would be inventing dirt about me, so Wanda could do her worst when we had the Atlantic between us.

Now she pouted and said, 'I suppose you're right. But it'd do Andy good.'

They still have the power to amaze me! I said, 'Believe me, honey, you don't do husbands good by telling them you've been screwing around!'

'I'm not screwing around,' she flashed. 'I'm screwing you. Anyway, he treats me more like a child than a wife.'

'Don't knock it,' I said earnestly. 'He dotes on you. He got you into movies!'

My appeal to her worse instincts failed.

'He got me in, but I'd have got straight out if it hadn't been for you,' she said. 'It's you who's got me acting, Sam. It's you who's explained things so I know what's going on.'

I closed my eyes in despair. In my experience a grateful woman can be even more dangerous than a scorned one. Pride can keep them quiet about scorn, but gratitude turns most of them into blabbermouths.

Next day, happily, there were once more plenty of diversions to keep Adamson busy.

Firstly, the weather changed to precisely that sort of bright and blustery spring day which he had attempted to create artificially with his lights and wind machine. The trouble was that, without these dull grey skies and still trees in the background, the striking effects of the earlier shots vanished completely. Adamson and Jake Allen spent half the morning experimenting to see how they could by art deliberately recreate in nature the effects they had previously achieved by art accidentally!

Then Mickey Defoe, whose mind becomes even sharper when honed against the prospect of making a lot of money, rang the BBC and got an area weather forecast which promised a return to the previous conditions within twenty-four hours, so that solved that.

Meanwhile Dick Morland, whose first version of the new dénouement was set out of doors, had produced an alternative indoor version. Adamson decided to film this anyway in case the weather forecast was wrong. This threw Wanda into a great tizzy. She'd been puzzling away with my help all morning at the new ending. Now to be told that the same afternoon Adamson proposed to film another version with, of necessity, different moves and different lines, was almost too much for her.

This was their first public quarrel and the audience of cast and crew settled back to enjoy it. All except me, of course. Women love a comparison to beat you with. What man hasn't had the whole of his male acquaintance cited as shining examples of something or other during marital altercations? I guessed it wouldn't be long before Adamson was being assured that Sam Stuart knew how to treat a lady film star.

But before this point was reached, there came a new diversion.

Dick Morland appeared, pursued by the bearded novelist who was beating him over the head with what looked like a rolled-up copy of the script. Among the thick-crowding oaths, words like 'monstrous travesty', 'sue', 'injunction', and 'hospitalize' were scattered like little flowers in the grass. By the time order was restored by the forcible removal of the novelist, the marital quarrel had been reduced to the status of a preliminary bout. I took Wanda by the arm and steered her quickly away, leaving Adamson and Defoe discussing whether the publicity attendant on bringing charges against the novelist would help or hinder the film.

'Listen, honey,' I said. 'Don't start rowing with your director till you're a star, not even if he is your husband.'

'The bastard won't be *that* for long,' she gritted.

I hastily urged her away from this disturbing line.

'And you were completely in the wrong too,' I said.

This brought her up sharp.

'Yeah?'

'Yeah! You've got two hours to prepare the new scene, and two hours is a long time in movie-making. I mean, how many of the most famous scenes in film history have been written in at the last moment? Songs too, composed on the set while the orchestra's tuning up.'

'How many?' she asked, not satirically but with genuine interest.

'A hell of a lot,' I said firmly. 'Come on. Let's get this

scene worked out before your lord and master comes and tells us how *he* wants it done!'

That proved the right carrot and by the time Adamson joined us we were making some sense of the scene.

He was not in a good mood but his anger had been re-channelled.

'Some stupid bastard must have gone straight to that lunatic and told him about the re-write,' he said. 'If I could get my hands on him . . .'

'Probably one of the crew let something slip in the local boozer,' I said placatingly.

'Maybe,' he said.

I guessed he shared my suspicion that the man who'd primed the novelist had been the highly disgruntled Gordon Griffin, desperate for a sympathetic ear.

'I'll find out,' he said. 'Meanwhile, let's have a look at this scene, shall we?'

It didn't go well. The scene itself was partly to blame. Briefly, Pascoe, having worked out that Ellie is the killer, goes to confront her with the evidence which includes the revolver she used for one of the murders. She doesn't deny it, but taunts him with his stupidity. But her taunts are only a desperate attempt to conceal her love and her despair at what might have been. She tries to leave him, he aims the gun and orders her to halt. She turns, looks at the gun and begins to laugh. It is her laughter which makes him squeeze the trigger. He goes to her. She has an envelope in her hand. It is addressed to him. He opens it. It contains a suicide note in which she declares her love.

There's only one way to deal with such full-blooded melodrama and that's with great panache. Outside with the wind-machine blowing and the dark clouds lowering above the sighing trees, Andy Adamson and Jake Allen might just about get away with it. Inside, it was always likely to sprout ears of pure corn and things weren't helped by Wanda's difficulty in remotivating herself as a murderess, and still less by the way in which Adamson pushed at her relentlessly in a manner totally at odds with his previous precious-porcelain handling of her.

In the end he said irritatedly, 'OK. Let's pack it in. This is getting nowhere. Maybe we'll do better outside. I hope to hell we do. There's no hope of a hit if we end with a whimper instead of a bang. Think about it, Wanda. Wouldn't you rather end with a bang than a whimper?'

His savage tone drew attention. Everyone sat back hoping for another row.

Wanda said, 'I'm sorry, Andy. It's a question of motivation . . .'

'Listen how she's got the jargon already!' mocked Adamson. 'What's with this motivation crap? Pascoe finds out you've been making a fool of him. You have a row. He produces a gun and blows you away. Who needs motivation? It's like sex, honey. When he pulls it out and points it at you, just fall on your back and stick your legs in the air!'

With this extraordinary outburst, he turned on his heel and strode away. Mickey Defoe looked accusingly in my direction, then went anxiously in pursuit.

Only Wanda didn't seem at all concerned about the incident. She was too wrapped up in this absorbing new game of being an actress.

'You'll rehearse me, won't you, Sam?' she said right out loud. 'You're the only one who can steer me right.'

Jake Allen exchanged glances with the lighting man and they both doubled up in laughter.

Things were getting out of hand.

I said, 'Yes yes,' in some irritation and went off after Defoe and Adamson, determined to do all I could to pour oil on the waters. I realized now that I wanted this film very much, and I wasn't going to let it slip from my grasp at the eleventh hour.

Mickey Defoe was coming down the steps of Adamson's trailer. He shook his head at me without speaking, took my arm and led me away.

'I wouldn't bother him just now,' he said when we were out of sight of the trailer.

'What's going on, Mickey?' I demanded.

'I don't know, Sam. All I know is what Andy *thinks*

153

is going on, and that's that you're screwing Wanda.'

I denied it half-heartedly and Defoe said, 'Yeah, yeah. Listen, Sam, your private life is between you and your privates. You can be getting off on underage hens for all I care. But this is serious. Andy's got himself so worked up, he's threatening to dump the picture!'

'He can't do that! We're almost finished.'

'Finished is finished,' said Defoe. 'And almost's nowhere. What am I going to do? Sell a fill-in-your-own-ending movie round the networks? If Andy says stuff it, Jake Allen will probably say stuff it, and a lot of the rest of the crew too. He commands a lot of loyalty, that Andy.'

'Money commands loyalty,' I said.

'You think so?' he said, looking at me closely. 'Well, it's not just loyalty, Sam. There's other things, like wanting to put one over on you.'

'Me?' I said in amazement.

He laughed humourlessly.

'You don't do much to get yourself loved, do you? he said. 'And there's a lot of people might reckon it was a pretty low trick making a play at Wanda when Andy so obviously doted on her. Not to mention that it puts all our livelihoods in jeopardy, especially mine. I'll not take it kindly if this lot folds under me now, Sam.'

He glared at me with such unconcealed dislike that I had to turn away. That night I ate alone, not feeling like company. Later I went to the phone booth in the college admin building and tried to ring Estelle, but I couldn't get any answer. She'd probably gone round to one of her friends and taken the baby with her.

On my way back to my room, I glimpsed a movement in a car parked on the driveway to the bar. Someone got out of the car. The opening of the door turned on the courtesy light and I saw it was the bearded novelist. At the same time I recognized the car as Gordon Griffin's. The novelist shut the door and the car drove off towards the bar. The novelist seemed to sense my presence for he turned and looked directly towards me for a few seconds, then he faded away into the shadows.

There at least went one guy who'd be perfectly happy if the film folded.

When I got back to my room, Wanda was there before me, in my bed. I ripped back the bedclothes. She was naked.

I said, 'Wanda, you'll have to go.'

'Andy's locked me out,' she said.

'Oh shit! Why? You didn't tell him anything, did you?'

She shook her head so violently that her breasts trembled in a unison which was anything but negative.

I said, 'Wanda, look, this is no good. I'm not just talking about the film. I mean, you and me.'

She said, 'You mean your wife and kid, is that it?'

'That's it,' I said.

She smiled.

'Don't worry about a thing, Sam,' she said. 'Honestly, there'll be no fuss. Trust me.'

She reached her slim white arms up towards me. It didn't seem worth while protesting.

I was awoken by her finger digging in my side. I opened my eyes and saw from the light that it must be very early in the morning. At first I thought she must be wanting me again and I had serious doubts as to my ability to meet the demand.

But she said, 'Sam, you awake? I couldn't sleep much. I'm so worried about this scene.'

'Jesus Christ!' I said. 'What's to worry? We'll probably never shoot the thing anyway.'

'No, I reckon Andy'll do it,' she contradicted me. 'But he won't be any good at helping me to get it right. Sam, look, it's getting light. Let's go rehearse.'

'Out there, you mean? You're joking!'

'Please, Sam,' she urged. 'He'll be wanting to start first thing. This will be our only chance. Please help me, Sam.'

In the end, I gave in. As I got washed and shaved, she disappeared. She must have had a key to the props and costume stores, as she reappeared a little later with our acting clothes and also the pistol Pascoe used.

155

'You don't do things by halves,' I said.

'You've got to do it properly, even in rehearsal,' she said. 'You didn't object that time you screwed me?'

We both smiled at the memory. I felt a pang of genuine affection for the kid. She had a lot going for her. But not me. Not on a long-term basis. No way.

Like a pair of youngsters breaking out for an illicit moonlight bathe, we stole away. The morning mist was still rising from the college grounds and the campus buildings were dark and sleeping.

'Over here is where he's going to shoot it, I think,' said Wanda.

'I hope it warms up a bit by then.' I shivered.

At least the wind had died away and it looked as if the forecast was right and we were going to return to the earlier settled weather.

We worked our way through the scene stage by stage. Wanda was now giving as well as taking, and some of her suggestions were useful, even brilliant.

Finally I said, 'OK, Wanda. Let's try the whole thing, shall we?'

'Yes, Sam,' she said. 'Let's try the whole thing.'

I am striding along the path which leads to the Hall in which Ellie has her room. It is evening. There is no one around. The wind tousles my hair. My face is grim and set. Then I glimpse a figure moving diagonally away from the Hall across the grass heading up a slope towards the bordering woodlands.

It is Ellie.

I call out, 'Wait!'

She hears me, turns, stands silhouetted for a moment with her hair streamed out in the wind, then begins to move away.

I break into a run shouting, 'Ellie!'

She is almost in the woods when I overtake her.

Now she stops and faces me.

For a moment we stand in silence.

Finally I say, 'I know, Ellie. I know.'

156

She doesn't reply. I pull out the revolver and hold it up for her to see.

She says, 'You know? What do you know? My God, it's taken you long enough to find out what a backward child could have guessed in minutes! As for *knowing* anything, Peter, really *knowing* it, you never have, and I doubt if you ever will.'

'Ellie,' I plead. 'Listen to me. I need to talk to you. I want to help.'

'Help? You mean you're going to do a cover-up and keep it all quiet, even from that fat mate of yours?'

'No!'

'What, then? You'll put in a word for me with the judge if I cooperate? Is that it?'

'No!' I cry again. 'Ellie, I want to understand!'

'Understand what? How you could have let yourself be fooled, is that it?'

'No!'

She makes a dismissive gesture and turns away.

'Ellie, I love you.'

'Love? How can you love what you don't know?'

'Ellie, you can't go. You have to stay.'

She looks back at me and says, 'You mean I'm under arrest, is that it? Or do you mean you're so desperate to have me stay with you that you'll forget all that law and order crap you've been spouting and ride off with me into the wild blue yonder to live happily ever after? Which is it Peter? *Which*?'

'There has to be a way,' I say helplessly.

'Yes, there has to be. But you'll not find it, Peter. That's why you're a policeman, so you can tread a nice clear path. It's a beat you want, Peter, not a life. But I loved you! Believe that.'

She starts to move away.

I cry, 'Ellie!'

She turns a tear-stained face towards me. I have raised the revolver and levelled it. She begins to smile and then to laugh.

'No,' she says lifting up her hand with a white envelope

157

in it. 'Oh no. Not that! That's too absurd. Too absurd!'

I pull the trigger.

The laughter freezes on her face. She looks down at her chest. A red stain is spreading across her white blouse.

She looks up at me once more.

'Too absurd,' she murmurs. And falls to the ground.

I let the gun fall and run forward crying, 'Ellie!'

Her sightless eyes gaze up at me.

The envelope is still held gently between the fingers of her outstretched hand. I see it has my name on it.

I take it up and open it.

Dear Sam, When you read this, I'll be back home with my folks. Enough's enough. It didn't take me long to realize that everything people had said about your egotism, bad temper and violent nature had a lot of truth in it, but I loved you and I thought that little Fiona would be the key that changed you for good. I've done everything I can to please you, even submitting to your most perverse demands. But this is too much. That you should start having an affair with that rock-and-roll whore is bad enough. That you should be so reckless about it shows how little you care for my feelings. And that you should boast that you're going to dump me, but hang on to little Fiona, well, that proved to me you're close to insanity. You'll be hearing from my lawyers, Sam. Little Fiona will be kept safe and surrounded by love. Also, in case you get any stupid ideas, she'll be surrounded by trained guards which my daddy has arranged for. I don't want to see you ever again, Sam. I'd like to say it was fun. But it wasn't. Estelle.

I reeled as though struck. This was incomprehensible. What did it signify?

'Wanda,' I said. 'Wanda, what's going on?'

She did not reply. She was lying very still. I looked down at her. A moment before as I fired and saw the red rose blossom on her breast, I had had to suppress a smile at the kid's enthusiasm at getting herself fitted up with a blood-bomb just for an unofficial rehearsal. Now in my state of bafflement, not far beyond which lay the beginnings of great pain, I just felt irritated at her stupidity.

'Make-believe time's over,' I said, reaching down to grasp her shoulder.

I shook it. She didn't move. I shook harder. So totally immersed was I in my reaction to the letter that the truth still eluded me.

'Wanda!' I said. 'For Christ's sake, *Wanda!*'

And then at last I began to realize.

'Getting the message at last, are we, Mr Stuart?' said a voice behind me.

I spun round. There a few feet away was the bearded novelist.

He said, 'Come on.'

'Come on where?' I demanded. 'Wanda . . . !'

'She's dead,' he replied. He stepped forward, reached down and closed her eyes.

'Oh Christ!' I said. 'We must get help.'

'We won't get it by standing around here, will we?' he said. 'Come on.'

Still disbelieving I stooped and touched Wanda's brow. It already felt chill. The novelist had set off down the hill, and fearful now of being left alone with the dead girl, I followed.

'What's going on?' I demanded. 'What's happening?'

'You're upset, Mr Stuart,' he said in a kindly voice. 'That's understandable. Give yourself a few moments and you'll find it's all pretty obvious.'

I tried to get control of my thoughts as I almost trotted along beside him in my efforts to keep up with his long stride.

'Someone must have put a real bullet in the gun,' I said. 'Oh God. What an awful accident.'

'Accident?' he laughed. 'Come on!'

'You mean . . . ? But who . . . ? Why . . . ?'

'Who'd want to kill Wanda? And why? Well, what about Adamson? He finds out she's been screwing you, what more natural than that he should kill her. And, being a director, might he not see it as peculiarly apt to arrange things so that her lover did the killing?'

'Christ!' I said, appalled. 'The bastard!'

159

'Now don't rush to condemn,' he warned. 'It might not be him. There are plenty of other suspects. Mickey Defoe, for instance. Remember when you were talking to him over dinner, back on page 137 I think it was, he said something about shooting one of his stars to claim the cancellation insurance? Well, that puts him in the frame, doesn't it?'

'But why should he want to claim on the insurance when he thinks he may have a big hit on his hands?' I demanded.

'Only if the film's finished,' said the novelist. 'But if Adamson walks off, as seems likely, the film won't get finished. And these insurances are pretty specific. A star dies, they pay out. A director walks out because his wife is playing around, they laugh all his way to the divorce and bankruptcy courts.'

'But I can't believe that Mickey Defoe would go to that extreme!' I protested.

'All right. How about Gordon Griffin? There's nothing in the film for him any more, is there? His part's been cut to the bone and he's not even on a percentage.'

'But that's hardly a motive for murder. What's Gordon got against Wanda, for Christ's sake?'

'Nothing against Wanda,' said the novelist. 'But against you, that's different. He hates your guts! He's never forgiven you for taking Annie from him, you must know that. But he detests you even more for what you did to her, and for not caring what you did!'

'What I did to her?' I said. 'I let her divorce me, that's what I did, and a pretty penny it cost me! So what's she got to complain about?'

'Nothing. She's dead. There, you didn't know that, did you? Back on page 131 when you were making those cracks about her, you didn't know she was dead, and Griffin's been nursing her these past three years, and that's why he's been out of sight and is almost bankrupt!'

I was so shocked by this that I halted in my tracks. The novelist had led me not back towards the main college buildings but to the rectangular block of the drama hall which stood some way apart.

I said, 'My God! Annie dead? It wasn't in the papers.'

160

'Her only claim to notice was that she was once your wife. I doubt if Griffin wanted her passing to be published in those terms. In here.'

He opened the door of the drama hall. Obediently I went in. It was dark in there but a moment later the lights came on and I found myself standing in front of the set of Ellie's flat.

'What the hell are we doing here?' I demanded.

'You wanted to telephone,' he said.

'Oh yes.'

I advanced and picked up the telephone, then said, 'Shit! You idiot, this is a dummy!'

'I think you'll find it's connected,' he said.

I listened. He was right; there was the dialling code loud and clear.

I dialled 999.

'Which service?' said a voice in my ear.

'Police,' I said, thinking they could fix up the ambulance.

I got through to the police instantly.

I said, 'I want to report a death. A woman, Wanda Sigal, rather Mrs Wanda Adamson. At the college—you know the college? She's up by the edge of the wood on the eastern boundary. Yes, dead. No, shot dead. With a revolver. Who fired it? Well, I did, but—all right, yes, I'll be here.'

I put the receiver down.

'They're coming,' I said.

'Good,' he said. Over here.'

I obeyed him. I was in such a state of shock, it seemed easier to follow his instructions than to think for myself.

'It might be as well to take a look in here,' he said.

He was standing by the door of the drama store room which our props man had taken over.

'Why?' I asked.

'Someone got in here and fixed the gun,' he said. 'Did they break in or what? There're only two keys.'

'Don't be a nana,' I said. 'Why should they break in? Look!'

I pointed at the key in the door.

'Wanda must have left it there when she got the gun,' I said.

'But was it there before?' he asked.

'How the hell should I know?' I asked in irritation.

I turned the key and went inside. Everything looked to be normal, which in the case of a props store means chaotic. I came out again.

'Better lock it and keep the key,' suggested the novelist. 'The police will want to have a look round there, I should imagine.'

A new thought had occurred to me.

'Could Wanda herself have loaded the gun with a live round?' I asked as I locked the door behind me and pocketed the key.

For the first time I felt I had the initiative over the novelist. He regarded me thoughtfully and said, 'That's very ingenious. But why?'

'I don't know,' I said. 'Suicide? A joke that went wrong?'

He laughed.

'Some joke! And she didn't strike me as the suicidal type. No. It's an interesting theory, useful for a bit of diversion, but it falls down on motivation. That's the important thing, Mr Stuart. I'm a writer; I know. Motivation is the lifeblood of a novel. It's the divine breath which gives it life. You start mucking around with motivation, forcing it, ignoring it, and you are maiming, perhaps even destroying, a living creature. That's what you and Adamson and the rest of you were doing with my book, of course. Oh, I know you can say you'd tidy things up retrospectively, make it all look possible. Yes, we can all do that. It's very easy. But it's a cheat, Mr Stuart. It's an offence against nature and against art. My Ellie, the Ellie Soper I created, could no more be a killer than ... I was going to say, than you could, Mr Stuart!'

'But it makes a better movie!' I protested.

'We'll never know that, will we?' he said with a smile.

Suddenly a dreadful suspicion was born in me.

I said, 'There's only one person who really has a motive for killing Wanda, for getting this film stopped, for destroy-

162

ing all the work that's gone into it these past few weeks!'

'Yes, Mr Stuart? Yes?' he said encouragingly.

'You! It was you, you bastard, wasn't it?'

To my surprise he didn't look shocked or frightened, merely disappointed.

'Oh no,' he said. 'Not me. Except perhaps, of course, as the first author of the work which brought you all here, I could be said to be responsible for all that follows. But that's a mere metaphysical conceit. Try that on the police and they'll refute you with rubber truncheons, I shouldn't wonder. No, Mr Stuart, I thought for one moment you'd got there by yourself, but I see you need a push. The police are simple souls, except for the odd Pascoe, of course. They'll ask simple questions. Such as: Who shot Wanda Sigal?'

'I did, but . . .'

'Who rang them up and confessed to shooting Wanda Sigal?'

'I did, but . . .'

'Who got the gun from the props room?'

'Wanda!' I cried.

'So you say. But who has the key?'

'I have, but . . .'

'Most important of all—who has the best motive for killing Wanda?'

'Not me!' I said. 'Certainly not me!'

'But the letter you received, the letter from your wife saying she was leaving you and taking your daughter, what about that?'

I had forgotten about the letter in the turbulence of the past few minutes. Now the pain of that greater loss overcame me once more.

'How could she? How could she?' I moaned. 'But that's nothing to do with this business. I didn't see the letter till after Wanda was dead.'

'It's open, and in your pocket,' he pointed out. 'It arrived yesterday, I think you'll find. The question you must have asked yourself was, who told your wife?'

'It could have been anyone. The bastards, they all hate me and resent me!' I said.

'But most likely of all is Wanda. Don't you remember coming into your room and interrupting her on the telephone? She looked guilty and banged the receiver down. Don't you remember that?'

'But that wasn't Wanda!' I protested. 'That was Ellie! It was in the film.'

He looked disconcerted momentarily, then said, 'No matter . . . If necessary, there can be a re-write. But I doubt if it will be necessary. Just look at yourself. You're the perfect murderer. Weapon, motive, opportunity and above all, character.'

'Character! Me? You're joking!'

'Hardly,' he said. 'Consider. Remember the things your first wife said about you, there's a mention of them on page 129. Perverse, violent, mentally unstable. As for Annie, you actually attacked her publicly. It's all there on page 130. Then there's your third wife. She's just briefly referred to on page 137 but once they start digging, they'll find the story as before. What about Estelle? From what she says in that letter, she'll be happy to stand up in court and confirm what the others felt about your personality. You're in real trouble, Mr Stuart!'

I began to edge away from the man. It was dawning on me that I was in the presence of a real lunatic. What they had done to his precious novel might have pushed him over the edge, but he must have been quietly insane for a long time before this. All this talk about what happened on page this and page that! He was treating the whole crazy tragic business as if it were a bloody script!

In the distance I heard the siren of a police car. I heaved a sigh of relief and turned towards the door but he was there before me. I was tempted to rush at him and force my way past, but it hardly seemed worth the risk of possible injury with my salvation so close.

'It's nearly over, Mr Stuart,' he said, taking a step towards me.

What he meant, I didn't know. But I decided not to wait and find out. I turned and ran back across Ellie's flat and through the door facing me. It was a stupid thing to do, I realized at once. It led nowhere but into a tangle of support scaffolding against an internal brick wall. I turned back. He was standing framed in the door of the set.

'What do you want?' I demanded, trying unsuccessfully to keep my fear out of my voice.

'No need to run from me,' he said gently. 'You must know I couldn't harm you directly.'

'I know no such thing!' I retorted. 'I've seen you attacking Morland, remember? That looked pretty direct to me!'

'Only with a rolled-up script,' he said, as if that made sense. 'And in any case, Morland is to some extent part of myself, isn't he? The cynical, grasping, commercial bit. No, you've nothing to worry about from me, Mr Stuart.'

Against my will, I let myself be reassured. If his lunacy had rules of non-violence I wasn't going to complain. Besides the police siren was very near now.

I said, 'OK then. What *are* you going to do? What for instance are you going to say to the police when they arrive?'

'Me? Nothing. I shan't even be around,' he said, faintly surprised.

'You mean you're not going to give them all that crap about me deliberately murdering Wanda?' I said, getting bolder.

'No need to,' he said. 'It's all there for them to discover. It could take them a few chapters. And it may need a bit of tidying up in the re-write. But they'll get there in the end.'

Suddenly I was no longer afraid of this idiot!

I said to him, 'You know, old chap, I really do wish you'd hang around and have a talk with the police. I think my best insurance against suspicion would be for you to have a heart-to-heart with the officer in charge. I mean, why not take him aside and tell him all about my past, with page references, of course, and then tell him about the future you've got plotted out for me. Will you do that? Please!'

I laughed as I spoke and after a while he began to laugh too. We laughed together for a while, then I stopped.

He went on laughing.

'It's not *that* funny,' I said suspiciously. 'What the hell are *you* laughing at anyway?'

'I'm sorry,' he spluttered. 'It's just occurred to me. You haven't twigged yet, have you? You're talking about the future. *Future!*'

'What's so funny about the future?' I demanded. 'It'll happen, that's for sure. And it'll happen the way I want it to happen.'

'No, I'm sorry,' he said. 'It *has* happened. It *is* happening. Haven't you realized? You're in a flashback. That's what's so funny. This has all been a flashback.'

'Nothing in this story is what it seems,' said the judge. *You should remember that, members of the jury. These people you have been listening to, accused and witnesses alike, they are not ordinary everyday people like yourselves. Or even like me.'*

He paused, sat back, adjusted his red robe, scratched beneath his wig, then resumed.

'They dress up, they play roles, they climb on to stages and address themselves to captive audiences, and very rarely are they interrupted or mocked. They are in a sense shadows, creating and inhabiting a world of words, a universe of the imagination. All this you must take into account as you ponder what you have seen and heard in the past few days. You have been patient; you have been attentive; now you must be just. Let me remind you of what has been said. Let me review for you what has been here performed . . .

It's a comfortable enough cell I'm in. The screws are friendly and helpful too. They tell me they like to keep their lifers in good heart. It makes it easier on everyone in the long run.

Long run! That makes me smile. Unless my appeal is successful, this could be the longest run of my career! I made this joke to one of the screws and he laughed. He's a nice chap. I told him that when (I refuse to say *if*) I get out, I'm definitely going back on the stage. That's where the real world is. I should never have left it. You can stuff the cinema for me!

Last night I woke up, about two or three in the morning, I suppose. I found my cell door wide open, so I took a little walk. I went right to the end of the long tiled corridor which runs by the door till I came to the corner at the end.

Round the corner there was nothing: no tiles, no corridors, no cells; only darkness. I stood still for a while and, as often happens, eventually my eyes adjusted and gradually shapes began to emerge from the dark.

I saw the sharp angles of mike-booms, the smooth tangles of cable, the eclipsing discs of arc-lamps, the staring blocks of cameras. I looked up, but whatever ceiling or sky arched overhead remained impenetrably black.

I didn't go any further, but turned round and came back. They're not catching me like that! I'll just go on sitting quietly here till I get the cue to make my appeal.

Then we'll see!

Then, we'll see.

POOR EMMA

Emma Knightley, handsome, clever, and rich, with a comfortable home and happy disposition, seemed to unite some of the best blessings of existence; and had lived nearly forty-one years in the world with little to distress or vex her.

Except for her husband.

'Poor Emma,' her father would sigh when forced to a reluctant admission that George Knightley's presence at Hartfield was by right of marriage rather than of neighbourly visit. It was not that he thought ill of Knightley. Had the Prince Regent himself won his daughter's hand, old Mr Wodehouse would still have thought his daughter to have fared badly, which indeed few might have disputed, as the Prince Regent already had more wives than was customary in this part of Surrey.

But against Knightley no such objection, or any objection at all, could be raised. In rank and wealth, as the owner of Donwell Abbey and its flourishing estate, he was the unchallenged first man in the hierarchy of the little township of Highbury and its environs. In character, he was sensible and resolute; in taste, he was sober and moderate; in conversation, he was pleasant and serious; in person, he was manly and handsome.

It was only in the matter of age that any reservation of total approval could exist, and it was generally agreed that the eighteen years by which he was her senior merely gave him a maturity of experience which perfectly complemented a certain lightness and even frivolity in Emma's own still unformed character.

So when Mr Woodhouse sighed and said 'Poor Emma!' the company responded with gentle amusement, recalling how Emma's governess and friend had become 'poor Miss Taylor' the moment she married the widowed Captain Weston, and Emma's elder sister had become 'poor Isabella' even before she married Knightley's younger brother, John.

To be 'poor Emma Knightley' was a fate which every maid and not a few matrons in the neighbouring countryside envied heartily.

How well the marriage had started! Emma indeed had at first hesitated to accept Knightley's proposal. Her father's delicate constitution had already suffered such nervous damage at the defection of poor Miss Taylor and poor Isabella, that she feared to administer it a third blow. To abandon him at Hartfield was unthinkable; and any plan to carry him with them to Donwell Abbey would almost certainly prove fatal to one who would by preference never make any journey longer than the perilous trip between his bedroom and his parlour.

But Knightley with that keenness of intellect and nobility of action for which he was justly famed had solved the problem by proposing that he and Emma set up house in Hartfield, leaving their transfer to Donwell Abbey until a time of more convenience. This last phrase was a way of avoiding direct reference to what had seemed imminent for many years, Mr Woodhouse's death. A fair age already (he had not married young), and by temperament even older, he had led the life of an invalid for so long that it seemed probably that even this gentlest of blows would quickly drive him down.

But the expected event (expected by all except perhaps Emma, and doubtless Mr Woodhouse himself) was not quickly forthcoming. The years went by. Knightley rode daily to Donwell Abbey to oversee the affairs of his extensive estate. But in truth there is a large difference, though subtle to perceive, between a man's rising of a morning, and throwing back his curtains and looking out, and saying 'All this is mine! I must not neglect to tend and improve it!' and a man's riding to work like any common factor and riding home again at night. Gradually the visits ceased to be diurnal; at first they still occupied the larger part of a week, but eventually Knightley discovered he could take care of Donwell by the application of his energies there on two afternoons solely.

Hartfield offered even less challenge to his powers of

organization. His stables he had already transferred there from Donwell and these he set about developing, soon acquiring a reputation for having some of the best mounts in the country, a reputation he was not unwilling to support on the hunting field. From hunting to racing horses is a short step, and here too he did not care not to be predominant.

Emma did not share his love of equestrianism. To her a horse was the motive power of a carriage or a plough, no more, no less. But she was content enough with her role as Mrs Knightley, mistress of Hartfield and Donwell, and beyond any doubt first in precedence in Highbury. Only once was this right to the primacy challenged. After about ten years of marriage, the even tenor of life in Highbury was disturbed by the death of poor Miss Taylor's husband, Mr Weston. He was a man impossible not to like and Emma mingled her genuine tears with her friend's.

The funeral was to be a large affair and the solemn anticipation of the event was somewhat disturbed by the news that Mr Frank Churchill was definitely going to attend. As Mr Frank Churchill was Mr Weston's own son by an earlier marriage, this may have seemed an event more to be marked by its omission than its occurrence, but he was a man whose early arrival had always been more forecast than forthcoming. Brought up by his uncle and aunt in Yorkshire, who had sufficiently loved him to give him their name and make him their adoptive heir, he had married Miss Jane Fairfax of Highbury at about the same time as Emma and Knightley were wed. Since then little had been seen, though much had been said, of the young couple. Mr Weston's paternal pride burnt all the hotter for being fuelled by absence and neglect, and his delight in the news that Churchill had at last come into his inheritance caused Emma to say, 'He talks of it as a deed so noteworthy that one might almost think Frank Churchill had actually murdered his adoptive parents for their money!'

That there had been a very great deal of money Mr Weston did not spare to broadcast far and wide. And though he himself was naturally not in a position to see it, the evidence of wealth was ostentatiously (Emma said 'vulgarly') displayed in the magnificence of the Churchills' carriage and the sombre richness of their mourning dress. Jane Churchill's tall slender figure, stately bearing, and pale almost translucent skin, were as well suited to the occasion as any stage tragedienne's (and perhaps the means were not dissimilar, murmured Emma). In the procession, during the service, and by the graveside, there was no denying her and her husband their right of precedence, and Emma accepted her demotion with a becoming meekness.

After the funeral they all returned to Randalls, the Westons' house, and gathered in the hallway, conversing in low tones, while Mrs Weston went ahead into the drawing-room to make sure all was prepared for her guests' refreshment. After a short interval a servant opened the double doors to reveal Mrs Weston at the end of the room, and invited the guests to come forward.

Jane Churchill began to advance but in a second Emma was by her side, smiling brilliantly.

'Nay, Jane Fairfax,' she murmured sweetly. 'Among the dead, you have undoubted precedence, but now we are back among the living, you must give me leave.'

And glancing coyly at Frank Churchill, who smiled so broadly it was nearly a grin, Emma advanced to comfort her grieving friend.

About this time, Mr Knightley began to take an interest in politics and being offered a nearby seat in the gift of a Tory lord, he was soon a Member of Parliament. This meant that during parliamentary sessions he spent two or even three days a week in London, some sixteen miles away. At first he stayed at the home of his lawyer brother, John, but not finding the large brood of his nephews and nieces conducive to mature political thought, he soon rented a small house for himself in a location convenient for Westminster. The effect of his presence on affairs of state was not visible to Emma except in so far as her husband grew daily more opinionated. Also, as political debate seemed impossible unless accompanied by vast quantities of food washed down by copious draughts of wine, Knightley's already portly figure grew softer as his opinions grew harder.

Soon Emma began to feel within herself a growing disgust with both her husband's person and his manner, but not much more than her observation told her most wives felt for most husbands, so she saw no reason to let it spoil the even tenor of her life.

There was another cause for unease, however. Mrs Weston, after a decent period of mourning, was expected by her friends to settle into an easy widowhood not much different, except of course for the unavoidable absence of Mr Weston, from her married existence. Instead of this, her grief continued unabated, and eventually she declined into religion, to such an extent that it came as no surprise, though an incalculable shock to all decent people, when she embraced the doctrines of Rome. It was not that there was a general prejudice against the Catholic Church in Highbury, but there are limits to everything, and Mrs Weston leapt over hers with a positively unhealthy fervour. Randalls she completely neglected, except for her husband's study which she turned into a memorial shrine.

'My dear Miss Taylor,' protested Emma. 'Your personal faith is your own affair, but dear Mr Weston died and, we must presume, remains a Protestant. Think of how bewildering to his poor spirit all this drapery, silverware and candlewax must be!'

Mrs Weston was not to be moved to even the ghost of a smile by her friend's wit and Emma departed 'so thoroughly impregnated with incense,' she told her father, 'that I dared not go into Ford's to purchase a string of beads I have fancied lest the assistant there should imagine I wanted a rosary!'

But it was not just the incense and Mrs Weston's increasing oddity which slackened the bonds which tied them. Emma's openness of character needed a confidante, but her pride needed the assurance of perfect discretion, and having met Mrs Weston's personal confessor, a soft-skinned, brown-eyed priest with insinuating eyes, she had no desire to risk having her own problems incorporated in her friend's confession.

This left a gap in her life, for it is difficult and dangerous for

172

a leader to create that equality which is the basis of trusting friendship. Mrs Weston had never been her social equal, but her position as governess for so many years had created a relationship of interchangeable authority which levelled out as friendship. Who was to take her place? Mrs Elton, the vicar's wife, would have leapt into the breach, but she was a woman of such a grating manner and such ineradicable natural vulgarity that it would scarcely have been possible to tolerate her as a housekeeper, let alone a friend.

Only one other woman fitted the part and that was Emma's own sister, Isabella. But Isabella, married to Mr John Knightley, was resident most of the year in London, and that was sixteen miles away. At least a short visit was possible, and she proposed to her husband that she should spend a couple of nights in his town house in Westminster. He seemed oddly reluctant to allow the possibility of this, advancing a whole battalion of objections as if attacking an opposition bill in the committee stage.

'Besides, who is to look after your father if you come to London?' he concluded.

'That is all taken care of,' said Emma tartly. 'You do not imagine I would not ensure my father's comfort before all else?'

'No, I do not imagine that,' sighed Knightley.

'Good. Then I shall come to London and stay at my sister's house as usual, though what she may think, knowing as she does that we have a house of our own in town now, I cannot imagine.'

So it was arranged. But when Emma arrived at John Knightley's house in Brunswick Square, she found her welcome not what she was used to, and the change had nothing to do with her husband's house in Westminster.

'We are ruined, dear Emma. Ruined!' cried Isabella. 'What is to become of us, I do not know!'

Emma, used to her sister's emotional hyperbole, settled herself comfortably in a chair and prepared to hear some tale of a mislaid purse, or a burnt dinner, or at the worst a law-suit in which John Knightley's advice had proven ineffective.

Instead she was retailed a truly distressing tale. It was not just John Knightley's advice which had proved ineffective, but his management of a large trust fund which had been in the care of his firm for many years. It was not John's fault, Isabella assured her sister tearfully. The day-to-day management of the fund had been in someone else's hand, but his had been the ultimate responsibility. When it had come to his notice that large sums of money from the trust had been most injudiciously invested in doubtful shares, he had acted quickly to remedy the error. Too late! The shares had already collapsed, and though it was only through John Knightley's efforts that the losses incurred were not more severe, there was no gratitude to be expected from the guardians of the trust.

John Knightley himself arrived as Isabella concluded her tale of woe. He was a thin, scholarly-looking man, restrained of speech and manner, and while his wife could make a spoilt meal sound like a cataclysm, his dry, even speech made disaster sound dull. But it was confirmation of disaster he brought.

'First,' he said, 'I must personally make up the losses. It is my duty, my dear, and if it were not, the guardians have made it clear that they will sue me for negligence, against which suit I would have no defence.'

'But the money, John, do we have it? What will it leave us? Answer my question, I beg you!'

'Two questions, I think, and so, two answers. Yes, we have it, answers the first. Nothing, answers the second. It will leave us nothing. No, please, wife, before you give yourself over wholly to the vapours, hear me out. There is worse. Word of this failure has spread quickly. Already the firm is beset by queries from clients fearful that I have embezzled every penny in the City! My reputation is quite vanished. I shall never get work as a lawyer in London again. Emma, you are better suited than your sister to deal with such emergencies, I think. I beg you to stay with her and offer what comfort you can.'

This was the nearest to a compliment that her brother-in-law had ever offered Emma. At the time of her marriage, he had made it clear that he felt his brother was acting foolishly. As the years went by, and George Knightley's character had decayed as Emma's had formed, John had been more tender towards her, but Emma had never accepted his attempts at *rapprochement* since this would have involved an admission that her situation deserved sympathy, and her pride could not permit that.

Now she held her weeping sister in her arms and suddenly she saw an answer to all their problems, her own as well as the John Knightleys'.

'Sister,' she said firmly, 'cease your weeping, for all is to be well. Your husband will have work to do, your family will have shelter, and you and I shall visit and talk to each other daily, as it has long been my wish for us to do. You shall have Donwell Abbey!'

Isabella stopped crying immediately and looked at Emma with dawning hope.

'What do you mean?' she asked.

'The house stands empty, the estate lacks stewardship now that Knightley is so much in Parliament,' said Emma. 'Why should you not live at Donwell till Knightley himself requires the house again, which if Papa continues healthy may not be for many years yet?'

'Emma! Is it possible? Oh, too marvellous! Though I know it must be Henry's one day, and it would seem very fitting that he should grow acquainted with the estate . . .'

Isabella's voice died away in sudden awareness of her solecism. The fact was that Donwell Abbey was entailed, and in the event of George Knightley's dying without an heir, the estate would pass first to his younger brother, John, and after that to John and Isabella's eldest son, Henry. The one flaw in Isabella's delight at her sister's marriage had been her awareness that Emma's first male child would deprive her own son of his inheritance. But more than ten years had passed with no sign of a pregnancy and Isabella had come to believe there would not be one. This present time, in the face of her sister's kindness, however, was not the best occasion to be voicing this belief.

175

Emma laughed, understanding her sister's thoughts.

'Don't look so distressed, Bella,' she said. 'I am not offended. And to show you so, I will go this very instant to Knightley's Westminster house and get him to put all matters in train.'

Emma hated to waste time once her mind was settled and she sped round to Westminster as quickly as might be. A footman opened the door and tried to keep her waiting in the hall while he went to inform his master of her arrival.

'Fool!' she said. 'I am Mrs Knightley,' and swept by him into a very prettily furnished reception room, calling her husband's name. He appeared within a few moments, looking black-faced and displeased, like a great Friesian bull.

'Emma, what are you doing here?' I told you that I would call on you in Brunswick Square this evening if my duties permitted.'

'I know you did, Mr Knightley, but emergencies alter circumstances. Have you not heard of your brother's misfortune?'

'Something of it has reached my ears,' he said negligently. 'The silly fellow has been dipping his fingers in other people's salad bowls, so they say.'

'Not so! It is a most tragic situation!' protested Emma. 'I wonder you can take it so lightly. Let me explain it, and my solution, to you.'

She did so, rapidly but with all necessary detail. When she had finished, she paused like an actress expecting applause.

'What's this!' cried Knightley. 'Let John and your giddy sister and their monstrous brood into Donwell? You must be mad, wife! What little I can spare to relieve hardship they shall have. I am a Christian and know my duty! But Donwell! Not while I live! Think on, Emma. When the old man dies, we shall return there ourselves. And what shall we do if the John Knightleys are camped all round the place, like the lost tribes of Israel!'

Emma was taken aback. She had not expected such opposition to her plan. She turned away from her husband

and stood leaning against a pretty little marquetry table with a jewel-encrusted lady's fan on it.

'I have promised Isabella,' she said.

'Then you must unpromise her as soon as may be!' said Knightley firmly. 'Go at once and undo this mischief as quickly as you can.'

Slowly Emma turned. In her hand was the fan.

'This is a very pretty ornament,' she mused. 'Is not this Lord Upton's coat of arms I see engraved on the handle?'

Lord Upton was the Tory peer who had sponsored her husband. Himself gross of flesh and torpid of character, he had a wife whose appetites were reputedly so voracious that even elderly clergymen spared to be alone in her company.

'No ornament,' said Knightley flushing. 'Lord Upton and his wife called on me this morning. Her ladyship must have left it behind. Give it to me and I shall return it to his Lordship in the House.'

Somewhere above them a board creaked, and Emma sighed and said, 'A careless lady indeed. I should like to make her acquaintance. Give me her address, and I shall return the fan myself. It will distance my mind and occupy the time, husband, for to tell you the truth, I do not look forward to being the bearer of such bad news in Brunswick Square.'

'Give me the fan!' thundered Knightley.

'Gladly, if I were to be speeding back to tell Isabella all is settled. But you know how I hate to bring ill tidings. I have not seen your house, Knightley. Will you not conduct me round the upstairs apartments?'

Husband and wife faced each other for a long moment, he gross and frustrated and scarlet, she slim and erect and smiling.

'They shall have Donwell till John sets himself up once more,' growled Knightley finally. 'But I'll have an agreement! They shall not think themselves settled there forever!'

'Of course they shall not!' said Emma, gracious in triumph. 'I will bring John back within the hour to make arrangements. Here is this beautiful fan, husband. Take care to see her ladyship has it restored to her at once. I doubt she will not rest secure till she can shade her delicate skin behind it once more!'

Now followed a period of much happiness in Emma's life, for she was always at her happiest when she felt herself the mistress of events and relationships. She did not doubt of her husband's infidelities, but so long as he kept them to the environs of the Palace of Westminster, and no rumour of them reached Ford's shop in Highbury, she would not pretend an outrage she could not feel.

Besides, it pleased her that his carnal passions were engaged elsewhere as she herself had long ceased to anticipate Knightly's corpulent embraces with anything but horror.

The John Knightleys were soon installed at Donwell, and the arrangement quickly proved satisfactory to everyone, even to Knightley. His lawyer, Mr William Coxe of Highbury, and John Knightley, acting for himself drew up a note of agreement covering the terms of John's stewardship of the Abbey estate. For several years, following Knightley's growing neglect, the revenues had steadily declined and the house itself had begun to assume a somewhat dilapidated appearance. Now all was changed. Under John's stewardship the estate prospered again, and the revenues soon equalled, then exceeded, their previous levels. Within a twelvemonth Knightley was congratulating himself gleefully on having got a first-class manager, free of charge, as though the whole arrangement had been his own stratagem.

Emma and Isabella, in the meanwhile, were rarely out of each other's company and usually in temper in it. It was true that from time to time Isabella put on airs as if she were the true mistress of Donwell, and Emma felt constrained to remind her of her real situation. Isabella was immediately and genuinely contrite, though secretly she comforted herself with the thought that one day she might be in fact what she was at present by favour, and that certainly her beloved son, Henry, must eventually become lord of the estate. If she felt guilty at the thought that this could only be achieved by her brother-in-law's death, his treatment of Emma soon assuaged the guilt. In any case, hers was such an easy, sunny temper, taking pleasure—or pain—from the present with little real planning for the future (*that* was her husband's prerogative) that George's death only occurred to her as part of nature's course, never man's interference.

Emma, on the other hand, with a mind made for analysis (albeit often wrong) and a constitution for conspiracy (though frequently flawed) could not conceive of a desired end without a premeditated means, and she watched speculatively as Isabella pressed another large helping of venison pasty on her bulging brother-in-law; or sent to the cellar for another bottle of port to help the poor insomniac Member of Parliament to a healthy slumber; or spoke of a wild young stallion offered for sale at Esher horse-fair which only the best rider in the county could hope to master.

But whatever her suspicions, Emma had to admit that her husband needed little urging to pursue his excesses. Nor did retribution follow. He drank more port, and did not die of an apoplexy. He bought more horses and failed to break his neck. He spent time in London even when the House had risen, and he did not appear either diseased or debilitated.

But it was in the end his excesses which brought the two families to a new point of crisis.

As the years passed and Donwell prospered, the rising income from the estate was steadily matched and frequently overtaken by Knightley's increasing expenses. He kept no check, merely sending all his private accounts to his brother for settlement. John Knightley was not a man to act precipitately. He guessed that his brother would, after these many years in Parliament, hardly be susceptible to reason. Besides, he had his own large family to think of. It would not do to speak without preparation. If crisis there were (and a crisis there must be, of that he was sure) he would delay it until the time and occasion were of his own choosing. So he laid his plans.

First he dropped hints that he was thinking of returning to London to renew his legal practise. Alarmed at the thought of losing so excellent, and so cheap, a manager, George protested, arguing the uncertainty of the move, the unhappiness of the family. John considered. George pressed. John allowed himself to be persuaded. And George was so relieved that he raised no objection to signing a new note of agreement confirming John's stewardship of Donwell.

Six months elapsed, and one day as George was visiting the Abbey, his brother called him into the room which he used as his management office. His face was stern and he wasted neither time nor words.

'Brother,' he said, throwing a sheaf of papers on to the table between them. 'These bills upon the estate, they are out of all proportion!'

'Out of proportion, John?' replied Knightley, taken aback. 'What does that mean? Is there no money to meet them? Does not the estate prosper?'

'Indeed it does, brother. But only because of the labour and the care which your nephew, Henry, and I myself bestow upon it. Think on, brother. Is it just that we should see the fruits of our labour so wildly dissipated? That you are entitled to a good competence we do not deny. But that we should toil to pay for your pleasures while our own family suffers neglect and deprivation, where lies the justice of that?'

Knightley struck the table a blow which came close to splitting it.

'Dear God!' he cried. 'Neglect and deprivation, you say? When all the county knows 'tis only my care and kindness that has kept you and your gipsy brood out of the workhouse! Will you deny me what is my own, sir? You are at Donwell on sufference! It is an act of my charity that you loll here at your ease while better men toil for a pittance. My property, sir. Recall that we are talking of my property!'

'And a pretty property it would be, brother, if it had stayed in your care!' cried John Knightley, becoming passionate beyond his customary cold and restrained nature. 'What would it have been like if I had not so managed it these many years? Yes, it is your property, surely, but not yours without condition; it is not yours to pillage and neglect! It belongs to our family, sir. It is yours only in entail and upon your death it will pass to me. Or if I do not outlive you, sir, which the hard work and long hours I expend on Donwell makes not unlikely, then it will be my son's, and his after him. These bills are outrageous, sir. You must moderate your excesses or find other sources of finance for them. The law will be on my side in this, I promise you!'

'Other sources . . . ! the law . . . !'

George Knightley rose to his feet, stuttering and staggering, so that it seemed for a moment as if the argument were to be resolved by his instant death. But then he recovered and strode out of the room crying, 'We shall see, sir! Other sources . . . the law . . . we shall see!'

Isabella, warned by her husband to keep herself and the children out of the way during George's visit that day, had naturally placed herself in a situation from which she could hear all, not a difficult task as the volume of the dispute attracted the attention of men in the fields two furlongs away.

Now she rushed in to her husband, pale-faced and alarmed.

'John!' she cried. 'I have never heard your brother in such a rage. He will surely return with dogs and bailiffs to throw us out!'

'Let him try,' said John Knightley. 'Let him try.'

'You are sure of what you said?' demanded Isabella. 'You are sure the law will be on our side.'

'I believe it to be so,' replied John. 'These entails are complicated matters, but their aim is always to stop the debauchers of one generation depriving the next of its rightful due. Also, the note of agreement George signed has given me something of a trustee's standing in this. Besides, to test my position at law might cost him half of what the estate is worth anyway! He will scarcely risk *that*!'

He spoke confidently, but he knew that the battle was not so easily won. His brother might now appear as a hard-drinking, hard-riding, grossly self-indulgent and mammothly overweight country squire, but he had proved for many years of his adult life that he was a man of sharp judgment, well versed in affairs. He might not be willing to enter into the expense of time and money involved in legal proceedings, but he would certainly spend a bit of both in taking legal advice.

This was precisely what Knightley did, after a brief interval in which he raged around Hartfield, drinking brandy and threatening fratricide, to the disgust of his wife and the dismay of old Mr Woodhouse, who feared that the rapid cooling consequent upon such an overheating must surely bring on a cold, if not a tertian fever.

Emma, when her husband had cooled into coherence, drew out of him an account of what had passed at Donwell.

As she listened, she found herself uncertain as to what her own feelings on the matter were. Indignation that Knightley should have been refused immediate access to the revenues of his own estate warred with understanding of her brother-in-law's motives. She herself regarded the waste of money upon pleasures she did not share with some horror, and would dearly have loved to find some device to limit her husband's expenses. But her pride in her position as wife of the owner of the largest estate in the district required that the John Knightleys be put in their place. As her husband sent for his lawyer, Mr Coxe, she began her own campaign by sending a servant up to the Abbey, rescinding an invitation to dinner at Hartfield the following day, with the cold excuse that it was no longer convenient.

William Coxe came quickly. Twenty years ago he had been a pert young lawyer. With age had come a superficial gravity, but beneath it he was as light and lively as ever, with a love of litigation which went far beyond simple profit.

His first advice, which was to sue John Knightley for back-rental for the Abbey estate, a course of action which, if admitted, must surely end with the incarceration of John and probably all his family in the Fleet, was rejected. Also rejected were his proposals to send a posse of bailiffs backed by militia into Donwell, and to swear out a warrant of distraint before the local magistrate (who was George Knightley) against the said John, on suspicion of embezzlement, mismanagement, and general malfeasance.

'Come, man!' cried Knightley, his anger now finding a nearer target. 'What? What? Do you tell me I should commit my own brother to the common jail? Is this your best advice, Lawyer Coxe? You show me your comb in this, sir, for it is a coxcomb's advice!'

Pleased with his pun, he allowed himself to be mollified by the lawyer's apologies and when the man asked, 'Then what is it you wish to learn of me, Squire Knightley?' he replied, 'How to get my money, that is all I wish. This damned entail's at the bottom of things. All would be well if I could sell off the damned place and have a capital sum to live off.'

Coxe now began to study the problem in a more moderate manner and within a few days returned with news, both good and bad. The bad was that it appeared that the note of agreement between John Knightley and his brother, might indeed be seen as investing in John full authority for the discreet disposal of estate revenues. In other words, George could not take out of these revenues more than the superfluity after all expenses were met and a reasonable amount set aside for re-investment in the estate's future.

The good news was that the entail, drawn up nearly a hundred years before, could be interpreted as applying only to the estate as it existed then, and not in its expanded form a century later. Three generations of Knightleys, including George himself in his younger, steadier days, had made wise purchase of fertile land and productive farms on Donwell's boundaries, till the estate had doubled in size with much of the most profitable acreage being in the most recently acquired portions.

'These are yours by common inheritance,' argued Coxe, 'and are therefore disposable as you wish, either by testament after your death or by sale within your life.'

Now the dilemma which John Knightley had gleefully forecast for his brother was his own. To test the validity of Lawyer Coxe's judgment in the courts could eat up the entire value of the disputed land, and more.

Emma joined in her husband's triumph, and when she encountered her sister in Ford's shop, she was ready to greet her with all the condescending generosity of victory, but Isabella had gathered her younger children around her with a low cry of, 'Behold your aunt who would rob your poor brother!' and swept them out of the door.

A farm and five acres was selected to be offered at auction. All the countryside understood this as a test case, and waited with the excited interest of spectators at a prize-fight to see how John Knightley would react. The general opinion was that he could not sit back and do nothing, there must be an injunction against the sale sought in a court of law, and William Coxe sat back in happy expectation of a long, complex and profitable case.

But John Knightley was not a man to let emotion rule sense. A few days before the proposed sale, he rode quietly down to Hartfield one morning, and presented himself before his brother with an expression so mild and conciliatory that George's instinctive wrath was stayed in his bosom.

Emma, made aware of his presence in the house, had no such balm to her agitation as, with straining ear, she engaged her father in their daily session of backgammon. The sound of furious dispute would scarcely have calmed her feelings, but the silence that proclaimed its absence disturbed her so much that she quite lost track of the game and defeated her father three times in a row, bringing on one of his nervous headaches.

In the library meanwhile, the two Knightleys were circling each other like wary animals.

'Brother,' said John, 'this is an ill business and I am sorry for it.'

'I am sorry for it too,' said George, 'but it is not of my making.'

'No,' admitted John. 'I acknowledge I am much at fault.'

George was quite nonplussed by this.

'No, well, that is to say . . . Brother, will you not sit and take a glass of madeira against the chill air?'

'Thank you, I should like that.'

John sat, George poured, together they drank, offering no toast, but implying a truce.

'Brother,' resumed John,' 'I come to tell you there is no dispute between us on any important issue. Beyond doubt the estate is yours, while you live.'

Instantly George was ready for wrath, but even more quickly John disarmed him.

'If it is your wish that I and my family leave Donwell, then of course we will depart within twenty-four hours,' he continued.

'No!' protested George. 'What talk is this? Shall I thrust out my own brother, and my wife's sister, and my dear nieces and nephews that I love?'

'It would look ill,' agreed John, with no trace of satire. 'But, brother, in this business of selling the farm, there we must look to all our interests.'

Again George bridled. Again John was quickly a calming influence.

'It may be that you have the right of it. Or may be not. But let me ask you this, brother. What is it above all else that you want?'

'Why, nothing but what is mine!' declared George.

'Which nobody shall deny,' said John. 'We are close bound together in many ways, brother, and the one of us scarce can move without disturbing the other. There is the entail on Donwell; no one will deny your rights there, but the heir must have his rights too, don't you agree? And then there is—' he made a gesture with his wine glass— 'Hartfield. This is no small estate, brother, our two wives the sole heirs, and mine the elder sister, just as you are the elder brother. A strange cross-relationship, when you think of it.'

'There is no entail here,' proclaimed George. 'It will be left equally, I have the old man's word on it.'

'Equal shares is how estates decay,' murmured John. 'It is the wasting disease that entails were devised to cure. Brother, think of this. If I die tomorrow, my Henry becomes your heir, and is of an age and ability now that he could run Donwell as well as I, were he called upon to do it. When you die, he will have to do that, of course, and he will care for his mother and brothers and sisters too, till they can care for themselves. But what of your Emma when you die? Suppose the old man to have died first. Then half of Hartfield is my Isabella's which means it is mine, to do with as I will.

I am no tyrant, and I would consult my wife's desires, but sisters do not always live in that rational accord that brothers achieve. There is no such difficulty in dividing up and selling off Hartfield as exists in regard to Donwell, is there?'

The threat, or rather the complex of threats, was presented so mildly that George Knightley knew a solution must be close on its heels, so he kept his temper once more, and said, 'Continue, brother. I am listening.'

He listened for half an hour, spoke himself for the other half, then both men went from the house and rode into Highbury together. John Knightley, feeling that in this case it would be neither wise nor diplomatic to represent himself, had summoned Mr Ackroyd, a lawyer from Esher, to represent him, and he was already waiting in William Coxe's chambers.

'By God, brother, you were sure of your powers of persuasion!' said George with some irritation.

'Not so, brother. I was sure of your powers of reason,' replied John.

The lawyers got to work. They would have preferred weeks, but driven by the two Knightleys, who, each in his separate way, were not easily to be denied, by the end of a long afternoon, they had hammered out an agreement inscribed it on paper, had it signed, countersigned and witnessed, and had copies made for each party's safe-keeping.

The terminology was long-winded but the terms were simple. In brief, George Knightley invested the management of Donwell in his brother's hands during his lifetime, and after that in his nephew, Henry's. In return, he, George would receive a fixed income from the estate revenues, and in consideration of this agreement, John had signed an undertaking on his wife's behalf to renounce all her future interest in the Hartfield estate in favour of her sister, Emma.

Each of the brothers presented this agreement as a triumph. Each of the sisters received it as a disaster.

'You fool!' cried Emma. 'Before, you had the largest estate in the district, and half of the second largest in fee, with the use of the whole of it in practice. Now you have given away

Donwell, where we would have lived after my father died, with half of Hartfield at our disposal also!'

'You fool!' wept Isabella. 'Before, we had the expectation of owning half of Hartfield in our own right. Now we own nothing!'

The brothers urged their own cases, talking of what would happen when this one died and that one died, but hypotheses of mortality are of little comfort to female pride. Emma and Isabella both felt themselves demeaned by the brothers' agreement, though only Emma felt enraged by the law which permitted her husband to treat as his own what was in fact hers.

Not the least unhappy outcome of this agreement was a permanent coolness of relationship between Emma and Isabella. On the surface, much of the old familiarity between the two households was renewed, but gone forever was that old easy trust which a shared childhood creates.

Emma suffered the worse for it. Isabella had her large family to occupy her mind and emotions. Emma had only her ailing father, her absent husband, and no one else besides. Mrs Weston was plunged even further into her unhealthy devotions, and Emma did not care to make a friend and confidante of anyone else in Highbury's small society.

Also the whole question of the brothers' agreement continued to rankle with her much more than with her more easy-going sister. Indeed, as time passed, Isabella came to applaud the wisdom of her husband's action. She was, in all but legal fact, the mistress of Donwell, and her brother-in-law's decease, which his ever-increasing intemperance promised could hardly be long, would confirm her in this station.

Emma, on the other hand, had no advancement to look for. She had always considered herself the mistress of Hartfield since before her twentieth year; and marriage to Knightley, which had promised so much, looked as if now it was going to give her nothing but what had always been hers. This she might have come to accept, but there was a worse alternative threatening.

The trouble was that George Knightley's income from Donwell, though more than generous, for John was at pains to appear just in the eyes of the county, soon proved inadequate to his needs. To this income was added an allowance from the Hartfield estate of which he was the titular manager, though more and more in recent years as her father failed and her husband floundered, Emma had taken over real control. Knightley applied to his father-in-law for an increase which Emma permitted to the limits of what the estate could bear. But when her husband within a twelvemonth demanded more, and in terms which sent poor Mr Woodhouse into one of his trembles, she threw off any pretence that the decision was not in fact hers, and said coldly, 'Mr Knightley, this will not do. You have foolishly given over one estate which was yours. You shall not drag down another which is not. What you receive now is enough for any to ordinary gentlemen. You shall have no more.'

Amazed, for though his wife was not above scolding him, never before had she berated him as a master might berate a servant, Knightley flew into a terrible rage and raised his hand as though he would strike her. Emma did not flinch, but regarded him with cool contempt till the hand fell once more to his side.

'Not mine!' he thundered. 'Not mine indeed, while that poor shadow still shivers on the threshold' . . . (this with a contemptuous upwards gesture at the bedroom to which Mr Woodhouse had retired with a bowl of soothing gruel) . . . 'but it *shall* be mine, madam! Oh yes. It *shall* be mine!'

He strode out of the house, crying for his horse and a moment later Emma heard the thunder of hoofbeats as he galloped away along the drive.

At that moment a wish that he might fall and break his neck drifted across her mind, like the first brown leaf that falls from the rich woods of summer. But it was hardly noticed, and soon all seemed green again as, warm with triumph, she went up to attend to her father.

In the months that followed, Knightley referred no more to money. Indeed his attitude, was on the whole more concerned and conciliatory than for many a year, and though there seemed little evidence that he had moderated his habits, it pleased Emma to think that he was somehow managing his affairs so as to stay within his means.

For her part, she now dropped all pretence that the management of Hartfield was carried on either by her father or her husband, and after an initial affectation of surprise, all those concerned with the estate were happy to acknowledge openly what they had long recognized privately.

It was this new openness that brought Lawyer Coxe into a conflict of loyalties. Hitherto the affairs of Hartfield and the affairs of Knightley had been treatable as one. Now that was clearly not the case, and though his first and natural inclination was to put his loyalty to the husband before that to the wife, in the end he felt he had to speak.

The simple fact of the case was that Knightley had for some time been financing his excesses by a series of post-obit loans. The moneylenders, seeing the richness of the Hartfield estate and the weakness of its aged owner, had not stinted their offerings. While the debts that Knightley was running up had remained within the compass of the estate to repay, albeit with much trimming and selling, Coxe who had made the arrangement had been able to quiet his conscience.

But now Knightley was negotiating a loan of such proportions that Coxe could see no way in which the total debt could be repaid without selling off the house itself, and at this point he was constrained to speak.

Emma listened in a silence which the paleness of her handsome face did not let him mistake for resignation.

'But these figures are not credible,' she finally interjected, 'My husband's excesses, even if he worked at them night and day, could not eat up such a sum!'

'There is the interest,' said Coxe.

'Interest?'

'Yes, ma'am,' said Coxe, and named a figure which turned Emma's cheeks, already pale, almost translucent with restrained fury.

'He agreed that much? Oh, the fool!'

'It is not an unusual sum,' said Coxe, defensive of his sex.

'Then there are more stupid fellows in the world than

even I had dreamt of!' snapped Emma. 'So, let me under-stand this. When my father dies and the estate descends to my husband and myself, these bonds fall due, and the law will require that Hartfield be sold to repay them?'

'If there is no other source of money, yes.'

'What if my father has in the meantime disposed of the estate elsewhere?'

'Why, then I fear Mr Knightley would end up in jail, where he would be like to spend the rest of his days unless the debt were discharged.'

'He would at least learn the art of frugal living there,' said Emma, frowning. 'And if he did die in jail, what then? Does the debt fail with him?'

'No. It is a charge upon his estate, and therefore upon his beneficaries, which is to say, yourself, Mrs Knightley.'

'That is a monstrous imposition!' complained Emma, whose rapid mind had been looking for ways to remove the value of Hartfield out of Knightley's way till such time as she might be able to enjoy it alone. 'Does that debt never die?'

'It would die with you,' replied Coxe. 'The law does not pursue beyond the first heir. And of course it would die if Mr Knightley predeceased your esteemed father. That is the risk the moneylenders take in these post-obits. They are careful to study the health of those concerned. In this case, the dangers your husband faces in the hunting field would be set against the age and reported frailty of Mr Woodhouse. The degree of risk to the lenders is, of course, reflected in the interest rate.'

Which was so high that the lenders cannot have been too impressed with Knightley's hopes of longevity, thought Emma. But it would have been higher had they known that Mr Woodhouse had continued in the same frail state of health for more than half a century now!

Perhaps after all her father would outlive her husband. And a little flurry of brown leaves drifted down from the summer trees.

And so Emma Knightley approached her forty-first birth-day, concealing beneath her still beautiful exterior the anxieties which would have scored ageing lines on weaker flesh.

She had instructed Lawyer Coxe to say nothing of their conversation to her husband, an imposition of silence he was all too happy to accept. She meanwhile made a visit to London where she consulted another lawyer who confirmed what Coxe had said, but assured her he could put all to rights with a deed of separation, linked by a codicillary convenant to a testamentary trusteeship, upon which she recognized him as a charlatan, eager to dip his own spoon into this rich country mess, and returned to Hartfield resolved to put no more trust in lawyers.

On her return with a trunkful of the new fashions which had been her excuse for visiting London, she found Highbury buzzing with the news that Mr Frank Churchill was soon to visit Highbury.

Nothing had been seen of Churchill since the occasion of Mr Weston's funeral, but news of such a celebrity could not fail to be brought to the town. Five years earlier, there had been general shock and sorrow at the news of his wife's decease. It seemed that the interesting paleness of Jane Fairfax's complexion stemmed not from the application of powder to cover disfiguring freckles, as some had suggested, but from a natural pre-inclination to consumption, which dreadful disease had struck her down. Mr Churchill (so it was reported) had long mourned her death, but finally his natural high spirits had been recovered and now he was touring the country to renew old acquaintance. What more natural than that he should visit his stepmother, particularly as Randalls would, by Mr Weston's will, become his on Mrs Weston's death.

It was not anticipated that he would find life at Randalls very congenial.

Mrs Elton, the vicar's wife, so eager to be first as to be always forward, had arranged a 'little evening assemblage' at the vicarage to welcome what she called 'the prodigal'. Emma had little mind to attend, till she heard that the John Knightleys were going, upon which she accepted the invitation, planning to stay only long enough to reconfirm the George Knightleys' precedence in Highbury.

They arrived late, and found the gathering already crowded with Highbury notables, loud in conversation, but Emma's appearance in the most daring of her new London. gowns was so striking that she was at once the object of all eyes. Mr and Mrs Elton she greeted with a charming condescension, putting them with a single smile both at their ease and in their place.

Frank Churchill was deep in conversation at the room's centre with Isabella and John Knightley. Emma and her husband joined the group. Within half a minute, by a turn of her shoulder, a flutter of her fan, Emma had put Frank Churchill face to face with her, and thirty seconds after that, they were having a tête-à-tête while the Knightley brothers and Isabella formed a quite distinct and, in Isabella's case at least, slightly disgruntled group a few yards away.

'You have not changed, Miss Woodhouse ... Mrs Knightley,' smiled Churchill.

'You must call me Emma,' she answered lightly. 'We are old friends, are we not?'

'Indeed I hope so. You have forgiven me, then, for pretending to be a little in love with you all those years ago?'

'I can forgive everything but pretence,' she replied.

'Then let me urge that it was not altogether pretence,' he said with a laugh.

'Then let me assert that you are not altogether unforgiven. Tell me now, what do you think of us at Highbury, you who are such a stranger here? Will you stay long among us?'

His face darkened. He had gone a little grey with the passing years, but he had retained much of his old slimness of figure and his face had lost none of its lively expressiveness.

'I fear not long,' he said. 'To tell the truth, Miss Woodhouse ... Emma ... Randalls is no place for a worldly fellow like myself to feel easy in. The only comforts my stepmother acknowledges are those of religion. But I should not speak so of one who is your dear friend.'

It occurred to Emma that he had probably already ascertained that she and Mrs Weston no longer remained on the terms of intimacy that once had existed between them.

She said, 'Alas, Mrs Weston is much changed from what she was when your father lived, certainly.'

'True,' he agreed, encouraged by her response. 'I fear she is so taken up with the joys of the next world that she has quite forgotten that one may be comfortable in this without mortal sin.'

'Or even with,' said Emma. 'So you will not stay long at Randalls?'

A new voice cut into the conversation.

'I have assured Mr Churchill that, should he desire to extend his stay in Highbury with greater convenience, Mr E and I will be delighted to put him up at the vicarage.'

It was Mrs Elton, exercising her imagined prerogative as hostess to interrupt.

Emma smiled at her and said, 'I fear that that would be merely to exchange the deficiencies of one religion for another. Pray, do not be offended, Mrs Elton. I merely mean that Mr Churchill has been telling me how much he regrets that his stepmother keeps no stable, and I know that your good husband and yourself have no need of more than Betsy, your old brown cob. But a gentleman must have his horses, so I have invited Mr Churchill to come to Hartfield, when he has finished his visit at Randalls, and enjoy the run of my husband's stables. They are quite the best in the county, I do believe.'

'So they are,' said Mrs Elton acidly. 'Mr K is a fine judge of horseflesh at least. There is a trifle of supper laid out in the dining-room. Mr Churchill, if you would like to lead the way.'

'Willingly,' said Frank Churchill.

He reached for Emma's arm but hesitated when he saw his hostess's arm proffered to him. Then with a smile he said, 'I shall be delighted to try your husband's mounts, Mrs Knightley. Thank you.'

And led the slightly mollified Mrs Elton in to supper.

Less than a week later (and it was thought a credit to his good nature that he endured Randalls so long) Frank Churchill took up residence at Hartfield.

Knightley, who had never cared for Churchill in the old

days, was soon won to a change of opinion by the younger man's enthusiasm for hunting which almost matched his own.

'Says I've got the best string of horses he's seen anywhere in the county,' he said complacently. 'Matured into a man of judgment, that young fellow. Always knew he would once he settled down.'

Churchill for his part was even more struck by the alteration in Knightley, though he would never have ventured to speak openly of it without Emma's encouragement.

'Knightley feels you are much improved from what you used to be,' she told him when they were alone one day.

'I'm flattered, I think,' he answered with a smile.

'And what think you of Knightley? Is he not much improved too?'

'He is certainly more . . . weighty,' said Churchill, glancing at his hostess anxiously, in case his witticism offended.

Emma laughed.

'You have a keen eye!'

Encouraged, Churchill continued.

'And yet he is less weighty too! He was such a fearsome fellow to us young scallywags in the old days. I was always afraid he was about to lecture me on my ill manners, or my lightness of thought, or my flimsy morals! Now, though he is as firm as ever in his opinions on all matters of note, yet he is no firmer than any country gentleman might be expected to be who has received his father's notions, and his notions before him, without feeling any need to submit them to the test of his own reason!'

He paused, fearful once more he might have spoken too boldly, but Emma offered no reprimand of word or look and he went on, 'On judgment of horses and wine-shippers alone does he show any of that true moral passion which once informed his very cough!'

'In short, Mr Churchill, you feel my husband has changed from a variety of preaching prig into a type of toping centaur!'

Frank Churchill was truly shocked to hear Emma speak so freely, though what she said expressed his feelings precisely.

And with the shock came another more pleasurable feeling of sensuous complicity in the closeness implied by her openness with him.

'Emma,' he said, taking a step towards her.

But before that small step could be followed by a second much greater one, the door burst open, and a maid rushed in crying, 'Madam! madam! come at once. It's your father, madam! The old gentleman is close to dying!'

For forty years at least Mr Woodhouse had seemed so close to dying that his actual and necessary approach to that condition had passed almost unnoticed. Now at last, to Emma's horror, he had taken a positive step.

He had suddenly cried out, half risen, then fallen back into his chair unconscious. By the time Mr Perry, the apothecary, arrived, he had recovered consciousness but was unable to speak or move his limbs.

Mr Perry diagnosed a seizure, spoke learnedly of a sudden rush of blood to the head, and called for a bowl and towel so that he could open a vein. Emma, looking down at the pale skinny frame of her father, thought to herself that he looked to be suffering more from a lack of blood than an excess of it, but Mr Perry had been treating the old man for many decades now, and for once she was ready to bow to expert judgment.

Frank Churchill, however, whose adoptive father had died of the same cause (which he suspected to be excessive bleeding as much as the seizure itself) urged caution; and Perry, who was an intelligent, gentlemanlike man, prepared to admit (to himself at least) that many of his treatments owed more to custom than to knowledge, readily put up his knife, and prescribed stillness and warmth instead.

At this point the front door of the house burst open and footsteps were heard making up the stairs. It was Knightley, who had been out riding while all the excitement took place. Apprised of the events by the groom who took his horse, he now burst into the bedroom and cried, 'What? Is the old man dead?'

To Emma, there seemed more of eager expectation than

grief in his voice, though a moment's thought would have told her that her father's death could be as little welcome to Knightley as to herself. But she did not spare the moment, and replied angrily, 'No, sir, he is not dead, though he is like to be if such a noise as you make further disturbs his poor mind. This is not a stable yard, sir, nor a tap-room!'

Discomfited, Knightley stammered, 'No, Emma, I only meant . . .' and retreated before her angry gaze.

Within twenty-four hours Mr Woodhouse recovered his speech, though it remained slow and somewhat indistinct. And over the next few days his power of movement returned fully to his left side, though his right was still partially paralysed.

These recoveries Emma credited as much to Frank Churchill as to Mr Perry. In many ways, the gratitude of a beautiful woman is more dangerous to a man than her love, for love can be irrational, while gratitude, being based on reasonable cause, makes him think the better of himself, and for a man it is always self-importance that lines the bottom of a dangerous liaison.

Emma was delighted with her father's progress. Curiously, the old man after a lifetime of alarums and crises based on such inconsequentials as sitting in a draught; rising too early or too late; over-exertion by walking; too rich a diet; too lively a company; too long a supper; or too short an afternoon nap; seemed to treat this very real ailment as a trivial and temporary inconvenience. Emma was ready to be encouraged by this to hope for a complete recovery, but Mr Perry was far less sanguine. Fearful of approaching Emma direct, and distrusting Knightley's ability to be a gentler bearer of bad news than himself, he decided to confide in Frank Churchill. What he had to say chimed perfectly with Churchill's own knowledge of the subject. At Mr Woodhouse's age, such a seizure as this was almost invariably the precursor of a more severe attack. It might come in days, it would certainly come in months, and it would beyond all reasonable doubt be fatal.

Churchill passed a sleepless night uncertain of his best course of action. Should Emma be prepared for the worst, or should she be permitted to enjoy her father's few remaining weeks in the bliss of ignorance? He had almost decided for the latter course when he rose next morning and rode down to Highbury to see Lawyer Coxe on a matter connected with Randalls. Though left wealthy by his adoptive parents, Frank Churchill had neglected his investments in the years immediately following Jane's death, and had suffered considerable losses. He had retained enough to live on, but not to be careless with, and he had been distressed to see the dilapidated state into which Mrs Weston was allowing his future inheritance to fall. His stepmother had been unmoved by his suggestions for repair and he had consulted Coxe to see what might be done to force her to maintain the property.

Coxe's researches had been fruitless. Nothing could be done.

'Except perhaps, if you, sir, would care to invest a little of your own money.'

'What do you mean?' inquired Churchill.

'It might be possible to persuade Mrs Weston to convert, let us say, the old stables into a Roman Catholic chapel. Once on the premises, the constructors could at your expense, and unbeknown to Mrs Weston, examine and make good any large defects in the main building.'

Coxe's subtle, complexity-loving mind was delighted with the scheme, but Churchill was less enthusiastic.

'It smacks too much of subterfuge,' he said. 'Besides, what should I want with a house that has a Romish chapel and no stable?'

'In architecture at least, apostasy is as easy as conversion,' said Coxe. 'And it is better than having no house at all as is like to be the case if Mrs Weston's neglect continues. Poor Highbury! Randalls crumbling, Hartfield like to follow, what sad days have I lived to see!'

'Hartfield? What say you of Hartfield?'

Mr Coxe had said too much, but was soon persuaded, under oaths of secrecy, to say more, and Randalls was completely forgotten as Churchill rode back to Hartfield.

His agitation was so great that he confronted Emma directly with a demand to know the truth of the matter and, after an initial anger at Coxe's indiscretion, she replied as frankly.

'So it is true,' said Churchill. 'With your father's death, Hartfield, and all that goes with it, must be sold to pay your husband's debts. Monstrous! Monstrous!'

'It is monstrous indeed, Mr Churchill, but a monster not to be feared yet awhile. My father mends daily and, who knows? he may yet live another twenty years.'

She laughed gaily, and he understood her laughter was a prayer. He tried to laugh with her, or at least to smile, but it was an effort hard to make, for he found his dilemma increased tenfold. To tell her the truth of her father's condition now would not be merely to deprive her of the hope of years of life for a beloved parent. It would also be to tell that by the year's end she could be homeless and penniless.

This agony of decision had better be endured in private. But before he could excuse himself, Emma spoke.

'Mr Churchill,' she said, 'you're strangely rapt. What is it that so moves you?'

He had forgotten how perceptive of reaction, how sensitive of nuance she was.

'Emma,' he said, 'will you not call me Frank?'

'If you will be frank, that is what I shall call you,' she rejoined. 'So tell me why you seem so troubled.'

There was nothing else for it. He told her.

'I am no apothecary, you understand,' he concluded. 'I speak but from observation.'

'And you have discussed this with Perry too?'

He admitted as much.

'There are other physicians,' she said.

He never admired her as much as at this moment. Knowing the turbulence of emotion that must be raging through her breast, he looked in vain for any sign of it on her face or in her voice and could find none, except perhaps a little not unbecoming pallor around the eyes.

There *were* other physicians. She consulted them discreetly, and even contrived to have one of them examine her father under pretence of visiting Hartfield to look at a gelding her husband wished to sell.

They confirmed unanimously Perry's judgment that this present seizure was but a harbinger of a much larger attack, almost certain to be fatal in a man of Mr Woodhouse's years and constitution. There was some disagreement on timing, but not a one of them would stake his professional reputation beyond six months.

Poor Emma wept, but she wept alone, and only Churchill guessed at the agony of spirit in which she passed the next few days. Such nobility confirmed him in his next move. He had already at the time of revelation of Mr Woodhouse's true condition been moved to recognize in himself a deep, almost worshipping love for Emma. Now he knew that come what may, he had to tell it. If she repulsed him, then that was merely the end of his own worthless life; but if, even in the repulse, there was the slightest sign that her awareness of inspiring such a deep, unselfish love might bring one iota of comfort to her wounded soul, then the sacrifice was well worthwhile.

He spoke. She was astounded.

'Mr Churchill . . . how can you speak so . . . ? You are a guest in our house . . . you alone know my present unhappiness . . . this is not the act of a gentleman, let alone a friend!'

Horribly chastened, he yet did not withdraw.

'Emma, forgive me. It is my care for you as much as my passion that makes me speak. How shall I bear to think of you, orphaned, friendless, in poverty? Emma, I cannot provide against the loss of your dear father, but friendship I can supply; and what I have of wealth is yours to dispose of. Emma, I beg you, let me help . . .'

'You are too familiar, sir,' she said angrily. 'You overreach yourself!'

'Emma!' he said, reproved. 'Miss Woodhouse . . .'

'*Mrs Knightley*, sir!' she cried. 'You forget. I have a husband.'

And she strode magnificently from the room.

It is not to be imagined that Knightley was so far removed from the realities of life as to be unconcerned about the future. At the moment his debts were huge and, with the punitive interest thereon, steadily mounting. But with the greater part of the latest (and so far as the security of the Hartfield estate was concerned, the last) post-obit advance still in his hands, plus his income from Donwell Abbey, he was for the moment comfortable enough. But old Mr Woodhouse's seizure had been a nasty jolt to his spirits. Like all who knew him well, he too had come to consider his father-in-law would live forever, and had indulged in some self-congratulatory mirth at the way in which he believed he had deceived the moneylenders.

Now suddenly the old man had showed he was mortal man.

The consequences of his death were unavoidable and Knightley now faced up to them for the first time. Hartfield must go in its entirety, house, land, stables, horses, everything. There was no avoiding it. All that would remain to him of this, the crowning glory of Highbury, was its fairest jewel, Emma.

It was small consolation. He could not think of his wife without anger. He compared himself now with what he had been twenty years before. *Then* he had been rich and respected, a fine figure of a man in the prime of life, dignified of mien, weighty of speech, sage and serious, the acknowledged exemplar of all the best qualities which went into the composition of an English country gentleman.

Now (suddenly the last infirmity of despair, which is honesty, was upon him) he was fat, corpulent, *gross*; a toper, a sot, a grotesque gourmandizer, who thought more of his horses than his human household, neglected his duties both public and private, and was, all in all, a laughing-stock throughout the county.

And what was the significant, the catalysing difference between himself twenty years ago and himself now?

Marriage!

He had married a vain, posturing, empty-headed girl nearly twenty years younger than himself in the arrogant belief that he could influence her development, and alter her make-up, to fit his mould. Yet how had they started?

By the abandonment of his own elegant country seat,

Donwell Abbey, to set up house here at Hartfield in order not to fret or inconvenience old Mr Woodhouse!

And later, whose voice had it been that urged upon him the propriety, the advantage, the *necessity* of admitting the John Knightleys into Donwell? Emma's, of course! Talking of the needs of her dear sister, the care and comfort of her dear nephews and nieces! Thus had he admitted his own brother, that cold, calculating, subtle Cain of a brother, into a situation to which he had no rights and few expectations.

'I have sold my birthright for a mess of potage!' proclaimed Knightley, whose Christian thoughts turned more easily to the violence of the Old Testament than to the gentler virtues of the New.

So he sat, tracing the course of his decline over two decades, and every downward step seemed to have been carved out for him by Emma.

By the time he had finished his tragic autobiography (and his third bottle of port) he felt it almost as a consoling justice that his wife was going to lose forever her beloved Hartfield.

But if that were just, then even juster would it be for himself to regain Donwell, and this was what he now set his mind to.

It was, or had been a steady mind, and a clear mind, but even before it was corroded by port wine and shaken out of its foundings by the bumping jog of a horse, it had never had the cold sharp edge of John Knightley's. John had long been aware of the extent of his brother's borrowings. In fairness, if there had been anything he could have done either by word or deed to stay the sad decline, he would have spoken or acted. But judging rightly that no interference of his would be allowed to influence events, he had looked ahead to their necessary conclusion and set about preparing his defences accordingly.

The outcome was inevitable. Soon Lawyer Coxe had to admit defeat to George Knightley. His brother was as firmly fixed at Donwell Abbey as if he were there by right of primogeniture. The very best that Coxe could hope for was to establish his client's right to a share in the occupation of a house which he had once possessed with a clear and undeniable title.

Donwell was a large mansion, but John Knightley had a large family, and also little desire to have a drunken brother and a sister-in-law he had never cared for living under the same roof. For the first time he spoke to his wife of these matters. Isabella, who had come to accept the gaining of Donwell as a fair compensation for the loss of her share in Hartfield, at once flew into a rage at the thought that her father's estate had been lost entirely to the moneylenders to pay for her brother-in-law's pleasures. This eventually died, to be replaced immediately by an even greater one at the prospect of the George Knightleys coming to live at Donwell.

Her husband let her anger die. His wife's occasional emotional outbursts were a price he had been always ready to pay for her undisputed intellectual subordination.

'Be still, wife,' he said finally. 'We cannot have George and Emma to live at Donwell, there is no argument about that. But we are obliged by strong arguments of law, family tie, and public reputation, to see they are not destitute. There is a cottage on the estate out beyond Langham, a very decent kind of little house, which, with a bit of attention to the roof, will do very nicely for a childless couple with a single maid, no horses, and small inclination to entertain. My brother and his wife might live there very comfortably on his allowance from the estate revenues and we should still be able to maintain easily all that pleasant intercourse which the bonds of blood make necessary to us both.'

As this pleasant intercourse had been reduced in recent years to an exchange of visits every sixmonth, it did indeed seem that it would be easy to maintain. It was true that Mr Woodhouse's illness had caused a more frequent communion between the sisters, but Isabella's strong hint that their father's seizure might have been accelerated by worry and neglect had not brought them any closer together.

So it was that John and Isabella together drove down to Hartfield to say in a friendly, familial kind of way what Lawyer Coxe was already transcribing into the cold convolutions of legal English.

They did not find George at home. Urgent business of state had required his presence in London. Emma received them with a courtesy whose chilliness hardly showed.

John Knightley for his part was all fraternal concern, and Isabella all sisterly condescension. Emma received their proposal with smiling calmness. And as the sisters parted, (John having gone ahead), Isabella's sense of the totality of her triumph was so strong that there were genuine tears of affection in her eyes as she embraced Emma and said, 'Papa looks so well, sister, that he may, God willing, live for many years yet, and so delay this unhappy day. Forgive me, if my concern for him made me so forget myself that I ever hinted a fear that he was not receiving the best of treatment here. I know now what I did not know then, that you have cause even greater than a daughter's love to cherish his dear health.'

'Sister, you are a great comfort to me,' said Emma.

The tears flowed faster and Isabella said, 'And, sister, the best news I have still to give. It may be yet that Hartfield is not to be lost to our family.'

'What's this?' cried Emma, sudden hope filling her heart.

'John has already spoken to Mr Coxe. Our private investments have flourished these past years, and when Hartfield finally comes on the market to pay George's debts, it may be possible for John himself to purchase the house at least, and some of the estate also.'

'This is good news indeed, sister,' said Emma, suddenly full of shame for the hard thoughts she had entertained of the John Knightleys. It would not be pleasant to live as the object of her sister's charity, but it would be infinitely preferable to living in a cottage at Langham! 'Oh, good news indeed!'

But if John purposed to buy Hartfield, what need had there been to mention Langham at all? she wondered.

Her thoughts had distracted her from Isabella's prattling.

'Yes,' she was saying, 'such a nice girl, and though she has only twenty thousand, her breeding is such that we cannot doubt that she will make an excellent wife for Henry, and mistress of Hartfield . . .'

'Mistress of Hartfield!' echoed Emma. 'Sister, forgive me, of whom do you speak.'

'Emma, do you grow deaf?' said Isabella tartly. 'I speak of Miss Augusta Otway, of course, who is to marry your nephew, Henry, and, if all goes well with the purchase, to set up house with him here at Hartfield!'

The shock was so great that Emma could not speak and Isabella, happy to fill any silence with her own chatter, was able to depart in complete ignorance of the violent changes of feeling to which her sister had been subjected in the past half-hour.

Once alone, however, Emma gave vent to her pent-up feelings and raged around the room, restrained only from screaming aloud and hurling articles at the wall by her remembrance of her convalescent father upstairs. But her mind was tempestuous.

'First Donwell—now Hartfield—to take all—give it to that bumptious boy—Miss Augusta Otway—empty-headed ninny—cottage at Langham—daily visits—nothing changed—oh, the hypocrisy!—private investments—liar, cheat—Donwell revenues—oh, for money!—or someone with money—money enough to buy Hartfield when the time comes and keep it from those prating hypocrites—*anything*, I would give *anything*!'

The door opened and Frank Churchill came into the room.

Do not judge Emma too harshly. Distressed beyond all tolerance, all reason, all control; betrayed by those nearest to her, a debauched husband and a disingenuous sister; praying to God for deliverance at any price; and the door opens . . .

They were alone in the house. Frank Churchill saw her distress and came naturally to comfort her. She saw the light of his loving concern in his eyes and let herself be comforted. By what small degrees they moved from comfort to caress, the reader must judge for himself. What resistance, what persuasion; what interchange of vows more sacred than those of church or state; what soft endearments, what gentle pressing, what warm yielding; all these are for the

204

reader to imagine at whatever speed, of whatever proportion, and in whatever detail, best befits his conscience. Suffice it to say that Emma bestowed on Churchill what she had not bestowed on any man save her husband, and not on him for many years, and Frank Churchill felt himself blessed in the bestowal.

In that gentle aftermath, where pleasure is still more than a memory and guilt still less than vapour, Emma murmured, 'Frank, do you truly love me?'

'More than anything. More than life even. Ask what you will, I shall provide it.'

Emma said, 'What shall I ask? What do I require? Nothing! Except . . .'

'Except? Ask anything, dear heart.'

'Dear *heart*, you say? Let that be my cue. Heart . . . hart . . . Hartfield! That is all I ask.'

'What?'

Churchill's surprise penetrated Emma's languor.

'Do not misunderstand, my love,' she said urgently. 'I do not mean as a gift. Do not believe that I would ask for such a gift, or any gift at all. To ask for *anything* would be the action of a . . .'

She let her voice fade into an indignant silence.

Churchill said, 'Emma, my love, ask me anything I can give, and you shall have it with no one daring to make such an imputation. What? You are above reproach! But what is it you say of Hartfield?'

'All I mean, dear Frank, is, could you not buy Hartfield for yourself? A man of your wealth and standing needs an estate. Randalls is well enough, but like to be a ruin by the time poor Mrs Weston passes on. Whereas Hartfield is fit for any gentleman, and must be sold if my dear father dies. I would rather it passed into your hands than anyone else's in the world! And it would mean you would still be close by, when . . . when . . .'

'When what?'

In tears, she told him of John Knightley's proposal for their accommodation after Hartfield was sold.

Churchill's indignation was great.

'Has the man no soul to make such a proposition?' he thundered. 'And your own sister too ... oh, monstrous! Dear heart, I swear that if I had the means at my disposal, you should not lose Hartfield, no, not if it meant I had to rent it out to Knightley for a peppercorn!'

Out of all these fine and heartfelt emotions, Emma dextrously plucked the only significant word.

'You say "if", my love ...'

With genuine disappointment, but without shame, for he was in no way conscious of having deceived her, Churchill confessed how small his fortune was, how little of financial assistance he could offer to help her retain Hartfield.

With magnificent restraint, Emma began to rearrange her dishevelled clothing, resisting his attempts to delay her by pointing out it was time she took tea with her father. Her thoughts as she climbed the stairs were a bitter turmoil, but nothing of this showed as she greeted old Mr Woodhouse with a bright smile.

'How are you, Papa?' she asked gaily. 'Hannah will be here shortly with the tray and afterwards we will play a game of backgammon.'

The old man's mouth opened and shut but no words came. She approached close, took his hand and raised it to her cheek. Still he did not speak. Alarmed, she released the hand. It fell, resistless, on to the counterpane.

'Papa!' she cried. *'Papa!'*

It was bad, but not the worst. Perry, quickly summoned, confirmed there had been a second seizure, but by no means as severe as he had feared.

'However ...' he said.

'Speak freely, Mr Perry,' Emma urged.

'Forgive me if I do, Mrs Knightley. Weakened as he is now, a third seizure would certainly be fatal.'

'And is a third likely?'

'Almost inevitable, I fear, dear lady. And it may not be long delayed. Forgive me for giving such news!'

Emma took the blow well. Isabella was summoned to weep; the Reverend Elton was called to pray. By midnight, however, Mr Woodhouse was a little better, and took a little gruel before falling into a peaceful sleep. The vicar went to continue his prayers in the vicarage, Isabella took her tears back to Donwell, and Emma went up to her lonely bedroom where at last she could give way completely to her grief.

The future looked blacker than she had ever known it. For the first time in her life she contemplated her own death. Would it not be best for everyone if she were to follow her dear father quickly into that abyss?

When her dark musings were interrupted by a tapping at her door, and to her whispered call, 'Who's there? came the whispered reply, 'Frank', her first reaction was of outrage.

Then she took thought, and after a while she opened the door and said softly, 'Come in.'

Once more old Mr Woodhouse amazed everyone by the strength of his constitution. Once more, albeit more slowly this time, speech returned and paralysis departed, but the end now seemed certain, and soon.

Knightley returned from London, shook his head in perplexity at the sight of his stricken father-in-law, whose frail figure was all that lay between him and ruin, and went back to London to pursue whatever affairs of state occupied him there.

That night, Frank Churchill came to Emma's room again as was now his accepted practice, though Emma and his own conscience insisted on complete discretion. She seemed strangely distant, and after a while he asked if anything ailed her.

To his amazement, and also his exulting hope, she replied, 'I spoke to Knightley of a separation today.'

'What did he answer?' he asked.

'What do you imagine? He laughed, and said God had bound us, and only God could untie us. I asked him if he spoke of divorce.'

Churchill's hopes leapt even higher. Divorce was difficult but not altogether impossible, if both parties were energetic in its pursuit.

He said, 'And what said he to that?'

'He laughed even louder, and said no, it was not divorce he meant, but death. That was the only instrument he recognized to untie God's knot. Frank, I must see you no more!'

'No more?'

Now hope had gone and only shock remained.

'What do you say? Why should we cease our encounters?' he demanded.

'While I thought there was hope that we might one day be legitimately joined, I could ease my conscience,' she replied passionately. 'But now I know that there is no hope, I see this relationship for the sinful thing it is. We must part and see each other no more! No, Frank, do not plead or protest. My mind is firm. Go now, dear one. Go at once. And God bless you!'

And Frank Churchill found himself outside in the cold corridor, the sound of a bolt sliding home behind him with all the finality of the iron bar which signals to a prisoner that his life-sentence has begun.

That night he sat up long in a desperate speculation as to what his future might be, and before dawn arrived, he had left Hartfield and ridden away into the paling shadows.

The following night George Knightley was preparing for bed. He whistled quietly to himself as he did so, the tune of an old hunting song. He had discovered in himself of late a great capacity to live for the present pleasure, and let the future look after itself. Today had been a good day. He had spoken well in the House and won the applause of his Party's leaders. He had come back to his other Westminster house in the evening, and found the wanton Lady Upton waiting for him. They had shared a supper of cold pie and claret, and much else besides. Finally she had departed, promising him to return the following night.

'He finished off a half-empty bottle of wine and thought complacently of his performance. For a man of his age and his corpulence, he was wonderfully lissome. It was this unexpected combination which so attracted Lady Upton, she had told him. It was a shame a man so vital should not have gotten an heir on his own wife. That would have solved some of his problems perhaps, in giving him a clear and continuous title to Donwell. But it was too late now. Or perhaps not. Emma at forty was still a beautiful and vigorous woman. What a jolt it would be to his sanctimonious brother and that awful babbling wife of his, not to mention that moon-faced oaf, his nephew Henry!

Perhaps the future was not as dark as it seemed.

He finished the wine, nibbled a few crumbs of pastry from the half-eaten pie, yawned and went to bed.

Soon he slept.

A sound woke him.

His bedroom door was ajar and he knew he had closed it. A figure stood by his bed. He tried to struggle upright, but the sheets seemed to bind him tight.

Outside a cloud was blown away from the moon and its bright light fell straight through the half-curtained casement, illuminating the intruder's figure.

The first thing that struck Knightley was that the intruder held a large wedge of veal pie in his hand.

Then he raised his eyes to the man's face.

'You!' he said in amazement.

He would have spoken more, but there was no more time to speak. Into his open mouth the intruder pushed the wedge of pie and leaned all his weight on it, thrusting it deep, deep, down. Knightley choked and struggled, but the tight stretched sheets held his huge body supine with his arms pinned tight by his sides. After a while, the cloud blew back over the moon, or so it seemed, for darkness came drifting down through the fading casement.

The news came first to Lawyer Coxe who took it straight to Donwell Abbey. Pale and serious-faced, John Knightley and Isabella drove quickly down to Hartfield.

'Why, sister, I was not expecting you today,' said Emma. 'And brother John! Is it about some new cottage you have found for my occupation?'

'Emma, be strong,' urged Isabella. 'We bring sad tidings.'

'What? Must I make do with a barn, perhaps? Or even a byre!'

'Sister-in-law, be still and listen,' commanded John Knightley. 'Your husband, and my brother, George Knightley . . .'

'Yes, yes. I know him.'

'He is dead. Emma, George is dead.'

'Good lord,' said Emma. 'George dead, you say?'

She sat very still, completely expressionless.

'How dead?' she asked finally.

'He . . . he choked,' said John Knightley.

'Choked!'

'On a piece of pie,' interposed Isabella. 'He had been drinking wine with his supper, and eating a veal pie. He must have taken some to bed with him and continued to eat it as he lay there . . .'

'What a remarkable thing,' said Emma. 'Choked, you say? On a veal pie. What a remarkable thing.'

'Emma, let your grief come out,' urged John. 'Do not hold it back. Such retention is . . .'

He was interrupted by the sound of a horse, ridden at speed to the front door.

'That is probably Mr Perry,' said Emma rising. 'I sent for him. Forgive me. I will ask him to wait.'

'But why have you sent for Perry?' cried Isabella. 'Is Father . . .'

But Emma had left the room.

It was not, however, Perry, but Frank Churchill, that the maid was opening the door to. He had a wild pale look, with his hair and clothes somewhat dishevelled, like a man who had not slept much, but ridden fast and far.

'Will you step into the library, Mr Churchill?' said Emma, leading the way. 'Forgive me if I can give you little of my time today. I have just received distressing news. My husband . . .'

'. . . is dead!' Churchill concluded for her.

'News travels fast! You have heard?' she said.

'*Heard?*' he cried. 'I was . . .'

His words tailed off, then he resumed in a quieter tone.

210

'Yes, Emma. I have heard, and I have come post haste. Oh, my Emma! I know that in the eyes of others you must put on a show of grief; but for us, what a different emotion this news must rouse!'

'Mr Churchill, I do not understand your meaning,' said Emma.

'Emma! He is dead. George is dead! Now we may be together and none can say us no! I can take care of you as you deserve; despite my losses, I have wealth enough to keep you comfortable, dear, dear Emma!'

'Comfortable!' Emma laughed gently. 'Oh, I see your meaning. You are concerned for my comforts now I am a widow. Rest assured, dear Mr Churchill. There is no cause for concern. Did you not know that with my husband's death while my father still lives, all debts are cancelled, and Hartfield remains safe? But none the less I thank you for your solicitude.'

'Emma, what are you saying?' demanded Churchill. 'I am offering my heart. I am asking your hand in marriage.'

'Marriage? With my widowhood a matter of hours barely, of minutes only in my knowledge? Fie, Mr Churchill what are you thinking of?' reproached Emma coldly. 'Besides, did you not understand me? Hartfield is safe. Now that I have Hartfield, what should I want with another husband?'

There was the sound of another horse approaching.

Emma said, 'That will, I think, be Mr Perry. Perhaps you could admit him on your way out, Mr Churchill, and ask him to wait. Forgive me if I am short with you. You understand, there is much for me to do. Goodbye.'

Leaving the haggard, stricken figure behind her, she returned to the drawing-room.

'I'm sorry to have left you,' she said to the couple waiting there. 'It was not in fact, Mr Perry, but Mr Frank Churchill, come post-haste to offer his condolences. A truly gentlemanly act, I think. Perry has arrived now, I believe, but I have asked him to wait till we shall have finished our business.'

'Sister!' cried Isabella. 'Why have you sent for Perry? Papa is not worse, I hope?'

'No, indeed,' said Emma. 'Papa in fact is much better this morning. I shall keep the sad news of Knightley's death from him a little while, I believe, till he grows strong enough to receive it.'

'Then, what of Perry?'

'Perry? Oh yes. I must admit I have summoned Perry here on my own account.'

'Emma! You are not ill, my sweet?'

Isabella moved forward all concern, and John Knightley plucked a cushion from a chair, though what he hoped to do with it was not clear.

'Not ill, exactly, Bella,' said Emma, smiling coyly. 'Is it not strange how Providence arranges things? On this very day that you bring me this tragic news about George, I have summoned Perry to confirm good news, which is also about George in a way. Oh, fate is strange!'

'What do you mean, Emma?' cried Isabella, now alarmed far beyond mere concern for her sister's or her father's health.

'I mean that I believe; no, I mean I am *sure* that I am, if you will forgive the phrase, brother-in-law, *enceinte*. I am with child, dear Bella. Knightley is dead, the poor, dear man. But his name will live on, his *full* name, if, as I hope, pray, and begin to feel, it is a boy!'

And now John Knightley began to look as if at last he had decided what he would like to do with the cushion.

Emma Knightley, handsome, clever and rich, with a comfortable home and happy disposition; with a much loved elderly father and an adorable, strappingly healthy son; seems to unite some of the best blessings of existence, and appears preordained to pass her remaining years in the world with very little to distress and vex her.

CROWDED HOUR

At twelve noon there were three people in that house. By the time the clock struck one, two of them would be dead and the life of the third would have changed for ever.

When the front door bell rang, Daphne was sitting curled up on the sofa, reading *The Postman Always Rings Twice*. She tried to pretend she hadn't heard it. Frank and Cora had just started to make love by the body of Cora's murdered husband. It was a bad place for an interruption.

The bell rang again. With a sigh of irritation, she rose and went to answer it. As she passed down the hall she heard the church clock beginning to scatter all the quarters.

There was a man standing on the step, rather too close to the door. He was in his mid-thirties, tall, narrow-faced, with a good tan which showed off strong white teeth as he smiled and said, 'Mrs Davis?'

'Yes.'

'Is your husband in?'

He wasn't. Daphne was opening her mouth to say so when the shadow of the Golden Showers growing up the pseudo-Græcian column of the mini-portico moved. There was no wind. Someone was standing there out of sight.

It was probably all perfectly innocent but she had been sensitized by her reading and she heard herself saying, 'Yes. I'll just go and fetch him. Please wait.'

She began to close the door. He continued to smile but his foot was already over the threshold. She tried to slam the door and had the brief satisfaction of hearing him gasp as his expensive soft leather slip-on was crushed against the jamb. Then the hidden man appeared and flung his weight against the door. It burst open. She turned to flee. They caught her in two strides. She hit the floor heavily. The second man knelt astride her, his knees gripping her as tight as a lover's. From inside his loose-fitting blouson he dragged a shotgun, barrels and stock sawn off to reduce it to little more than eighteen inches. He pushed it hard under her chin and hissed, 'Keep quiet!'

She heard footsteps moving swiftly, doors opening and shutting. She glimpsed the first man passing on his way to the staircase. He carried an automatic pistol and he was no longer smiling.

Time passed; terror stretched it to an eternity. Then she saw him again, a tapering giant from her angle of view. He was pushing his gun back into an underarm holster.

'All right. Let her up,' he commanded.

The man astride her squeezed once more with his legs and rose reluctantly. The tall man offered his hand. She ignored it and rolled away from them both.

And as she pushed herself upright she heard the church clock complete its long recitation of the hour.

In the lounge they prodded her into a chair. The man with the shotgun glowered down at her while the other went to the drinks cabinet, poured a tumblerful of Scotch and brought it to her.

'Get that inside you,' he said.

'I could do with one of them,' said the other. He was much younger, stockier of build, coarser of feature.

'No way,' said the tall man. 'Come on, Mrs Davis, drink it up, then we'll have a little chat.'

Slowly Daphne drank. She hated whisky. Worse than medicine, she used to say. For some reason this seemed to exasperate Ted, so she stopped saying it. But now it *was* medicine and she needed it. Her whole body felt slack and weak. She was seeing this familiar room through a soft filter. Only the intruders came out sharp and focused.

'He keeps nothing here,' she said. 'It's all in the shop. You're wasting your time.'

She hadn't meant to speak but her voice was only as lightly in her control as her muscles. Words were jostling to get out. It wasn't contact she wanted but a barrier. There seemed to be some measure of safety in words.

The tall man said, 'Thank you, Mrs Davis, but we realize

that. Just you concentrate on answering a couple of questions and everything will be all right. Where's he gone?'

It was Ted they wanted. Ted and the shop keys. Her mind was racing like a squirrel in a wheel, the words were crowding her lips once more.

'He's gone out. He's lunching out. Business. He often has Sunday business lunches. He won't be back till this evening. He's bringing some people back for dinner. Business friends. All men. Half a dozen of them. They'll all be arriving together . . .'

The words felt as if they would come forever. She was amazed at her quickness of wit. Ted would be amazed too, Ted who was always putting her down for being slow . . .

Suddenly her hair was seized from behind and she shrieked as her head was jerked viciously to one side. She'd been concentrating all her attention on the tall man and hadn't noticed the stocky man's movements.

'Shall I knock the stupid cow about a bit?' he asked.

'Not yet,' said the other. 'She's only trying to be clever. That's a good sign. Shows she's got her wits about her. I can't bear hysterical women, Mrs Davis. So Ted's gone to lunch? Thing is, we've been watching the house for half an hour, ever since he finished washing the car. We'd have come in then, only your neighbour was deadheading his roses and it's silly to take unnecessary chances, isn't it? But we know the car's still in the garage and your husband hasn't come out of the front of the house. So where is he?'

Daphne didn't speak. Her head was forced further sideways till she was almost looking at the tall man upside down. He sat down on the sofa facing her. He noticed the open book lying there, picked it up, looked at the cover, read a little, smiled.

'OK, Tommy,' he said. 'Give her one. But take it easy. Just break her nose.'

Somehow that *take it easy* was even more terrifying than the shotgun swinging up over her face.

'He's taken Lady for a walk!' she screamed. 'Our dog. Lady. He's taken her for a walk.'

The shotgun stopped at the peak of its swing.

'Dog? No one said nothing to me about a dog,' said the man called Tommy.

'Tommy, I try to keep demands on your mentals to a minimum. No sweat. It's not a Dobermann, just a nice old friendly Labrador. Right, Mrs Davis?'

The tall man's detailed knowledge was disturbing, but the bit of her mind still in touch with thought observed that he himself had been disturbed. This was an upset to his plans and he didn't look like a man who liked upsets.

He rose from the sofa and went to the window overlooking the rear garden: patio and barbecue area, long lawn, small orchard, bounded by a briar hedge with open fields beyond.

'He went this way?'

'Yes. There's a gate in the hedge.'

'Then?'

'There's a path. Lots of paths. You can get down to the river. Or across to the golf course. Or through the woods to Little Morton. Please, can you make him let me go?'

He made a gesture and Tommy gave her hair a last vicious twist before releasing her.

'What now, Mac?' he said surlily. 'This ain't so bleeding clever, is it?'

He spoke with an indeterminate London accent. The tall man's voice had seemed flat and featureless till the name of Mac drew attention to a faint under-burr.

'No sweat,' said Mac. 'He'll be back for his lunch. We just sit in comfort and wait.'

He returned to the sofa. He looked very relaxed in his dark blue lightweight jacket, open-necked grey silk shirt and knife-edged light blue slacks. The outfit looked continental in style and very expensive. Tommy by contrast was straight off a chain store counter. Beneath the loose cotton blouson he wore a hooped T-shirt which strained over his barrel chest. Daphne tried to register every detail. She didn't want to seem stupid when the police or Ted were asking her questions. Also it was important to make herself believe in a time after this.

Tommy wandered across to the drinks cabinet.

'Come on, Mac,' he said. 'What about a drink? Little one won't do no harm.'

'Are you deaf or just stupid? I told you, no alcohol. You can get pissed out of your mind on your duty-free's later on. But I wouldn't say no to a coffee. Why don't you make us a cup of coffee, Mrs Davis?'

She wanted to say no but she wasn't brave enough. In any case, simple acts of defiance led nowhere. She had to think and it was terror that made you clever, not courage.

'All right,' she said, rising.

The door from the kitchen into the garden was open. Ted had gone that way and she hadn't locked it after him. There were bound to be people outside on a sunny Sunday. And even though the houses were some distance apart and well screened, her screams could not go unheard.

She didn't want to appear to be hurrying but in fact her legs proved to be so unsteady that she didn't have to pretend. She went out of the lounge, down the hall, into the kitchen; there was no sound of anyone coming after her; she was holding her breath as she moved to the sink and gazed out on freedom. Now she darted a look behind her. No one. She might not have to scream. A thirty-yard dash and she could be into the garden next door where there seemed to be a large and noisy party every sunny Sunday. She'd asked Ted to complain. He hadn't, of course. But now she would greet the revellers like dear friends and never be able to hear them again without thanksgiving.

She went to the door and pressed the handle and pulled. Nothing happened. She pulled harder. Still nothing. And knowing now it was all pointless, she pulled again and again, sobbing with effort and frustration. 'I just wanted to say, instant will do,' said the man called Mac. He was standing in the doorway from the hall. In his upraised hand was the back door key.

'First rule: plug all boltholes,' he said. 'Two spoons of sugar for Tommy. You've probably noticed, his metabolism's on fast burn.'

She thought she'd trained herself not to cry any more, but now the tears streamed uncheckably as she filled the electric kettle. By the time it had boiled, the tears had stopped. She stared out of the window again. There was still no sign of Ted and Lady coming over the fields.

She didn't know whether to be glad or sorry.

As she carried the tray of coffee cups into the lounge, she heard the church clock strike the first quarter.

They drank the coffee in silence. Tommy was still sulking at being forbidden a real drink, but silent inactivity was clearly not something that came easy.

'Look,' he said. 'What if he hasn't got his keys with him? They could just be lying around the house somewhere, couldn't they?'

Mac clapped twice.

'Great thinking, Tommy,' he said. 'Except that he won't take those keys off, no matter what he's doing, am I right, Mrs Davis? But it's not important anyway. It's him I need as much as his keys. A stranger can't just walk into a jeweller's shop on a Sunday, even if he knew where all the alarms were, which I don't. Too many eyes, too many mouths. They see Mr Davis taking a special customer in, that's OK, that's normal. Anyone else and it's 999, hello hello hello, in five minutes flat.'

'Yeah, all right,' conceded Tommy reluctantly.

'I'm glad I meet with your approval, Tommy.'

'But what if he don't come back?' persisted the other. 'We've not got all bleeding day.'

'For God's sake, he's just taking the bloody dog for a walk,' snapped Mac. 'Give your mind a rest, Tommy. It's not up to overtime.'

Daphne noted his reaction with interest. What had Tommy meant by not having all day? What was their hurry? It couldn't make any difference to getting into the shop if Ted didn't show up for another hour or more. So it must have something to do with afterwards . . .

A getaway, perhaps?

But it was hardly the crime of the century, was it? They wouldn't be jetting off to some South American hide-out on what they were likely to be getting from Ted's strongroom.

A couple of months on the Costa del something, perhaps . . .

And then it came to her: what if the Costa del something was already where they lived? Her eyes took in Mac's tan and his fancy clothes. It all fitted. What if they'd come across to do this job and were keen to get back to their sunny safety before anyone spotted them and started hunting out old warrants? They could have a nice safe flight booked back that afternoon. A package probably, less risky than a scheduled flight, and from Luton, only thirty minutes away for a quick driver.

It was a nice theory, marred only by the absence of real motivation. No one like Mac was going to risk his liberty for the contents of Ted's downmarket little jeweller's shop.

All the same, she found herself unable to resist testing it out.

She said, 'It must be hot living in Spain this time of year.'

She had the satisfaction of seeing a giveaway frown of surprise crease his face. Then he smiled and said, 'Having second thoughts, are we, Mrs Davis?'

It was an odd answer but she ignored it in the glow of self-congratulation. Ted would scornfully put her feat of inductive reasoning down to a diet of paperback thrillers and TV crime series. He had a way of diminishing everything she did. She didn't doubt but that he'd find some way of criticizing her reaction to this crisis. At least she was coping as well as he would. He had no skill for dealing with unforeseen complication. He'd always rather walk away from trouble than face up to it.

Well, he'd literally walked away from it today.

She realized that she was beginning to feel uncomfortable and stood up.

'I need to go to the bathroom,' she said in response to Mac's querying gaze.

'You're sure? I mean, if you've got any more daft ideas, forget it. You'll leave the door open and Tommy here will be standing outside. Still want to go?'

She looked at Tommy who pursed his lips and made an obscene kissing sound.

'I've got to,' she said. 'Only I'd rather you came with me than that animal.'

'You think I'm more of a gent, do you?' Mac laughed. 'That's the nicest thing anyone's said about me in years. All right. Let's go.'

He motioned her ahead of him. She went out of the lounge, turned towards the stairs. He said, 'No.'

'What?'

'I saw a cloakroom down here. It's got no windows to shatter or jump through. It'll do nicely. In you go.'

She went in. At first she was inhibited by the idea of his presence beyond the door but her need proved greater than her inhibition. When she came out she saw that she needn't have worried. He was sitting some distance away at the foot of the stairs. He looked tired. She readjusted her estimate of his age. The tan and expensively casual dress had deceived her. He was probably older than she was. Perhaps a bit of sun and styling would take her back from forty to thirty. Ted had tried to push her in that direction a few years ago but it had all seemed a waste of time and money. They would be celebrating their twentieth anniversary soon. Why try to look as if you got married at the age of ten?

Mac stood up rather wearily.

'Is it worth it,' she said. 'I mean, for what you're likely to get . . .'

He shook his head and said thoughtfully, 'I'm still not sure about you, Mrs Davis. They said you were a quiet little nobody . . .'

'They?' she said, absurdly piqued. 'This is the same "they" who didn't warn you Ted might go out the back way with his dog? I'd ask for a refund.'

'Maybe I will,' he said. 'All right. Enough talk. Get back inside. *Move!*'

The change of tone alarmed her.

She said, 'I thought I might make a few sandwiches . . .'

'Crap. You're starting to think because I don't flex my muscles all the time like Tommy, I'm the one you can work on. Don't. The only difference between me and Tommy is

220

I need a reason for breaking bones. But I'll do it if I have to, you'd better believe me.'

She believed him.

Back in the lounge, Mac returned to his position by the window. Tommy was sitting in an armchair as they'd left him, but when Daphne glanced at the drinks cabinet, she saw the stopper was out of the whisky decanter. Tommy caught the direction of her gaze and glowered at her as he drained what must by now be a cup of very cold coffee.

The church clock struck the second quarter.

The first sign they would see of Ted's return would be Lady. He always let her off the leash once in sight of the house and she would come bounding up the garden, as excited as if she had been away for weeks. Daphne hoped the two men would remember what they had been told and not mistake her enthusiasm for menace. Mac might think twice but she doubted if Tommy would think even once.

She wished she knew how tight their timetable was. Perhaps Ted wouldn't get back in time. Once it had been hard to get him out of his chair to throw a ball for Lady in the back garden, but in the past few months he had developed a taste for longer and longer walks. As he said, a big dog needs a lot of exercise . . .

'Where are you going?'

Mac's voice, harsh and authoritative, jerked her out of her reverie.

Tommy had risen from his chair and moved towards the door.

'Thought I'd take a look around,' he said. 'Even a bent jeweller wouldn't stick his old lady with bits of glass, would he? Might be some nice stuff upstairs.'

'Sit down, dummy. We've not come here for a few beads and bangles.'

'It might be all we get from the way things are going,' retorted Tommy. 'If he's not back soon, what the hell do we do? Leave a message saying we'll call again next week? Me, I want something to show for wasting my time, even if it's only a good luck charm.'

'You'll need more than *one* if you don't do as you're told,' snapped Mac. 'I don't want some nosey neighbour spotting you wandering round upstairs.'

'They'd just think the duchess here was spreading herself for her fancy man. Though looking at her, that might be a bit hard to credit.'

'Looking at you, it would be quite impossible!' exclaimed Daphne.

Common sense told her it was pointless rising to Tommy's gibes but it was out before she could think. Instantly she regretted it as he moved swiftly towards her and thrust the shotgun hard against her throat.

'Don't need to be no oil painting when you've got one of these, girl,' he said. 'Know what the worst thing about hanging around here is? I'm getting to fancy you, 'cos there's bugger-all else! So talk, you slag! If there's any way of getting him back here quick, spit it out or I'll carve you another mouth under your chin.'

You didn't get used to terror. It came up spring-fresh every time. She rolled her eyes towards Mac in desperate appeal. He came slowly forward and stood by the chair, looking down at her.

'You may have something there, Tommy,' he said. 'What do you say, Mrs Davis? Is there anywhere he might have called in? You mentioned the golf club . . .'

'Yes yes,' babbled Daphne. 'He might have walked across there. He's a member. He could have called in for a drink. He often does.'

'Right.'

He picked up the table with the telephone on it and placed it next to her chair.

'Right,' he said.

She didn't move, not out of defiance but terror.

Tommy reached down and squeezed her left breast till she shrieked in pain.

'Now ring,' he said, relaxing his grip to an obscene caress.

'What should I say?' she gasped.

'She could say she's sick,' said Tommy looking at Mac.

He shook his head and said, 'No. We don't want him

turning up with a doctor. Golf clubs are full of quacks. And we don't want him suspicious . . .'

He stared speculatively at Daphne.

'Spain,' he said. 'What does Spain mean to you, Mrs Davis?'

'Nothing. I don't know. Ahh!' She screamed again as Tommy renewed the pressure. 'What do you want me to say?'

He smiled.

'Just say there's been a phone call from Spain. It sounded urgent but the man wouldn't leave a message. He said he'd ring back soon, though.'

He glanced at his watch.

'On the hour, say. Tell him, on the hour.'

'But why . . . ?'

'Just do it!'

His anger was more frightening than even Tommy's threat. She dialled. His face came close enough for her to feel his breath as he listened to the ringing tone.

'Hello. Clubhouse. Steward. Can I help you?'

'It's Mrs Davis,' she said unsteadily. 'Mrs Ted Davis. Is my husband there, please?'

'I haven't seen him, Mrs Davis, but if you hold on I'll check.'

There was a pause of nearly a minute, then another voice came down the line.

'Hello, Daphne. It's Tony. I gather you're looking for Ted.'

'That's right. Have you seen him? He took Lady for a walk and I need to get hold of him rather urgently.'

'Nothing wrong, I hope?'

'Oh no.' She managed a poor relation of a laugh. 'Just that someone needs to get hold of him in a frightful hurry and they're ringing back. It's from Spain. Business, I think.'

'Ah, business, eh? Look. I've just finished playing and I did think I saw that labrador of yours galloping across the practice ground. Could be Ted's in the vicinity. I'll stick my head out and if there's any sign, I'll tell him to contact you tooty-sweet, right?'

'That's very kind of you, Tony. 'Bye.'

She put the receiver down and looked at Mac. She was sweating freely from nervous reaction. He said, 'Tony?'

'A friend. Of Ted's.'

'Locker-room friend, not one of your favourites?'

He was very sharp.

'No. Does it matter?'

'What do we do now?' interrupted Tommy, impatient of this meaningless exchange.

'We wait,' said Mac. 'Nothing else to do. But I think my money's on good old Tony finding good old Ted.'

The phone began to ring just as the church clock started to sound the third quarter.

'Daph, it's me. Tony's just dragged me into the clubhouse. Something about a phone call from Spain. What's it all about?'

She took a deep breath but words wouldn't come. She looked in appeal and fear at the tall man who returned her gaze neutrally, as if uncertain how best to respond. A threat would have finished her off. But suddenly he smiled and pointed at the mouthpiece and nodded encouragingly.

'Daph? Are you there? Daph!'

'Yes. I'm sorry,' she said. 'The line went faint. Look, it's just that there was this call, not a good connection and his English wasn't marvellous. He was very keen to get hold of you, I could make out that much. I said you were out but should be back any time and he said OK or perhaps it was *Olé*, he'd ring back on the hour. This was thirty minutes ago and I really did think you'd be back. But time went by and I began to wonder if you'd got stuck at the club, so I thought I'd try to get in touch in case it was something important. Is it important?'

There was a silence.

'Probably not,' he said. 'But I'd better get back all the same.'

'Yes. You should make it all right if you don't dawdle,' said Daphne.

'Yes, setting off now. See you soon. 'Bye.'

The line went dead. She put the phone down.

'That was good,' said Mac. 'You did well.'

'Did I?'

'Yes. I liked the *olé*. Nice touch. Funny, though.'

'What is?'

'When you were talking to Tony, you were nervous. Once you got going talking to Ted, you stopped being nervous. Why, I ask myself.'

Tommy who'd been listening in puzzlement broke in.

'Hey, you don't reckon the sly cow's been passing coded messages, something like that?'

'Try not to be stupid all the same, Tommy,' sighed Mac. 'Ninety-five per cent's quite enough. You're not close enough for codes, are you, Mrs Davis? In fact, you're not very close at all.'

'Close?' she echoed with great bitterness. 'Oh no. We're not even as close as the golf club.'

Mac's attention was diverted before he could reply. Tommy, his face tight with resentment, had gone to the drinks cabinet and poured himself a large glass of Scotch.

'What the hell do you think you're doing?'

'I'm sick of being called stupid,' said Tommy. 'If I'm so stupid how come you need me on the job?'

He downed the drink in one go.

Mac's anger was livid on his face but he controlled it.

'There's no time for this, Tommy,' he said. 'He's on his way. Get to that window and sing out as soon as you see any sign. And keep that great fat head of yours out of sight!'

Tommy looked ready to be offended once more, then Daphne said, 'I shouldn't worry, he won't be coming that way.'

Mac turned his attention and his anger to her.

'What's that mean?' he demanded. 'You'd better stop being clever with me, lady, or I'll rearrange your face.'

'No need for that. All I'm saying is that while it's only ten minutes' walk from the golf club, Ted's got further to come.' She felt herself amazingly calm. 'His dear friend Tony must have guessed or known where he really was and rung him up to warn him that I was trying to get hold of him urgently. So Ted rang me. But he got right through, you see. The phone at the club's a payphone.'

'So he wasn't at the club,' said Mac. 'Where do you think he really was?'

'At Little Morton, would be my guess,' she said. 'That's a village about thirty minutes' walk away. There's a woman lives there, Betty Stanton, a widow, very attractive, very expensive. I've met her a couple of times. She's always very friendly but we don't like each other. Now I know why. No, I think to be honest I've known for a while, but knowing and admitting aren't the same, are they? I took Lady for a walk over there a couple of weeks ago when Ted was away, on business, he said. When we got near the village, Lady ran off and I found her sitting on Mrs Stanton's doorstep. I went up the path to get her and a passing neighbour, thinking I was calling, told me Mrs Stanton was away for a few days. I think I knew then.'

'It's a hard life,' said Mac indifferently. 'So what you're saying is, he'll need a lift from there. Which will bring him to the front.'

'Yes. He'll probably say Tony brought him.'

'You reckon?' Mac consulted his watch. 'Five to. Could be here any time. Tommy, keep watching out the back just in case the lady's wrong. I'll take the front.'

He drew his automatic and went out.

'Thinks he's God, that bastard,' said Tommy. 'Where the hell do you think you're going?'

'Into the kitchen. I want a glass of water,' said Daphne.

'No way! You sit quiet, slag, or I'll give you a little tranquillizer with my fist. I shouldn't like to have to do that. You and me are going to be spending a bit of time together while Mac and dirty old Ted go off for the loot and I don't like my women unconscious.'

'That's the only way you'll ever get near me, you ape,' she said scornfully, and set off for the kitchen.

Her defiance took him by surprise and she was through the kitchen door before he caught up with her. Once more he grabbed her by the hair.

'They all talk brave to start with,' he mocked, 'but this

226

soon has them doing tricks their mummies never taught them.'

He tried to thrust the shotgun up her skirt. She shrieked and twisted round to claw his face. But he controlled her with his grip on her hair and forced her back against a waist-high kitchen unit. She felt as if its edge in the small of her back was going to break her spine and flung her arms sideways to try to thrust away from it.

His face came towards her, his mouth wide, red and slavering like a hungry animal's. Then Mac was in the doorway saying, 'What the hell's going on? He's just driven by with some tart. He'll be here any moment. Let her loose, you stupid bastard.'

Tommy relaxed his grip on Daphne's hair and turned to face Mac.

'I told you not to call me stupid!' he yelled brandishing the shotgun.

And Daphne's hand struck the wooden knife-holder she'd been half-consciously searching for, her fingers tightened round the handle of the big butcher's knife, she pulled it out and swung it with all her might to plunge deep into Tommy's right arm. His fingers splayed, sending the gun skittering across the tiled floor. The sharp blade sliced clear through the biceps muscle and drove into the ribcage, pinning his arm to his body. He screamed and pirouetted away from her as his left arm clawed vainly at the knife's handle which it could grasp but not withdraw. His staggerings brought him up against Mac who seized him round the waist, took a firm hold of the handle and ripped it out in one violent movement.

Tommy shrieked again, glared at Daphne with a promissory hatred and collapsed in his partner's arms.

Mac tossed the knife into the sink.

'Oh, Mrs Davis,' he said. 'They really should have warned me about you.'

'I didn't mean . . . I didn't . . . he . . .'

The front doorbell rang. She pushed the hair back from her brow, realized there was blood on her fingers, grabbed a tea-towel and began to wipe it off. Her tongue was loose again.

'That'll be Ted,' she said, 'he never has a key, only the shop key, he knows I'm always here, you see, the bastard . . .'

'Don't go hysterical on me now,' said Mac. 'Pass me that towel.'

He began to bind it round Tommy's arm.

The bell rang again.

'What will you do?' asked Daphne fearfully.

'What's to do? I can't leave Tommy to take care of you now, can I? And there's the fancy woman. She'll be parked a few yards up the road waiting to see if lover-boy comes flying out on his ear. In any case, the way things have turned out, I doubt if threatening you was going to have him exactly rushing to open up his safe!'

'What do you mean?' asked Daphne.

'I'll spell it out, though I'm sure someone sharp as you must have had some idea. He's bent, that husband of yours. Where do you think the money all comes from, eh? He's a fence and a hard bastard in a bargain too. Few months ago there was a whisper in Marbella that Ted Davis was buying himself a nice little villa up in the hills. Not a holiday place but permanent. Retirement, a life in the sun. Give us another towel, will you?'

'Retirement? But . . .' Her mouth was dry. She passed him the towel.

'I thought you knew all about it when you made that crack about Spain. But gradually it dawned on me you didn't. Well, you know now. You're well rid of him. I can't say I fancied him as a neighbour. Fences get rich off honest crooks' graft. Then we got another whisper he was planning to double his pension fund with a last investment in some dodgy industrial diamonds. So some of us decided it'd be fun to pop back here and take them off him. The joke is— or was—he couldn't complain, could he? So Tommy and I flew in this morning on a package flight and we're due out in two hours on another. Not long enough for there to be much risk of being clocked by the filth, see? Christ, he's an impatient sod, isn't he?'

The bell was ringing continuously now. Mac had made

a pad out of the second towel and placed it against Tommy's rib wound, then forced the hand of his damaged arm into his trouser pocket to hold the pad in place. The man was conscious though his colour wasn't very healthy. He groaned and swore at his partner's roughness, but lacked the strength to resist.

'What a big baby it is,' said Mac. 'Don't worry about him too much, Mrs Davis. I don't think you got the lung and I know a quack who owes me a favour.'

'I won't worry,' said Daphne. 'When was he going?'

'Was?' He raised his eyebrows. 'Week after next was the word.'

'Our anniversary week,' she said.

'Nothing like a surprise. I'll be off now, Mrs Davis. If you're ever in Puerto Bunus, look us up. Tommy will be delighted to see you. *Hasta la vista!*'

He unlocked the kitchen door and led his weak and staggering partner out into the garden. Presumably they had a car parked somewhere close. She didn't watch which way they went but turned towards the hall which was echoing to the sound of her name and the beat of her husband's fist against the door. Her foot kicked against something hard as she left the kitchen. It was Tommy's shotgun. She picked it up and laid it on the hall table as she passed.

She opened the door.

It was like looking at a stranger, like being looked at by a stranger.

She let her eyes slide by him. At the end of the drive she could see Lady, her tail wagging as she addressed herself to someone hidden behind the tall brick gatepost.

'Daph, what's happening? Why didn't you answer the door?' her husband asked fearfully.

He tried to step inside but she blocked the way.

'Why don't you fetch Mrs Stanton inside?' she said, meeting his gaze without blinking till he turned and went down the drive.

As he walked away, the church clock began to sound the quarters.

She went back into the lounge, picking up the shotgun en route.

After a little thought she sat on the armchair opposite the sofa, placing the gun between her thigh and the side of the chair and covering it with a cushion.

A few moments later she heard low voices in the hall.

'In here,' she called.

As they came into the room, she heard the church clock striking the twelve notes of noon.